THE LEGEND OF
ROBIN HOOD

Never was such archery seen in Merry Sherwood (see page 22)

The Legend of
ROBIN HOOD

Illustrated in Black and White

Cover illustration by Anita Nelson

J. G. Ferguson Publishing Company
Chicago, Illinois

Contents

Introduction   *viii*

How Robin Hood Became an Outlaw   1
Robin Hood Meets Little John   25
Will Scarlet Joins the Band   33
The Curtal Friar   41
How Robin Hood Dealt with Sir Richard of
   the Lea   51
The Wedding of Alan-a-Dale   57
How Robin Hood Won the Sheriff's Prize   66
Guy of Gisborne Seeks Robin Hood   76
Robin Hood Meets a Tanner   90
How the Sheriff Gained a Queer Servant   98
The Sheriff Spends a Night in the Greenwood   113
Robin Hood Meets George-a-Green and Then
   a Beggarman   121
Friar Tuck and the Bishop of Hereford   134
Robin Hood Meets with a Tinker by the Way   142
The Bishop Tries His Own Hand   155
Robin Hood Becomes a Butcher   164
How Robin Hood Saved the Widow's Sons   173
Robin Hood Meets Maid Marian in
   Sherwood Forest   182
Sir Richard of the Lea Pays His Debts   189
Robin Hood Sells Pots in Nottingham Town   207
How Robin Hood was Seized by the Sheriff   222
Will Stutely Falls into a Trap   250
King Richard Comes to Sherwood   259
Robin Hood Shoots His Last Arrow   270

Illustrations

Never was such archery seen in Merry
   Sherwood   Frontispiece

He floundered into holes and slid about
   on slippery stones   46

As he walked he ran his finger over the
   strings of his harp and chanted like a
   lark   59

The shaft hummed in at the window and
   struck into the table before him   75

Robin Hood stood looking down on the
   body of his prostrate foe   85

For a good hour Little John and the cook
   fought sore together   110

The doughty beggar leaned on his staff,
   and now began to laugh and jeer at
   poor Robin   127

The stranger smiled and opened Sly's
   wallet   147

He gave them as much meat for a penny
   as other butchers were giving for three   166

Right welcome did the wife of Alan-a-Dale
   make Maid Marian   187

A glittering stream of gold poured on the
   mantle   201

The sheriff slunk away, only too glad to
   find himself on the way with sound
   bones in his body   220

Robin Hood was shut up in a dungeon
   where only at high noon a little light
   came through a thick grating   229

So that night the sheriff made a great
   feast in honor of the king's messengers   241

No sooner did he see the abbot than he
   hasted to leap down from his horse
   and fall on his knees beside Little John   267

He smiled as the bow twanged full
   and deep   277

Introduction

Robin Hood is a legend that has been told since the 14th century. Whether there really was a Robin Hood is unknown. If he existed, it would have been during the 12th or 13th century. There are several theories about who Robin Hood might have been; he may have been a nobleman or he may have been a common man who had to flee the law.

From the 11th through the 14th centuries, there were many categories of social class. Lords owned land and held people as workers for the land. The people who worked the land were villeins. The villeins gave a large percentage of everything they gathered from the land to the landowner, or lord.

Most people in England were villeins. Another group of people commonly found in English villages were cottars, or owners of a small amount of land or a small business. Craftsmen who made wheels, horseshoes, bows and arrows were cottars.

The stories of Robin Hood center around men who rebel against the law of early medieval England. Because so few people were independent, there were many people who had barely enough food and money to support a family. Many people took to the woods, where it was difficult for the villagers and lords to find them.

Since the law labeled those who fled as outlaws, the outlaws would have nowhere to go except into the woods. They could not go to another village to buy property because they would have to prove they were freemen. If they were not freemen, they would have to have permission of their lord to be moving or travelling. As soon as the villagers notified the old lord, they would find out the person was an outlaw.

So it is from this group of outlaws living in the forest that Robin Hood found his men. Robin Hood himself was in trouble for shooting a deer in the King's forest. In those days, only royalty could hunt and kill deer in the forests of the king. Lords were allowed to declare forests in their territory their property, which then were only hunted by the lord and his family. Anyone else hunting deer in the forests did so illegally. The laws over hunting in England were the most hated by the people. It kept them from being able to feed their families.

Robin Hood and his men worked to even the wealth of the villages by taking the money of the land-owning rich and distributing it back to the poor. It is this aspect of the story that has made the legend so continuously popular for the past 700 years.

Robin Hood was first brought to life in songs, then stories were written about him. The tales that are told here are part of both—song and story. The spirit of the legend is kept in this edition of the story, with all of the characters, such as Little John, Will Scarlet, and the Sheriff of Nottingham, wandering their way, once more, through the legend that has made them famous.

How Robin Hood
Became An Outlaw

L ong, long ago, in the days when Henry the Second,
first of Plantagenet kings, was seated on the throne
of England, a youth was walking swiftly through the
forest of Sherwood. He was a tall, strong, comely lad,
wearing a woodland dress of green jerkin and hose and a
blue cap or hood on his head. At his shoulder swung a
longbow of great strength, at his side was his sheaf of
cloth-yard arrows, and hanging at his girdle was a short
woodknife.

The forest glade through which he strode was lined by
huge oaks, and once he stood still to watch a herd of antlered deer sweep by in swift and graceful flight. One
hand went to his bow, the other to his quiver, but he re-
strained himself and forebore to lay an arrow on the string,
for he knew that he was in a royal forest. These were the
king's deer, and to slay one was as much—nay, more—
than a man's life was worth. More than a man's life, that

1

seems a hard saying; but it is a true one. In those days one who killed a deer in a royal preserve had his eyes torn out and was mutilated in so dreadful a fashion that death would have been preferable.

The tall lad knew this very well; but another reason also caused him to stay his hand. He was on his way to Nottingham, hoping to enter the king's service as a forester, and it would ill become one with his hopes to lay a hand on the royal deer. He strode on, left the glade, and was crossing a piece of greensward, dotted by thickets of holly and coppices of hazelwood, when he was hailed by a harsh voice.

"Stand!" it cried. "Who art thou to march boldly through the king's greenwood?"

The lad turned and saw a group of five or six figures beneath the shadow of a wide-spreading holly bush. All were seated on the ground save one, and he was the speaker. At a glance the youth knew them for a band of the King's Foresters, men who guarded the royal preserve and the deer, and he saluted them with a motion of respect. Then he replied to the man who had accosted him, a man whose silver bugle horn showed that he was the Chief Forester.

"My name," said the tall lad, "is Robert Fitzooth, though many people call me Robin Hood. My parents are dead, and I am going to Nottingham."

"And why goest thou there?"

"I hope to become one of the King's Foresters."

The man laughed scornfully. "Easier said than done!" he growled. "Every landless man and masterless rogue

longs to join our goodly company. Of what use to us
would be such a stripling as thou art? We want a man,
but thou has naught save a man's bow."

"'Tis more than a man's bow," cried another forester.
"Look at the strength of it. I trow that slip of a lad can
never draw it."

"Draw it?" jeered the Chief Forester; "not likely. He
does but carry it for vain pretense."

Robin's bright eye flashed, and his fresh face colored.

"I will draw it at a mark with any man among you," he
cried.

"And what will you wager?" said the Chief Forester.

"I have no money," cried the fiery lad, "but I will lay
my head against your purse that I hit any target you
choose."

"Done!" cried the forester angrily, "there's your target."

He pointed across the greensward to the mouth of a distant glade. A herd of deer had swept into view and
paused at sight of the men. They were led by a splendid
hart, who now flung up his antlered head, snuffing the air
and striking the ground impatiently with one forefoot.
Robin Hood said nothing, but took his bow, tightened his
string, and chose an arrow from his quiver. Then he laid
his body into the bow in such fashion that the foresters
knew that here was no common archer, either in point of
strength or skill. The great bow bent and tautened amid
murmurs of wonder from the onlookers. Then Robin
showed that he had nerve as well as great strength and
skill. Just as he was drawing the steel head to the bow-
shaft the Chief Forester cried out suddenly:

" 'Tis your head you wager. Bethink thyself of that, my young friend!"

This was done to shake and disturb Robin just as he hung on his aim, but it failed. To all appearance the lad had heard nothing. His keen eye was glancing along the shaft, his brow was slightly furrowed in calculating thought, his lips were set firm; then twang! sang the bowstring, and the arrow hummed through the air like a great bee. At the next instant the great beast made a leap into the air and dropped on his side, dead, the shaft through his heart.

For an instant the foresters were dumb with amazement at the wonderful shot; then murmurs of wonder arose. Robin turned quietly to the Chief Forester.

"I have won the purse," he said.

But the man smiled an evil smile. "I will tell thee what thou hast won," he said jeeringly; "thou hast won the pains and penalties of the forest laws. Yon was a king's hart royal, and so good a bowman as thou are must well know what it means for a man to slay a deer in the royal forest. Seize him and bind him, my men."

Robin saw the fearful danger into which this hasty acceptance of the target had led him, and turned to fly. Too late! A couple of foresters had already sprung on him. He was tripped up and borne to the earth and, in a trice, his feet and hands were lashed together with bowstrings.

"Now we have a deer-killing rascal taken red-handed," chuckled the Chief Forester. "Twice or thrice of late the sheriff hath complained to me that deer be stolen from the coverts, and yet we bring no rogue to be charged with the theft. This day we can content him."

Robin's blood ran cold as he heard these words. The treacherous villain had drawn him into the trap of shooting the deer and now meant to give him up in cold blood as a common deerslayer, and to pretend that his capture was a proof of the keepers' vigilance.

The forester's speech was hailed with shouts of applause from his underlings.

"Ay," cried one, "and let us take him in as such a knave should be carried!"

"How, Hubert?" demanded the Chief Forester.

"Why, bound in the hide of the deer he hath slain!" cried Hubert.

"Good!" cried his leader, "off with the hide, lads, and tie the rogue in it."

The knives of the foresters made short work of stripping off the skin of the deer, and within a short time Robin was wrapped in the hot, greasy hide, the latter lashed across with spare bowstrings. The lad's head was thrust through an opening where the deer's neck had been, but of the rest of him there was but a shapeless bundle, enclosed in the soft dappled fur, which had so lately clothed the great stag. Robin's heart was bursting with rage and scorn for these mean traitors, but he was helpless. And the future was very black. The Norman sheriff would never listen to a word that he might say; it was clear that an example was needed, and that he was to furnish it, and the picture rose before his eyes of the market place of Nottingham and himself under the hands of the hangman who would carry out the dread sentence of the law. He had once seen a poor fellow suffer for this very offense that he was charged with, and he writhed again in agony to think that the punishment now hung over him. To hobble about for life, blind and a cripple, he who was now so young and strong, was too frightful a fate to dwell upon, and he twisted and turned in his bonds and struggled to get free. But every effort was in vain. He was bound too securely for that.

"How shall we carry the knave in?" cried one of the rangers.

"Marry, but I have just thought of that, Dickon," replied the Chief Forester. "Did we not see two or three Saxon hinds* cutting wood a short half-mile from here as we came along? List, we can hear them now."

There was silence among the band, and the sound of axes rang from a distance.

"Run, Dickon," said the leader to the man who had spoken, "and bring them hither with the sled they had with them for dragging home the logs."

Away went Dickon, and in a short time he returned with the woodmen and their sled.

"Take up this knave," commanded the Chief Forester, "fling him on your sled, and drag him before us to the town."

The woodmen were three in number, and two hastened to obey, the third following more reluctantly. All three belonged to the poorest class of workers and were dressed

---

*Laborers.

rudely in jerkins made of cowhide, with sandals and leggings of the same material, and no head covering on their matted shocks of hair. Two were old men, and these were swift to obey the command of the forest tyrants whom they feared; the third was a strongly built, square-shouldered fellow of some thirty years of age, who, as has been said, moved more slowly to obey the command. Among them, however, Robin was taken up and swung onto the sled, a framework of planks set on two wooden runners, the latter shaped from pieces of ash, which curved up naturally towards the fore part. Then the three hinds seized the ropes with which the sled was drawn along, and the rude carriage slid easily across the short, crisp grass.

Within half a mile they gained a rutted track, along which they turned, and now the sled bumped and jumped and tossed the deerhide bundle, with its human contents, from side to side. Robin was not flung completely off, because a row of posts stood up on either side of the sled to prevent a burden being dislodged, but he was banged and bumped from side to side, utterly unable to help himself, while the brutal foresters roared with laughter at the hopeless plight of their captive. The hide, too, was cramping Robin's limbs in dreadful fashion, and as it drew tighter moment by moment, he could have cried out in agony. But he shut his teeth and maintained silence, knowing that his groans would be music to the ears of his brutal captors.

Suddenly the course of the jolting sledge was interrupted. The Chief Forester sprang forward and brought his bowstave down with tremendous force across the shoulders of the young woodman.

"Ha, knave!" he cried, "thou dost not pull with a will. What, would'st thou show thy Saxon sullenness to us, the keepers of the forest!" And he rained a shower of blows on the man's head and shoulders.

The woodman's hand dropped to the handle of the short broad-bladed knife thrust in his girdle, but at a cry from one of the old men he withdrew it, and pulled as if he had been a horse which had felt the urging lash.

"Will, lad!" cried the old man, in trembling tone; "pull! pull! anger not the forester."

"Aye, old man, you speak sooth," said the tyrant, with a savage laugh. "That advice is good, indeed. 'Twere well that Will should not anger the forester. Pull, Will! Pull, dog of a Saxon!" and the forester laid half a dozen hearty blows again on the young woodman. Beneath the fell of matted hair, the Saxon's eyes gleamed redly, but he bent his head to the storm, and pulled with a will in the most humble and obedient fashion. Presently a turn of the way brought them to a small hamlet of half a dozen huts, the largest of the houses being decorated with a bush hanging before the door.

"A tavern! A tavern!" cried Hubert. "What say you to a halt here, comrades! I trow I could empty a flagon after our long walk through the forest."

The others were of his opinion, and the sled came to a stand at the door of the little inn, while the foresters called for wine.

As they stood there drinking, one of them suddenly raised a great shout.

"Look!" he cried, "yonder comes a band of our comrades, and see whom they have taken!"

Through the trees five more foresters were approaching the hamlet, and among them marched two men, with hands bound and ropes fastened to their arms.

"Good, good!" cried the Chief Forester, in delight. "They have seized two of the outlaws who lurk in the forest. What with yonder rogues and the young scamp we have seized, the sheriff will be heartily content. Bravely done, lads, how did ye seize them?"

Eager to hear how the outlaws had been taken, the Chief Forester and his men swarmed forward to meet the newcomers. They did not fear the escape of Robin Hood, lashed tightly in his wrapping of deerskin, and they did not dream that the Saxon woodmen would dare to make a movement without their permission.

Yet it was the old man who had called upon the younger woodman to be patient who was the first to flee. When he saw the foresters turn aside, he dropped his rope and fled softly away on his sandalled feet, like a dog that runs from the lash. He sprang into a narrow passage between two huts, and vanished. The second old man saw nothing of this. His back was turned to his comrade, and he stood stupidly gazing on the crowd of foresters as they called to each other, laughing and talking, and some of the newcomers drinking from the flagons held out to them.

The young woodman, Will, made at first as if to follow his older companion, then cast a glance at the sled. Robin said nothing, lest he should call the attention of the foresters, but his imploring eyes spoke for him. In reply Will dropped on one knee beside the sled, whipped out his broad, sharp knife, and slashed the bowstrings through with a few swift sweeps of the keen blade.

Robin was free. His bow and arrows had been laid beside him on the sledge to be brought in witness against him before the sheriff, but now he caught them up, shot between two of the upright posts, and leapt after Will, who was dashing into the narrow passage between the huts.

"Hobb! Hobb!" called Will as he ran. "After us, man! After us!"

Hobb was the third woodman, the old fellow who stood gazing like an ox at the meeting of the foresters. The warning cry drew his attention, and he looked round with a slow gape of wonder to see his comrades in flight. Unhappily, the voice of Will had caught ears for which it was not intended. The Chief Forester whirled on his heel, and gave a yell of anger at the sight which met his gaze.

"The knaves are fleeing!" he roared, in a voice of thunder, "and they have freed the captive. Back, lads, and seize them, alive or dead!"

He clapped an arrow on his bow as he spoke and drew the string to his ear. Hobb was now lumbering after his friends, for at last his slow-moving wits had grasped the fact that a flight to the forest was the safest thing for him. But the grey-goose shaft was too swift by far. It hummed after him with the tremendous speed of an arrow just leaving the bow, struck him squarely between the shoulders, and he pitched forward on his face and lay still, the grey-goose shaft quivering as it stood upright from his back.

When Robin ran through the narrow passage between the houses he came to a small courtyard, over the further wall of which Will the woodman was already climbing: the old man had completely disappeared. Robin bounded across the little courtyard, put his foot on a crossbar of the wooden paling which formed the wall, and was over in a twinkling. Beyond lay a stretch of open ground, and across that the old man was running nimbly, with Will some distance behind.

Robin followed them at full speed, running hardest for the shelter of the wood toward which his companions were making. He was just on the edge of the trees when he heard a shout behind him. He glanced back and saw five or six heads spring to sight over the palisade. The foresters were after them: but Robin shouted back a gay defiance, for among the woodland it would be difficult to track him, and he knew that he was within arm's length of safety.

He darted in among the trees and saw Will a little before him, waiting for him to come up.

"This way! This way!" called the woodman, and Robin followed. At the next moment Robin saw the old man trotting along a narrow path, and the two younger men ran after their guide for some ten minutes. The old man led the way to a swamp, where he leapt from tussock to tussock of grass, warning the others to jump exactly where he did, or they would sink in the miry bog and be lost. Then they gained firm ground again, and the old woodman paused beneath a huge oak, and sat down to rest on a great root.

"Where's Hobb?" he panted.

"Dead, father," replied Will; "the Chief Forester took him with a shaft atween the shoulders. Hobb was slow to move."

"Ay, Hobb was always slow to move," returned the old man. "Well, well, his fate will be ours if e'er we come in reach of a forester's longbow again. Ay, Will, I thought it was all up wi' ye when ye dropped your hand to your knife. Yon Chief Forester is indeed a hard and cruel man."

"It was naught but your words, father, that kept me quiet," replied Will. "It's hard to be beaten like a dog for nothing at all."

"Ay," said the old man, "we that once were holders of the land are treated as dogs, and worse than dogs, by our Norman masters. But we can never show our faces in the village again, Will. We must take to the forest, and hide there, or we shall soon be lodged in Nottingham jail, waiting for the rope and Master Hangman, as an example to all Saxon hinds who dare to disobey their masters."

"And that, or even worse, would have been my fate, had it not been for your brave and friendly deed in cutting me loose," cried Robin, seizing Will's hand. "A thousand thanks to you, and a thousand thanks again!"

"'Twas naught," said the woodman. "I did but give a slash or two with my knife. But how fell ye into their hands?"

Robin told his story, and the Saxon woodmen nodded grimly. "'Tis all of a piece with their cruelty and treachery," said Will. "Any trick will serve to lure us into their clutches."

The old man sprang up from the root where he had been resting.

"Well," said he, "we are out of their hands now, and must take care to keep out. Follow me, lads, and I will be your guide to a safer part still of the greenwood."

But Robin did not move.

"By my faith, friends," he said, "it goes hard with me to think of the two poor fellows still in their grip. I fear their fate is certain if they be carried to Nottingham."

"As certain as gallows and rope can make it," cried Will the woodman, "for they are two of the outlaws who range the hidden depths of the forest. There is bitter feud between them and the foresters, and proud, too, will be the cruel sheriff to get a couple of them into his clutches."

"Ay," said the old man, "they be poor fellows driven from their homes by Norman tyranny and the harsh forest laws. Now they hide in the wood and live on the king's deer, and are lost men if they fall into the power of the law."

"Guide me to the path they must take toward Nottingham!" cried Robin.

"That can I easily do," said the old woodman, "or, for matter of that, my son could do it. But to what end? What can one man do against a whole band of the King's Foresters?"

"I know not yet what I shall do," cried Robin, "but I cannot bear to think of the poor fellows being carried off as I was being carried off, and I will gladly venture a stroke on their behalf if opportunity should offer."

"Well said, comrade," cried Will, "and I will be your guide. Father, betake yourself to the forest, and secure your safety. We will meet again at the Great Oak."

Upon this the little company broke up at once. Robin, led by Will, struck out by a new path back across the swamp, and the old woodman betook himself to the depths of Sherwood.

Within twenty minutes Robin and Will were approaching the little hamlet under cover of the trees, but on the opposite side from that by which they had escaped. Peering from the depths of a thicket, they were just in time to see the foresters march away from the hamlet with their prisoners in their midst. The search for the fugitives had been given up at the edge of the dangerous swamp, and the band was now returning to Nottingham. They were leaving the sled where it had come to rest, and near it lay poor Hobb, just as he had fallen.

"Rescue and revenge!" muttered Robin Hood; and Will nodded and repeated the words, but wonderingly, as if he could not divine in what manner they were to be fulfilled.

"Now, Will," said Robin, "describe exactly the road yon proud foresters must follow to reach the town."

Will plunged into the description, and Robin soon raised his hand. "Ay," said Robin, "that will suit me. A great open plain you say. Guide me there, Will, and let us gain it before the foresters have crossed it."

Will Stutely, for that was the woodman's full name, led

the way, and they hurried through the trees and gained
the open plain just as the foresters were in the very midst
of it. Then Robin Hood left Will among the trees,
stepped boldly into the open, and hailed the Chief Forester with a great shout.

"Ho, Forester!" he cried, "give up thy prisoners, or it
will be the worse for thee."

The Chief Forester could scarce believe his own eyes
when he saw that Robin had come back alone, as it
seemed, to face the great band of his enemies. But his
anger was such that he made no reply; he only hastened
to seize his bow and shoot the bold lad before he could
retreat into the cover of the trunks. He drew his bow with
all his strength, and loosed the shaft. But the distance was
too far, and the arrow stuck in the turf twenty yards from
Robin Hood's feet.

Then Robin showed them the power of his great bow,
and the wonderful truth of his eye, for he laid a cloth-yard
shaft on the string and shot it without hanging for an instant on his aim. Then a great scream burst from the Chief
Forester's lips, and he went to earth, dragging madly at an
arrow which had gone clean through his throat, and stood
out a hand's breadth behind his neck.

And while the foresters stood in wonder at that terrible
shot, again Robin's voice pealed out, "Loose ye the prisoners or hold them at your peril!"

He waited an instant and let another shaft fly, and this
went through the shoulder of one of the two men holding
the nearest prisoner. Scarce had the arrow alighted than

another shaft hummed among them and smote the man on
the other side of the prisoner; and the foresters saw that
no man could stand beside a captive and live.

Filled with fear at the deadly skill of this terrible young
archer, the two men holding the second prisoner sprang
away from him, lest a fourth shaft should light on one of
them. Their motion of flight set two or three of the foresters running, and the panic spread to the whole band.
Away they raced across the plain, for they feared to stand
before this mighty archer whose arrows struck them down,
while none of them could reach him.

"They fly! They fly!" shouted Will the woodman, in
huge delight, springing from behind a bush, whence he
had watched the whole affair. "By my faith, Robin Hood,
but you can draw a longbow in noble fashion. Now I will
lend a hand to the prisoners."

Will ran as hard as he could to the men, and cut their
bonds with his broad knife. In a few moments he was
back, the outlaws running with him.

The two men were full of joy and gratitude. They
thanked and blessed Robin Hood a hundred times, for
they knew very well they would have been hanged out of
hand as soon as they had been taken to Nottingham.

"It is a wonder the foresters did not slay ye at once
upon taking ye," said Will Stutely to them, "seeing that ye
bear a wolf's head,* and are a mark for any man's arrow."

"They had received the orders of the sheriff to bring in
any prisoners they might seize," said the younger outlaw,

---

*A term denoting an outlaw whom anyone might shoot on sight.

a broad, stout young man, with a fresh-colored face and a merry eye, "and as sure as my name is Much and that my father is a miller, I thought I should look out over Nottingham market place through a halter. But not this time will it happen, thanks to the finest archer that ever roved in greenwood," and he saluted Robin Hood once more.

"Whither now?" cried the second outlaw. "We must all to cover, and that right speedily. These foresters will raise the country on us without delay."

"True, true!" cried Will Stutely. "Come, Robin Hood, you must go with us, too, or your head will pay for this day's work if the sheriff's men can but once lay hands on you."

Robin Hood nodded, for he knew that the woodman spoke truth, and away they went at once into the depths of the forest. On their way they passed the Great Oak where old Stutely was waiting for them. When he heard what had passed, he shook his head. "This countryside will be no place for us any longer. Any man who has taken the least share of this stand against our tyrants will forfeit his life. I shall go to my daughter's house, on the other side of the forest, and hide. And you, Will, what is in your mind?"

"I am for the greenwood life, father," cried Will. "From this day Robin Hood is an outlaw, and I shall follow him."

Robin was standing a little aside, leaning on his great bow. An outlaw! The word struck to his heart with a chill. Yet it was, it must be, true. He would be outlawed for rescuing these prisoners and for withstanding the brutal foresters. Then his spirits rose, and he looked round him on the beautiful greenwood, the great branches of the trees tossing in the sunshine and wind, and thought of the bold, free life of the open woodland. "A thousand times better to be an outlaw whose hand must keep his head," thought Robin, "than to be dragged off and clapped into the sheriff's dungeon at Nottingham," and his heart became light, and he looked forward eagerly to the new life before him.

The outlaws led him and Will Stutely ahead once more, Much the Miller's Son being the guide. For two hours they marched at a swift pace through the forest, and though there was never once the least sign of a path, Much strode on through glade and thicket as if he were following a highway.

At length he paused in a small open space beneath a huge oak, and softly blew the horn which hung at his belt. It was at once answered, and he went forward again. Within three hundred yards the little party entered a clearing made by chopping away a holly and hazel coppice which had clustered thickly about the foot of a rocky wall. Here they were at once challenged, but upon the voice of Much being recognized, the challenger came forward, followed by half a dozen stout followers, every one with bow in hand and arrow on string, showing with what reception they would have greeted an enemy or a stranger.

The outlaws raised a shout of joy to see their comrades back again, for news of their capture had already been brought to the camp.

"Much and Wat are here again!" they cried. "Joy! joy!

brave boys! How did ye escape the fangs of the forest mastiffs?"

"List to me, comrades," cried Much. "I was saved by this youth, and in him I bring to our band the finest archer and the boldest heart that I have ever met." He told the story, and the outlaws shouted praise of the bold deed which had saved their comrades.

That evening the outlaws were sitting around a great fire, making a merry supper off a fat deer which had been shot that day, and washing down their feast of fresh venison with great draughts of ale. Suddenly, amid the laughter and chatter, Much the Miller's Son spoke up in a loud voice:

"Comrades," he said, "do ye not remember that it was but last night that we talked over the matter of making choice of a leader to govern our band so that we might have order in our doings?"

"Ay, ay," called out a stout yeoman, "and the choice as good as fell on thee, Much, my bully boy."

"Then it shall fall on me no longer," replied the miller's son, "for Much has met his master this day. I give my word and vote for Robin Hood!"

"And I," cried Wat, "and if any man dares to say nay to that, he shall feel the weight of my little switch of crab,"* and Wat took up a huge quarterstaff, fully six feet long, and brandished it about his head as if it had been the little switch, as he called it in jest.

But one outlaw, a tall, dark-faced man, shook his head.

---

*Crab-apple tree.

"I thought we half agreed that the best archer should be the captain," he growled.

"So it was said," cried Much, "but nothing was settled upon. Well, I am content to leave it there. Yonder sits the best archer within the bounds of merry England!" and he pointed to his deliverer.

"And how are we to know that?" grunted the tall outlaw.

But Robin Hood struck in at once. "Nay, Much," he said, "I will take no place here or elsewhere which I have not earned. It is true, then, that you had thought to make the best bowman the leader of your band?"

"We talked of it as a way of settling the matter," admitted Much.

"Then let it stand," cried Robin Hood, "and tomorrow we will shoot off our shafts man by man, and let the best shot win."

"Agreed, agreed!" cried all, and the tall man, whose name was John Ford, shouted with the rest. And so, when supper was ended, they wrapped themselves in their cloaks and lay down to sleep around the fire.

The next morning the band of outlaws carried out the trial of shooting without delay. In a sunny glade they set up such a mark as they were used to shoot at, and called upon Robin Hood to show his skill by putting a shaft in the center of it. But Robin shook his head.

" 'Tis no test at all" he cried; "anyone could hit that mark, and then several would succeed. Nay, nay, set up a mark, I say, which will end the matter once and for all."

"Set it up yourself, Robin Hood," cried John Ford, who

had hitherto been looked upon as the best shot in the band, and hoped to win the leadership.

"That I will," replied Robin Hood, "if it is agreed that I may do so."

"Ay, ay," cried the outlaws, "set up the mark, Robin Hood!"

So Robin took sprays of leaves and clusters of wild flowers, and wove a little garland or wreath. Then he bade Will Stutely take the garland and hang it from the bough of an oak at the far end of the glade.

"Now," said Robin, "I say that he is worthy of the name of an archer who can send his shaft through the ring of yonder garland, yet touch neither leaf nor flower."

The outlaws looked at each other in wonder. "Who could see such a mark?" cried one man. "It would need the eye of an eagle to take aim."

"Ay, and the strength of a horse to bend a bow to send a shaft to such a distance!" cried another.

"I am out of it at once!" shouted a third, "my bow will not reach so far."

In the end only John Ford was willing to try his chance at the garland, and he fitted a new string to his bow and chose the straightest, truest shafts from his quiver. The two competitors drew lots for the order in which they were to shoot, and John Ford had to shoot first. Each man was to loose three shafts at the mark.

Ford loosed his first shaft, but it fell a good ten yards short. He gave a grunt of vexation, and drew his string farther back, and shot higher, but still he fell short. A third time, and his arrow dropped under the garland.

"I have gone as near to it as I may," he cried. " 'Tis the most puzzling mark I ever tried at. No mortal man, I believe, will ever compass it."

"Shoot, shoot, Robin Hood!" cried Much. "I saw thee loose four shafts in wondrous fashion yesterday, but this is another kind of mark to a man's body," and the miller's son shook his head, as if in doubt that his champion had set up too severe a test.

Now Robin Hood stood forth, and the outlaws watched him in utter silence as he raised the great bow, laid his body into it, and drew the string taut. The shaft hummed through the air, and a shout of surprise burst from every lip as it was seen to dart through the very center of the garland and stick quivering in the trunk of the oak.

But the voice of John Ford rose above all. "Let him do it again! Let him do it again!" cried the tall outlaw. "It may have been a happy chance. Let him loose his three shafts!"

"Willingly," said Robin, and bent his bow, and sent a second shaft whistling through the garland, and then a third, nor did any one of the three touch leaf or flower.

The flight of the third shaft was followed by a great shout of applause from the lookers-on. Every man there was an archer of more than common skill, so that all could appreciate this wonderful shooting, though none could hope to rival it.

"Robin Hood forever!" they shouted. "Never was such archery seen before in Merry Sherwood!"

"Now," cried Much, "what say ye, comrades? Is not this

prince of bowmen worthy to be our leader and captain?"

"He is! He is!" they cried. "We will live and die under Robin Hood."

The outlaws swore to be faithful and true to their young leader, and the first of them to take the oath were Much the Miller's Son and Wat, the two men he had saved from the foresters. Next came John Ford, who had been wholly won over by Robin's wonderful skill with the bow, and then Will Stutely, his companion in the flight to the forest, and lastly the remainder of the band.

"Listen to me, my comrades," cried Robin, when all had given their fealty. "These be the laws that all in our band must follow: First, we will wage war on all the Norman tyrants who are enriching themselves with spoils torn from the rightful owners of the soil, our Saxon brethren. Second, we will offer no violence to any poor or needy man, but aid him with the wealth we may gain from Norman sheriff or baron or churchman. Third, that no woman, rich or poor, Norman or Saxon, shall have aught to fear from us. These be the laws of our fellowship."

And the outlaws agreed to obey Robin's orders in every particular. They were still gathered around the garland talking of the wonderful feat which had been performed when a small bent man came shuffling through the trees.

"Who is this coming?" cried Will Stutely, who was the first to see him.

"A friend," replied Much; "he is one Lobb, a cobbler of Nottingham. He watches for us in the town, and is a

sworn gossip of some of the sheriff's men. From them he
learns what the sheriff thinks of doing against us and then
warns us that we may secure our safety. How now,
Lobb?" he cried, as the little man came up. "What news
bring ye?"

"Look out for yourselves, say I," replied Lobb; "the
sheriff is drawing together a strong force of foresters to
march upon ye. He is in a terrible rage, for the Chief Forester and others have been slain in a fray yesterday, and he
swears that he will have the heads of three outlaws for
every man he hath lost. But most angry is he against
some stranger of whom I have never heard before. There
be notices set up in the market place offering a great reward for one Robert Fitzooth, also known as Robin
Hood. Whoever shall bring him in as a prisoner, or his
head, shall receive three hundred silver pennies."

"A great reward, indeed!" cried Much. "So you may
see what value the sheriff puts upon you, master."

He spoke to Robin Hood, and the latter nodded, but
made no reply. How strange it seemed to Robin that
Lobb had seen a notice offering a reward for his life! It
made him feel the reality of his outlawry. Then Much
raised his bow, and shouted, "Ho, for the merry greenwood! Ho, for our brave leader, Robin Hood, prince of
bowmen, and now in very deed prince of outlaws!" and
the rest of the band joined in the cheer. Robin's eye
flashed, and his face brightened. He might be an outlaw,
but with the vast forest open to him and a band of stout
fellows to be his support, he feared no Norman sheriff in
the land.

Robin Hood Meets Little John

THE news that Lobb had brought from Nottingham proved to be quite true. The sheriff sent a great band of well-armed men against the outlaws, a band so strong that the outlaws had to leave Sherwood for a time and seek refuge in another great woodland, that of Barnesdale in Yorkshire. But they loved their haunts in merry Sherwood above all other places and returned as soon as as they discovered that the angry sheriff had given up the chase.

Now, Robin Hood saw that his band was not strong enough to hold its own with the Norman rangers, and he looked about for stout men who would be a gain to his fellowship. Many men, driven to despair by harsh and cruel lords, wished to join him, but he took none but such as were proved to be bold, stanch, and trusty. If he heard of any man who was strong and clever beyond his fellows, he did his utmost to draw that man to him, and he very

25

rarely failed; so that, little by little, he gathered a powerful band of splendid archers about him, all picked men, of
whom it was said that one of Robin Hood's men was
worth four common bowmen.

Now it happened one day that Robin Hood went roving
through the greenwood, and a number of his men went
with him. They came to the border of the forest, and
looked out across the open country.

"Stay among the trees, my men," said Robin; "it would
draw attention if a company should be seen marching
across the fields. But I will go forward alone to see if any
adventure may promise for us. Perchance some rich
knight or abbot may be on the road this fine morning, and
we will lighten his swollen purse of its load. If I need ye,
I will sound my bugle horn."

So Much and Will Stutely and Wat and the rest stayed
in hiding in the forest, and Robin went on alone. He
walked down to the high road, but it seemed empty, and
he strolled along it. Presently he came to a place where a
brook ran across the road. Horses went through a ford,
but foot passengers could cross by a long, narrow, wooden
bridge without a handrail. Robin stepped on the bridge
to walk across, and at the very instant that he did so, a
huge fellow, a very giant of a man, stepped on the farther
end. Each moved forward briskly, thinking that the other
would give way, and they met in the middle of the
bridge.

"By our Lady," thought Robin Hood to himself, "this is
a noble yeoman. Would that I could win him over to my
side! I will see if he has mettle to match his size."

In truth such a man as the stranger was not often met with. He was head and shoulders taller than Robin, of immense breadth of shoulder and depth of chest, long-armed and long-legged, and appeared strong as a bull. He had a pleasant face and a bright brown eye, but there was a quiet resolution in his bearing which hinted that he would be a very awkward person to cross. Robin made test of him at once.

"Give way, my man!" he cried. "What meant ye by stepping on the bridge when you saw that I was about to come over, and that the bridge is not wide enough for two?"

The stranger carried besides his sword, a huge quarterstaff, full seven feet long, thick and heavy, a tremendous cudgel. He now quietly leaned upon it, and smiled as he said, "And why should I stand aside for you, archer? Let me tell you that I have never stood aside for any man yet, and see no reason to begin this day."

"What!" cried Robin; "you bandy words with me, do you? I'll show you some right Nottingham play, my fine fellow, big as you are," and with that Robin Hood slipped an arrow on the string of his bow, and drew it to his ear.

"Now," went on Robin, "back with you, I say! Your life is in my hands. I could sent this shaft through your heart before you could lift your staff to fetch a single blow at me."

Robin did this to see if the stranger would show fear, but the tall man listened as calmly as if Robin had been giving him good day.

"A coward's trick that would be," replied the stranger.

"Here stand I with but a staff in my hand, and you threaten me with longbow and grey-goose shaft. A coward's trick, I say!"

"Nay," quoth Robin, "I will gladly meet thee on thy own terms."

So Robin laid aside his great bow of Spanish yew and his quiver of sharp-pointed arrows, ran to a thicket beside the stream, and cut himself a stout staff of ground oak. When he came back with his stick the stranger was still resting on his quarterstaff in the middle of the bridge.

"Here will we fight where we have met," cried Robin Hood, "and the man who knocks the other into the stream shall be the winner."

"Agreed!" cried the gigantic stranger, and the two combatants faced each other warily, setting their feet cautiously on the narrow planking and grasping their staves about midway of the length in order to be ready for assault or defense.

For a few moments the two champions whirled their sticks about, feinting, striking, parrying, each searching for an opening in the other's guard. Robin was the first to get in a body blow. He pretended to strike at the stranger's head; the latter raised his staff swiftly to parry, and Robin, changing his hold and the direction of his blow with wonderful speed and dexterity, caught his opponent a tremendous thwack across the ribs.

The giant give a growl of anger, and replied with such a terrific slashing cut that no man could have stood before it. But Robin dodged it nimbly, and replied with a smart rap across the shoulder. But even as this fell, the stranger whirled his staff in his hands, and launched a shrewd stroke at Robin's head. Nothing but Robin's quickness saved him from being knocked headlong into the stream, and as it was he did not altogether escape. The big man's staff glanced across his head, cut his crown, and caused the blood to stream down the side of his face.

This put Robin in such a rage that he dealt a whole shower of blows at his opponent with such swiftness that the tall man was kept entirely on the defensive. He was forced to parry, parry, parry all the time.

Time and again Robin's quick staff got home on the big man's body, but the tall fellow never gave way an inch, but fought stoutly on. Suddenly the giant repaid Robin Hood's many thwacks once and for all. Gathering all his tremendous strength, he brought down his great staff with all the power of his long arms and mighty body. Robin parried, but though his stick was held correctly, he might as well have tried to parry a thunderbolt. Down came the crashing blow. It broke Robin Hood's staff in two, it fell with but little diminished force on Robin's body, and hurled him flying into the brook.

Beneath the bridge was a deep pool, and in went Robin Hood head over ears. In a moment he came up gasping for breath.

"Ha, ha, Master Archer!" laughed the stranger merrily; "where art thou now?"

"By my faith," replied Robin Hood, spluttering and blowing, for he had swallowed a good deal of water, "methinks I am in the brook fairly enough, and thou hast won the bout. But I'll freely say thou hast won fairly."

Then Robin Hood waded to the side and climbed onto
the bank, pulling himself up by the aid of a whitethorn
bush which grew at the waterside. As soon as he was on
the bank, Robin set his horn to his mouth and blew the
lusty notes which formed his own bugle call.

Scarce had the valley ceased ringing with the echo of
the horn than his stout bowmen came in sight, Much and
Wat and Will running ahead of the rest in their eagerness
to gain the side of their leader.

"Why, master," cried Will Stutely, as they ran up to the
place, "what is the meaning of this? You are wet to the
skin, and the water is dripping from you. Have you been
in the brook?"

"Ay, that I have, Will," replied Robin Hood, "and there
stands the man who put me there," and he pointed to the
gigantic stranger.

"Then in he goes, too!" cried Will, and Much and Wat
shouted, "Ay, ay, 'twere foul shame to let him go scot free
after treating our leader so. In with him, lads!"

The stranger prepared to resist, but even his great
strength would not have availed him against the crowd of
angry yeomen, had not Robin Hood called upon them to
desist.

"Hold your hands, my lads," said Robin, "ye shall do no
wrong to this bold heart. It was a fair fight, and he won,
and I owe him no grudge for it. Rather would I be
friends with so stout a striker. Come," and now Robin
turned to the stranger, "join us, and be one of our band."

"First," said the stranger, "who are ye? I have sworn to
enlist under one man, and one man only, and in search of
him have I come."

"I am Robin Hood," said the leader.

"Robin Hood!" cried the other; "oh, happy day! It is he for whom I search, and to Sherwood Forest am I making my way to enter his goodly company, if I may."

"Thou may'st in very truth!" cried Robin, "and gladly will I receive thee. Methinks such a recruit is not picked up every day. And what shall we call thee?"

"My name is John Little," replied the stranger. "I'll serve thee well and faithfully, and here's my hand on it."

When Will Stutely heard the stranger's name he began to laugh. "John Little!" he cried; "by my faith, that name ought to be changed, and as he is a newcomer to our band, let him be christened anew. I will name him."

"And what wilt thou call him, then?" cried Much.

"Why, seeing that the infant is so puny, his name shall no longer be John Little, but he shall be called Little John."

The outlaws laughed at the idea of calling this giant Little John; but the jest pleased them, and the name was given to the new recruit.

"Now for a jolly feast to finish off the christening," said Will Stutely; "it is not every day we get such a stout companion in our band, and we must have a revel in honor of it."

So they went back to the forest, and soon two fat does had fallen to their keen shafts and were being carried to their hiding place, the great cave in the rock, which was their secure retreat.

Here they built a great fire, roasted their venison, and feasted on the rich meat, washing it down with mighty draughts of nut-brown ale. When the feast was over, they

sang to the music of the harp, and danced, and enjoyed
the frolic to their heart's content. High above them all
rose the head of Little John, he who was to prove so
stanch of soul and stout of hand, whose name was to fill
the ballads with a renown second only to his great leader,
Robin Hood.

Will Scarlet Joins the Band

ONE day, soon after Little John had joined the band, he and his master, Robin Hood, took their bows and went in search of a fat buck, for the hollow oak which formed their larder was empty.

About midday the two outlaws saw a fine herd of deer before them at the far side of an open grassy space in the forest.

"Yonder is the buck we want, Little John," said Robin Hood.

He pointed to a noble stag, feeding quietly at a short distance from the herd of which he was the lord and master.

"Then this is the best way to take him," said Little John. "The wind is blowing from the herd toward us. I will work round till the great hart can scent me on the breeze. He will rush in this direction, and you will then have an easy shot."

They agreed upon this plan, and Little John was just

about to move away when he stopped short and pointed, but said nothing. Robin Hood looked and saw a young man step into the open space from a forest path. The stranger wore a gay dress of scarlet and carried a longbow, while a stout broadsword hung at his side. No sooner had he left the narrow path than his glance fell upon the herd of deer, and the great stag, which now raised its head and tossed its antlers at the sight of this scarlet-clad figure, stamped on the earth.

"Who can this gay spark be?" said Robin Hood.

"I do not know him," replied Little John, in low tones. "He is not of the forest."

"By my faith, I should say not," returned the leader; "yonder suit of scarlet shines like a fire among the trees. It were better for him to wear a dress of good Lincoln green if he wishes to walk in the forest. 'Tis some fop out of the town come to walk in the greenwood."

But just at this moment the two watchers saw a feat which brought a murmur of admiration to their lips.

The stranger had strung his bow, snatched an arrow from his quiver, and laid it on the string. The movement had startled the stag, and he had given the alarm, and the whole herd was fleeing silently and swiftly. Several hinds had gathered around the mighty hart as if to protect their lord, and it seemed hopeless to think of getting a shot at him. But just on the edge of the trees the stag bounded out and headed the herd for a moment. That moment was enough. The string twanged, the arrow flew, and the stag pitched forward headlong, and lay still, the shaft buried up to the feather in his dappled side.

"By our Lady, a noble shot!" murmured Robin Hood. "This is no fop from the town, Little John. Do you stay here while I go to speak with him."

So Little John remained in hiding in a thicket, and Robin Hood walked up to the stranger, who now stood beside the great deer which he had slain.

"Well shot! Well shot!" said Robin, as he marched up to the place. "Yon shaft was loosed in the very nick of time, stranger!"

The young man in scarlet looked coolly at Robin but made no answer.

"I love a bold bowman," went on Robin Hood, "and draw to me all that I can. Wilt thou become a yeoman of mine, stranger?"

"And pray who art thou?" said the young man in scarlet, and his tone was rather scornful. "And why should I become thy yeoman? It seems to me thou art some kind of forester."

"Ay, truly am I!" replied Robin.

"And herd the deer for the king?" went on the young man.

"Aye, truly—for the King of Sherwood!" chuckled Robin.

"Whether King of England or King of Sherwood, it is all one to me," drawled the gallant; "take thy own way, good forester, and trouble me not. I want naught to do with thee."

"And if I am not of a mind to take my way, what then?" demanded Robin.

"Why, by my faith, thou wilt remain at peril of a beating," returned the other.

"This seems a cool fellow," said Robin to himself; "I will make trial of him and see if his courage is as great as it seems."

So while the young man in scarlet began to examine the horns of the deer he had shot, as calmly as if no one stood within a mile of him, Robin secretly slipped an arrow on the string. Then he gave a great shout, "Ha!" and stamped his foot. The young man turned, and saw Robin's bow bent, and an arrow laid full upon his heart. But he changed not his color and gave no start, only said in rather a vexed tone, "Get thee gone, forester! What means this fool's play?"

"Call you an arrow between your ribs fool's play?" growled Robin Hood. "I am an outlaw, and the enemy of all such gay sprigs as you. Fling down your purse at my feet, and quickly, too, lest I loose the string."

"Aye, you are of that company, then?" said the young man in a tone of mild surprise. "Well, well, there is strong argument in a grey-goose shaft," and he turned as if to unloose his purse from his girdle.

But instead of unloosing the purse, he clapped an arrow to his own bow and bent the latter with wonderful speed; so there they faced each other, both in act to shoot, and Robin, who had never dreamed of letting his arrow fly, saw that he was likely to be paid back in his own coin.

"Hold thy hand!" cried Robin; "hold thy hand! We are likely to slay each other, and there is no advantage in that."

"None at all that I can see," replied the stranger, coolly, "but the game was of thy beginning, not mine."

"Then I end it," said Robin Hood, and took his arrow from the string. The stranger did the same, and stood waiting.

"You carry sword and buckler," said Robin; "so do I. 'Twere shame for us to part without seeing who is the better man."

So they betook themselves to a flat piece of turf beneath the wide-spreading branches of a mighty oak, and each man arranged his buckler on his left arm, and took his good broadsword in his right hand.

Then to work they went, cutting and thrusting, feinting and parrying. Clash! clang! went the heavy broadswords time and again on the stout bucklers, as the blows were deftly caught and warded off. So equal were the combatants that they fought for a good half-hour, and neither had been touched, nor had either of them given way for an inch before the other.

At length the combat was ended by a lucky stroke made by the stranger. He cut at Robin's head, and the outlaw's buckler did not entirely check the blow. The point of the gallant's sword snicked Robin along the top of the forehead, and the blood poured down and filled his eyes so that he could no longer see to fight.

As soon as Little John saw that his master was disabled, he sprang from his hiding place, and ran up to the spot.

"Give me your sword!" he cried to Robin Hood, "and he shall try a bout with me, master. I can play with sword and buckler."

"Nay, nay, Little John!" cried Robin Hood, wiping the blood out of his eyes; "there has been enough sword

play. 'Twere shame to set a fresh man on one who has
fought so long and so well. And a fair and honest fighter,
too. He hath never offered a stroke while I have been at
disadvantage."

"I am bound to obey!" grumbled the big fellow, "but I
like it not that this gay spark may brag to his cronies that
he drew blood from Robin Hood, and went unscathed
for it."

For the first time the gallant in scarlet began to show
interest.

"Robin Hood!" he cried eagerly; "and have I met Robin
Hood and fought him and yet not know him?"

"Why should you know me?" cried Robin. "Who are
you?"

"Who am I?" laughed the youth in scarlet. "Why, a
few years ago you would have known me at once, and I
you. Robin, have you forgotten Will Gamewell?"

"Forgotten my only cousin!" said Robin Hood. "No,
never. But can you be he? Are you the lad I used to go
birds'-nesting with and whom I taught first to draw a
bow? Yes, I know your smile now, and your voice. Well,
to think we should have fought each other."

The two cousins shook hands heartily, and then Little
John took Gamewell's hand in turn.

"But what are you doing in the forest, Will?" asked
Robin Hood.

"Looking for you, Robin," was the answer. "You must
know that I am an outlaw, too. I have fled to the forest
with a man's blood on my hands, though it was not shed
willingly. You remember old Grimm, the steward?"

WILL SCARLET JOINS THE BAND   39

"Aye, that I do, the scurvy old knave," replied Robin; "if it was he you killed, you had good reason for it, I warrant."

"You shall hear," replied Will. "You know that our lands run with the chase of Baron de Lacy, our Norman neighbor. De Lacy has long coveted our estate to round off his great possessions, and as my father is now old and has no children except me, the Norman thought to slay me and then get a grant of our lands as being without an heir."

"The rascal!" said Robin. "But the trick hath been played before, and with success, too. Well, how did you fare with him, cousin?"

"I was out shooting with the bow the other day," went on Will, "and Grimm came with me. I was waiting at a gap for a deer to pass, when some feeling—I know not how it sprang up in my heart—caused me to turn, and there was Grimm, bending his bow, the arrow laid upon me. To save myself, I loosed a shaft at him, and we shot together. His arrow tore my doublet, but mine went through his body, and he was a dead man within five minutes. Yet in that time he confessed that he had agreed with De Lacy to slay me for a great reward and a high position in the Norman's household."

"Foul Norman treachery!" cried Robin Hood. "They are ever ready to strip the Saxon by any means, and the fouler the practice the better they like it. And what happened to you then, cousin?"

"Why, as ill-luck would have it, the manner of the steward's death came to the Norman's ear at once, and he set the sheriff speedily on my track. You see, his purpose would have been just as well served if he could see me strung up by a rope for what he called the murder of the rogue Grimm."

"Ay, ay," replied Robin Hood, "that is easy enough to see. So you fled to the good greenwood, cousin? Welcome to Sherwood and to our forest company! This is Little John, the biggest of us all, and second in our band."

Will Gamewell and Little John shook hands again, and Robin went on, "But we will drop your old name, Will. 'Tis best to put aside a name for the owner of which the law is in hot pursuit; you come in scarlet, and Scarlet you shall be called. Will Scarlet art thou from this day, my cousin!"

"Good!" cried Little John. "Will Scarlet he shall be in our band, master, and with a new name he shall be a new man, and free of the forest."

So Will Scarlet entered Robin Hood's company and swore to be true to the forest laws and the forest ways. "And I will give you the great stag as my first footing," laughed Will Scarlet. "Let it be for a feast of friendship on my joining your goodly company."

Robin Hood laughed and applauded the speech. "We were in search of venison when you appeared, Will," he said, "and I had marked down this hart which fell before your strong bow. Now we will carry it to our meeting place, and it shall be as thou sayest. We will feast high today on this rich venison."

The Curtal Friar ꙅ

ONE fine day when the forest was at its greenest and loveliest, and the sun was casting a pattern of light and shade on the smooth greensward, Robin Hood's men were in so joyous a mood that they resolved to make holiday. They ran races and jumped like so many merry schoolboys, they played with the quarterstaff, they wrestled, they danced, they practiced every sport of the forest. At last they came to the sport which was nearest and dearest to their hearts, the use of the good longbow. They might try their hands at this or that, but in the end they were certain to betake themselves with new delight to their beloved archery.

Several parties went into the forest in search of deer, and one party was formed of Robin Hood, Little John, Much the Miller's Son, and Will Scarlet. Soon they saw a herd pasturing at a good distance, and Robin Hood said, "Which of you can kill a buck or doe five hundred feet away?"

Instantly Will Scarlet killed a buck, and Much killed a doe, but Little John drew his great bow and loosed a mighty shaft and sent it humming through the heart of a big stag more than five hundred feet away.

"Good shot!" cried Robin Hood. "God's blessing on thy heart, Little John! I would go a hundred miles to find the man who could match you with the bow."

Will Scarlet began to laugh, upon hearing this flattering speech.

"You need not go a hundred miles, Robin," he cried. "You can meet his match nearer than that!"

"I know not where to go," replied Robin Hood.

"Why, to Fountains Abbey!" cried Will Scarlet; "there you may find a curtal* friar, who can draw a strong bow with any man. He will beat Little John, ay, or you either."

Robin Hood pricked up his ears when he heard this. His master passion to draw a stout fellow to him awoke at once, and he vowed that he would seek out this famous friar without delay. So he made himself ready for the journey and away he went. Robin was well armed, for the country into which he meant to venture was a dangerous one for him if he should become known. He wore a coat and cap of steel, a good sword at his side, a buckler on his arm, a sheaf of arrows slung at his belt, and his trusty longbow at his shoulder.

At last he rode into the beautiful dale where Fountains Abbey stood—and where its ruins stand to this day—and

---

*Short-frocked.

saw the river calmly gliding, a band of silver, through the sweet valley. He drew rein to glance over the scene and, as he looked, he saw a figure walking at the waterside.

It was a strange figure, for though it was wrapped in the robe of a curtal friar with a cord round the waist, a steel cap was on the friar's head, and a sword and buckler were at his side.

"By my faith," thought Robin, "this should be my man. If he be a friar, he has the air of a fighting friar, and he must be the man I seek. Now will I make trial of him."

So Robin sprang down from the saddle, tied his horse to a thorn, and went to meet the curtal friar. Robin followed a path which ran down straight to the river and then appeared on the other side. "There is a ford there," thought Robin Hood, "and I am in mind to cross it dry shod, and the friar shall take me over. Now where is he?" for the burly form of the curtal friar had disappeared among the bushes that fringed the stream. Presently Robin saw him coming back; the friar was pacing to and fro on the river bank, reading from his missal; as he came he began to chant a Psalm, and his voice was like the bellowing of a bull. Suddenly the friar's voice stopped in mid-verse: he had gained the point where the road ran into the river, and there stood a stranger whose bow was bent, and whose shaft was pointed full upon him.

Such a sight as this would have dismayed many, but the curtal friar took it very calmly. His round, red, plump face lost not a shade of color, his little, pig-like eyes, almost hidden in the fat of his cheeks, were filled more with amusement than alarm, and he thrust his steel cap back and scratched his bald, shiny noddle with one forefinger.

"I' faith," he said, "ye may put down that bow and arrow, my son. If your purpose be robbery, 'tis useless. Not the smallest coin have I about me, and 'twere trying to dine off a dry bone to rob a curtal friar, a man vowed to poverty. And if your purpose be not robbery, I know not why you should point a shaft at me, since never before have I set eyes on your face."

"Nay, friar," said Robin. "I seek neither thy life nor thy money. I do but wish to have thy aid in crossing this ford, for I see that the water runs deep after rain. Therefore, take me on thy back and carry me over."

The friar said nothing, only pulled a wry face in so comic a fashion that Robin Hood had much ado not to burst into a fit of laughter. But the holy man carefully laid his missal down and prepared to take the outlaw on his broad, burly back.

Robin Hood leaped merrily to his perch and silently the friar strode into the water and soon they reached the other side.

When they were over the stream, Robin Hood sprang nimbly from the friar's back and turned to thank him. But as he was doing so, he felt himself seized in a grip of iron, and saw a dagger at his throat.

"What means this, friar?" he cried. "What, would you shed my blood? Know you not that a churchman is forbidden to shed blood?"

"The blame will rest on thee, my son, if blood be shed," replied the friar with a grim chuckle. "Obey but my simple commands, and your skin is safe. Refuse, and I will slit your windpipe three fingers deep."

"And what dost thou ask?" cried Robin.

"I have left my missal on the farther side," said the curtail friar. "Lend thy aid, I pray thee, to convey me over this rude stream that I may recover it."

This was a bitter pill for Robin to swallow, to be obliged to carry the friar back, but there was no dodging out of it; the knife was at his throat, and the curtal friar had the strength of a bull, as well as the voice of one.

So Robin was compelled to bend his back and take up the enormous weight of the stout friar, who was almost as thick as he was long. It was a long time before Robin Hood forgot that trip across the ford with the curtal friar on his back. It seemed as if no mortal man could be such a frightful load as the friar proved. Robin was bent two-double under it, and every bone in his body seemed to crack under the weight of the friar's burly form. Then Robin knew not the ford as the other did, and he floundered into holes and slid about on slippery stones, and time and again was within an ace of going down headlong into the stream.

But the friar tugged his hair, jerking him up when he appeared about to fall, and pounding him with both heels like one urging a reluctant steed across. At length Robin, panting and gasping, came to the farther bank, and the friar leapt lightly down, for, unwieldy as this churchman looked, he was as nimble as any. But as the curtal friar bounded to earth, Robin Hood caught him by the ankle and tripped him up, and the friar came to earth with such

He floundered into holes and slid about on slippery stones

a bang that all his breath was driven out of him in an odd sound which was something between a squeal and a grunt. Then Robin Hood whipped out his sword and bestrode his fallen opponent, whose helmet had flown three yards away.

"Now friar," he cried, "I think the game has turned my way again. I am still in mind to reach the farther shore. Promise me that you will once more carry me over, or I will cleave your bald noddle in twain!"

"I promise," gasped the curtal friar as soon as he could draw a breath, for he liked not the look of the heavy, shining blade, flashing above his bald crown.

So once again the friar took Robin upon his broad back and strode into the stream.

But in the middle of the stream the friar paused for a moment. Robin thought the holy man had halted to gain fresh foothold, and he laughed to think the friar and not he was floundering over the slippery stones this time. But his laugh was cut short. The curtal friar suddenly gave a tremendous jerk of his huge shoulders and shot Robin Hood head first into the river.

"Now," roared the curtal friar, "choose ye, my fine fellow, whether you will sink or swim!" Saying this, he turned and bustled back to his own side of the stream.

Robin Hood was washed to the other side by the strong current, and he caught hold of a bush of broom whose long branches swept the water. Now he dragged himself to the bank and scrambled ashore. He turned at once to see where his cunning opponent was. There stood the burly friar, laughing all over his fat, red face to see Robin Hood climb to land with the water pouring from every stitch of his clothes.

"I'll soon make thee laugh on the other side of thy mouth, Jack Priest!" shouted Robin Hood, who was hopping mad after this great ducking.

He caught up his bow and let an arrow fly with tremendous force. But it never reached its mark, short as the distance was, and so true the aim; for the friar raised his steel buckler and caught the arrow very deftly in the middle of it; and this he did time after time, until Robin had emptied his quiver and never touched the fat friar once. Then the friar sang, in his great, roaring voice, like a bullfrog in a pond:—

> "Shoot on, shoot on, thou fine fellow,
>   Shoot as thou hast begun,
>   If thou shoot here a summer's day,
>   Thy shaft I will not shun."

"Nay," shouted Robin when his last arrow was sped, "if I cannot reach ye with a grey-goose shaft, friar, I will show ye a trick or two with the broadsword," and with that he drew his sword, swung his buckler up, and leapt into the river. Seeing that the outlaw meant to assail him at close quarters, the curtal friar ran for his steel cap and clapped it on his round, bullet head, and took sword and buckler himself. As he turned to the fray, Robin sprang to the bank and was upon him at the next moment. Then began a fierce and obstinate battle. The great broadswords flashed and glittered as they were swung on high to deliver mighty strokes, and the steel bucklers rang again as the heavy blades were caught and turned aside. Up and down the bank the combatants swung to and fro as they struck at each other, Robin leaping nimbly from side to side to seek some unguarded point of his opponent's defense, and the doughty friar turning and turning and meeting him face to face all the time.

For a full hour swords struck and bucklers rang. They fought on the bank, in the water, waded ashore again, lunged, parried, smote, warded, lashed at each other with might and main. At last they were fain to pause and lean on their swords, so weary were they with the stern battle.

"Beshrew me, friend!" said Robin Hood, "thou art to the full as bold a companion as I expected to find. A boon, a boon, I beg of thee."

"What boon dost thou ask?" said the friar.

"Naught but this," replied the outlaw. "Hold thy sword while I put this horn to my mouth and blow three blasts."

"Blow as thou pleasest," replied the friar, "I care not for thy horn."

Robin Hood smiled, for he knew what his horn would bring. Then he set it to his mouth and blew three mighty calls. The third blast was still echoing among the woods when fifty yeomen, their bows ready bent, came racing over the lea.

"What men are these," cried the friar, "who come so hastily?"

"These are my men, friar," replied Robin Hood, "and they hasten to their master's aid."

"And who art thou?" asked the friar.

"Men call me Robin Hood," quoth Robin, "and these bold archers are my companions in the greenwood."

"What is thy name, bold friar?" said Robin Hood. "Thou art a man after my own heart."

"I am called Friar Tuck," said the curtal friar, "and these seven years have I kept this vale and beaten every man who hath ventured into it against my will."

"Come with us to Merry Sherwood," cried Robin, "we need a priest, that we may not live like heathen in the greenwood. We are outlaws and dare not venture to church in the town. But if you would join us, thou couldst sing us a Mass and read us a service, and 'every Sunday throughout the year a noble shall be thy fee.' "

"I will come," cried Friar Tuck; "my heart leans toward your jolly brotherhood, and I will be your priest and father confessor. I will bring my dogs, and we will range the greenwood with them and hold many a fine stag at bay."

That was how the famous Friar Tuck joined Robin's band in Sherwood and came to have his share in many a song and story.

How Robin Hood Dealt with Sir Richard of the Lea

A FEW weeks after Friar Tuck joined the gay band of
outlaws, Robin Hood, wrapped in deep thought,
was leaning against a tree one hot noontide. Presently
Little John came up to him.

"Master," said the great fellow, "it seems to me you
would be better making a good dinner than standing here
alone. And a dinner is making ready to which a king
might be proud to sit down. One man has brought in
vension, and another birds, until we enjoy such plenty that
a man may have what he wishes."

"True, Little John," said the outlaw, "but for all that I
have no mind to sit down to dinner alone. I wish you
could seize some baron, or bishop, or Norman knight.
Then he should dine with me, and afterward pay the
reckoning."

"That he should, master," laughed the giant; "and
however heavy his purse might be when he came, it
should be no load in his pocket when he went away."

"Take thy good bow in thy hand," said Robin, "and let Much and Will Scarlet wend with thee, and walk up to Watling Street and see whom you may meet."

So away went the three outlaws to keep watch on the great high road. First they saw a rich lady, riding a beautiful palfrey and attended by several servants, pass by. They knew her for the wife of a Norman baron, but the outlaws made no attempt to detain her, for every woman was safe from harm at their hands. Next passed some peasants who were returning from a fair where they had sold their cows.

Little John and his companions were hidden among a thicket of hazels, and heard the men talk of the silver pennies in their pouches.

But they only smiled at each other on hearing the simple husbandmen chatter together and let them pass. Robin Hood never laid a finger on a poor man's store. Then Little John raised his bow and pointed through the bushes. Much and Will looked and saw a knight riding slowly towards them. At first glance he did not seem worth stopping: his dress was in disorder, his armor was rusty, he had a most forlorn and hopeless air about him.

One foot was in the stirrup, the other hung limp and swayed as his palfrey ambled on.

But Little John remembered his orders. Here was a knight, and that knight must dine with Robin Hood this day. So he stepped forward and bent on one knee, and with all courtesy begged the knight to stay.

"Sir Knight," said Little John, "I pray you come to the greenwood. There you will be heartily welcome. My master has been waiting dinner for you this three hours."

"And who is thy master?" asked the sorrowful knight.

"His name is Robin Hood," said Little John.

"I had intended today to dine at Blyth or Doncaster," replied the knight, "but I care not where I eat. Lead on, good fellow. I will come with thee to that good yeoman. I have heard he is a friend to the poor and needy."

When Robin Hood saw his men and the knight coming through the trees he went to him, welcomed the knight to the forest in most courteous fashion, and invited him to be the chief guest at the noble dinner now ready. The knight thanked him, and both of them washed their hands and sat down to the feast. There were steaks and collops of rich venison, roasted swans and pheasant, game pies and pasties made of many small birds, huge flagons of ale, beakers of wine, and flat, round cakes of excellent wheaten bread.

The sorrowful knight was very hungry and ate heartily of this good cheer and, when he had dispatched his meal, he looked a little more cheerful than he had done.

"Gramercy, good Robin Hood," said he, "I have not eaten such a dinner this three weeks. If ever you come my way I shall hope to give you one as good some day."

"Gramercy, good knight," laughed Robin Hood, "your promise were poor payment for my dinner here. Surely you do not expect a mere yeoman to pay for the dinner of a worshipful knight. Wherefore, I must ask you to put down your purse ere you wend."

"That would I do at once," replied the knight, "but I am ashamed to offer you the very little money I have."

"Tell me the truth," said Robin. "How much have you?"

"No more than ten shillings in all the world," replied the knight. "Such money as I have is in the coffer slung at my saddlebow."

"Look to it, Little John," said Robin Hood.

The big fellow took the coffer from the saddlebow, spread his cloak on the ground, and emptied the coffer on to the cloak.

"The knight speaks truth," said Little John, when he had counted the money.

"Come!" said Robin Hood, kindly, to the sorrowful knight, "tell us how you prove to be in such low estate. Your clothes are very thin, your purse is all but empty, and you are very sad. Come, tell us your troubles. Have you been careless of your own interests, or have you spent your money in riot and waste?"

The knight shook his head, and sighed. "I will tell you all, and you shall judge, Robin Hood," said he. "I am in distress this day for a matter of four hundred pounds. And yet two or three years ago such a sum would have been nothing to me. Now I have naught but my wife and children and that poor ten shillings there."

"How lost you your money?" asked Robin.

"It was through my son," replied the knight, and sighed again, "a gallant lad of twenty, of high spirit, and greatly skilled in the play of sword and spear. At a tournament where he was jousting he overthrew a knight of Lancashire, who felt deep anger at his defeat. As my son was coming home, the knight and his squire attacked him in a lonely place, but my son slew them both. Now, the knight had powerful friends, and they were furious against my boy. To save him I have been compelled to spend all my money and to mortgage my land. The Abbot of St. Mary's lent me four hundred pounds upon my land, and today I should repay the money. But, alas! I have it not, and I must lose my home and land and become utterly ruined."

"And your friends?" said Robin. "Have they not come forward to your aid?"

"Friends!" said the knight, bitterly. "No man had more friends, as it seemed, than I in the days of my wealth. Now all fly from me, and take no more heed of me than if they had never seen me in their lives before."

"'Tis the way of the world, Sir Knight," said Robin Hood, and looked round on his comrades, whose faces were full of sorrow for the poor knight. All of them knew the rich Abbot of St. Mary's and knew well that land in his clutch was not easily released.

Robin beckoned to Little John and whispered in his lieutenant's ear, and Little John went away. In a short time the latter came back with a heavy bag, which clinked as he set it down.

"There are your four hundred pounds, Sir Knight!" said Robin Hood, "Never say there is no pity in the world. If you have not found it among your friends and the proud churchman who grasps at your land, you have found it among the outlaws of the forest. Count out the money, Little John!"

The money was counted, and the bag was found to hold

exactly the four hundred pounds for want of which the knight was so sad.

As for the knight himself, he was utterly dumb with surprise and gratitude. He could only stare at the bag and then at Robin Hood and then turn his eyes once more on the money in such wonder that he had no words to express.

When at last he found his voice, he poured out a thousand thanks and blessings on the men who had saved his home and the land on which he supported his family.

"His clothes are very thin, master," whispered Little John, "give him a good suit, I pray thee."

So from the well filled storehouse bales of cloth were rolled out, and Little John measured off a length of cloth. And right good measure it was, for Little John used his six-foot bow stave for a yard measure, and so gave double allowance. And they gave the knight a fresh horse, and a new saddle, and many other things, until he was as gallant and gay as before he had been shabby and sad.

When he was ready to depart, he said to Robin, "I am Sir Richard of the Lea, and I thank you from the bottom of my heart for this most generous loan. Now, tell me when shall I return it, if my affairs should prosper?"

"Meet me twelve months from today in this place," replied Robin, "and we will talk of the matter again."

So Sir Richard went his way, the happiest man in England.

The Wedding of Alan-a-Dale ∽

Aᴛᴛᴇʀ Robin Hood had seen Sir Richard of the Lea
started on his way, he took his bow and rambled
through the forest. As he stood in shelter of a bush beside
a forest road that led from one small town to another, he
heard a merry voice singing a merry song, and the rich
deep notes of a harp, very skilfully played, blended with
the strong sweet voice of the singer.

"By my faith," quoth the captain of the outlaws to himself, "this is a jolly blade. If his purse rings as golden as
his voice he should be a bird worth plucking."

He stood quite still, and presently the singer came into
sight.

"A strolling minstrel," murmured Robin to himself once
more; "gay enough to look at, but I'll warrant you nothing
at all in his purse."

The newcomer was a handsome young man, with flow-
ing yellow locks, on which a gay bonnet, with a cock's

feather in it, was perched. He was clad in a suit of scarlet, and as he walked he ran his fingers over the strings of his harp and chanted like a lark on a bright May morning.

Robin Hood was so pleased with the merry carol of the light-hearted young fellow that he let him pass scot free. "Shame were it to harass one who sings so joyously in the greenwood," thought Robin. "He shall go free for me," and he stood behind the bush, without moving, and listened until the last sweet note, softened by distance, died away among the trees.

Robin looked eastward and saw that the shades of evening were closing over the distant woodlands.

"The night is near," said he; "No one will pass again this day," and he returned to the meeting place, where a great fire was blazing in the quiet glade, and the yeomen sat about it laughing and talking with each other.

As it happened, the very next morning, Robin Hood, followed by Little John and Much the Miller's Son, went to watch the same road again.

After a little time had passed, Robin Hood espied the same young harper, but what a wonderful change had taken place in his appearance! His head now drooped, and with each step he sighed heavily.

"What's wrong now?" said Robin Hood to Little John. "I saw this fellow last night, and a gayer young spark you never beheld. He made the woods ring with his merry song, and now he looks like one who goes to a funeral. Fetch him to me. I would know the reason of this sudden change."

So Little John and Much stepped forth and bade the

*As he walked he ran his fingers over the strings
of his harp and chanted like a lark*

ministrel stand. But the ministrel was no coward. He
bent his bow and made ready to beat them off if they
should attack him.

"Nay," said Little John, "there is no need to shoot. Un-
bend your bow. We mean you no harm, but our master
wishes to speak with you. Look! he stands under the
greenwood tree."

So they brought the minstrel before Robin Hood, and
the latter greeted him most courteously, and said, "Oh,
hast thou any money to spare for my merry men and me?"

"Little enough money have I," replied the sad minstrel;
"but five shillings in all and this ring."

Robin took the ring, and looked at it.

"Why, 'tis a wedding ring," he said.

"Ay, truly," replied the minstrel, "and I have kept it for
seven years, and I thought to have used it today. But the
maid has been taken from me, and anyone may have yon
ring now. 'Tis of no use to me."

"Tell me all about it," said Robin. "Here is a change,
indeed! Last night you were as gay as a bird on a bough,
and now you are mournful and sad."

"What!" cried the minstrel, "you saw me last night?
Ay, truly, I was gay then. I thought I was about to wed
the fairest lass in all the North Countree, but today my
heart is broken. She is to be taken from me and given to
a rich old knight."

"She has changed her mind very suddenly," said Robin
Hood.

"Nay!" cried the minstrel, "she has not changed her
mind at all. She loves me as truly as ever she did. But
her friends will have nothing to say to me because I have

neither land nor riches. They will force her to marry the
old knight this very day," and he sighed again, as if his
heart would break.

"What is thy name?" asked Robin Hood.

"My name is Alan-a-Dale," said the man.

"Well, Alan-a-Dale, I am Robin Hood," said the famous
outlaw, "and if I help you and your true love what will
you give me?"

"Money I have none," quoth Alan-a-Dale, "but if thou
wilt help me I will swear ever to be thy faithful servant."

"Even so," said Robin, "a good and true man to serve
me is more to my liking any day than a purse of gold.
Now, where is this wedding to take place?"

"At the church beyond the wood," replied Alan-a-Dale;
"'tis but five miles from here."

"I know it well," replied the leader, "and Robin Hood
will be there."

He thought for a moment, then said to Alan-a-Dale,
"Give me your harp."

The minstrel handed it over, and Robin stripped himself
of all his weapons and gave them to Little John. Then he
whispered a number of orders into the ear of his lieutenant and hastened away.

When Robin came to the church he marched up the
churchyard path, plucking at the strings of his harp, and
fetching out deep ringing notes. This drew a stout figure,
in fine robes, to the door of the church. It was the bishop
himself, who was going to perform the marriage ceremony, for he and the knight were old friends and had been
boys together.

"I thought by the sound of the harp that the wedding

guests were coming," said the bishop. "What doest thou here, and who art thou?"

Robin took off his cap, and bent low before the bishop.

"Reverend father," he said, "I am a wandering harper, and there be those who say I am the best in all the North Countree. I heard of this wedding and hasted hither to make music on this happy day."

"Oh, welcome, bold harper!" said the bishop; "'tis the music I love best of all. Come, strike thy harp, and let me judge of thy gifts."

"Nay, not so, Lord Bishop," replied Robin, who, to tell the truth, could only twang the strings a little; "where I was brought up 'twould be thought to bring ill-luck to begin the music before the bridal procession appears."

"Well, prepare thyself!" said the bishop, "for here they come now."

At that moment an old, solemn, but wealthy knight appeared at the door of the church followed by a beautiful young girl.

The church was filled with people who had come to see the bridal, and when they saw the bride and bridegroom they looked at each other and began to murmur what a shame it was to wed this pretty young lass to the withered old fellow. The knight was not only withered and spindle-shanked, but he had only one eye and a great hump on his left shoulder; while the maid was as pretty as a rosy dawn and looked as sweet as newblown May.

But in the presence of the bishop in his robes and the wealthy old knight, no one there dared to speak his mind save Robin Hood.

"Well!" cried Robin, "many a bridal pair have I seen, but never a worse-matched couple than this."

"Silence, fellow!" said the bishop. "The bride is in the church, and the marriage goes on at once."

"You speak truth, my Lord Bishop," answered Robin, boldly, "the bride is in the church, and for all that has yet come and gone she shall choose her own dear."

"Prate not, fellow!" cried the bishop, angrily, "but strike up your music as the bride goes to the altar."

"Ay, that will I," laughed Robin, "but I must confess one thing to you, I love the horn better than the harp." And, saying this, Robin pulled his bugle horn from under his cloak.

He put the horn to his lips and blew three shrill blasts. In an instant, it seemed, twenty-four bowmen came running over the lea, and at their head as they entered the churchyard was Alan-a-Dale.

What an uproar and confusion there was when the four-and-twenty archers burst in at the church door! The bishop was purple with rage, and the old knight shook with rage and fear mingled, for he saw the bride make one rush to the side of Alan-a-Dale, and saw, too, that the minstrel had a strong band of friends. Then all eyes were turned on the mysterious harper whose bugle call had brought about this strange turn of affairs.

Robin lifted his hand, and for a moment there was silence in the church, for all wished to hear what he had to say.

"Alan-a-Dale," said the outlaw, "this maid is thy true love, as I hear say."

"She is, master," cried Alan-a-Dale.

"Then," went on Robin, "if she is willing to wed thee, the wedding shall go on, with a change of swains."

"Who art thou," roared the bishop, "to come hither in the guise of a harping knave and give orders like a king?"

"A true word, bishop," replied the outlaw, quietly; "king am I among these stout bowmen, and men call me Robin Hood."

Robin Hood! The sound of that famous name struck everyone dumb with surprise. The people in the church stared at the great outlaw with all their eyes, and the bishop and the knight were silent from fear.

"Now, bishop," went on Robin, "I bid you marry these young folk, who have plighted their troth."

"That I will not!" cried the bishop angrily; "for one thing they have not been asked in church, and that must be done three times, by the law of the land, as thou well knowest, Robin Hood."

"True, bishop," replied the outlaw; "it must be done, and it shall be done at once. Cry them three times, at once, Lord Bishop!"

"If you will not," calmly replied Robin, "I must e'en make a bishop of mine own. Pluck off his gown!" He pointed to the bishop, and the great man's gown was plucked off at once by two stout bowmen.

" 'Tis the cowl that makes the monk and the cope that makes the bishop," quoth Robin Hood, laughingly. "Now, Little John, don the bishop's robe at once, and take his place."

Little John grinned, and put the bishop's robe on. He looked so queer in it that everyone began to laugh.

"Now, up with thee, and cry this young couple in church the three times needed!" said his master, and Little John went into the choir. All the lookers-on shouted with laughter when they saw Little John in the bishop's robe and the bishop's place, crying the names of the young people in church, for he did it so comically and cut such an odd figure in his churchman's dress.

Little John took his task very earnestly and, for fear three times should not be enough, he went on and on until he had cried them seven times, amid great merriment. Then Robin called on him to come down, and turned to the bishop.

"Now, Lord Bishop!" he said; "choose ye and choose quickly. Will ye marry these true lovers or come to the greenwood with me as a prisoner?"

The bishop shook in his shoes at the idea of being carried off to Sherwood as a captive and quickly agreed to perform the marriage. When it came to the question, "Who gives this maid?" Robin Hood cried out:

> "That do I.
> And he that takes her from Alan-a-Dale,
> Full dearly he shall her buy."

So Alan-a-Dale and his true lover were married by the bishop who did not wish to do so, and in face of the knight who trembled with rage to see his bride taken before his very eyes; but none durst lift a finger against the mighty outlaw and his band of chosen archers.

How Robin Hood Won   ℚ
the Sheriff's Prize

After the wedding of Alan-a-Dale, the bishop posted off to Nottingham to make complaint to the sheriff against Robin Hood.

"Here you are, placed in authority by our noble king to keep order!" fumed the angry bishop, "and you permit that sturdy outlaw Robin Hood to rule the country as if he himself were king!" And altogether the bishop rated the sheriff in such a fashion that the latter became very uneasy, lest the matter should be brought before the king.

"If complaint is to be made to the king, and it looks very likely," said the sheriff to himself, "I had better go to the king myself, and explain what a difficult fellow to deal with is this Robin Hood."

So the sheriff posted off to London and told the king that he could do nothing with Robin Hood, for the outlaws were so strong and bold and knew every corner of the forest so well that his men could not catch them.

"What can I do?" cried the king. "Are you not sheriff, in order to deal with these matters? You have all the power of the law behind you to punish those who injure you. If you cannot meet the rogues with strength, bethink yourself of some way of drawing them into your power in other fashion. In any case, get you gone, and let me hear that you have put them down, or it will be the worse for you."

Seeing that the king was angry, the sheriff went hastily from his presence and took the road homeward. Day after day, as he rode north towards Nottingham, did the sheriff cudgel his brains for a plot by which he could hoodwink the outlaws, and at last he smote his thigh and laughed aloud.

"I have it," he said, to the new Chief Forester, who rode beside him. "I have it. I will draw those sturdy rogues into Nottingham town, as surely as the smell of roast meat draws a hungry dog."

"And how will you do it?" asked the Chief Forester.

"In this way," replied the sheriff. "Thou knowest that Robin Hood and the rascals who follow him brag and boast that they are the best archers of all that ever shot at butt or deer. Now I will proclaim a great shooting match to be held at Nottingham, and the chief prize shall be an arrow with golden feathers and silver shaft. And he who wins that arrow shall also be hailed as the greatest archer of the land."

"I see, I see!" laughed the Chief Forester; "a proper bait to draw those bragging rogues to your hand."

"A certain bait!" cried the sheriff; "it will prove that,

mark my words. For they will never submit to see that
title won without some of them making a trial to win it,
and then when they come into the town I will have men
who know them on the watch ready to seize them."

So the sheriff went home; and soon the day of the great
shooting match was proclaimed, and the news spread
fast. Lobb the cobbler carried the news to Sherwood and
told the outlaws that famous archers from all the country
round were coming to Nottingham to contest for the handsome prize and the famous title.

"And the winner is to be proclaimed as the best bowman of the land?" said Robin.

"Yes, master!" replied Lobb; "and it is said that all the
best archers of the shires will try for the prize."

"Why," said Robin, "I think we count ourselves as good
shots as any, and 'twere foul shame to let the title be
seized, and we make no effort to gain it."

"Have a care, master!" said one of his followers, a stout
bowman called David of Doncaster; "I have heard that
the match is but a trick to draw us into the town and so
beguile us."

"That is coward's talk," said Robin Hood; "trick or no
trick, I'll be there."

"Yes, we'll go," said Little John, "and I have a plan in
my head which will take us there in safety. We'll leave at
home our cloaks and doublets of Lincoln green, and dress
ourselves like countryfolk going to the match. Then the
sheriff's men will not know us.

"One of us will wear white, another red, another yellow,
another blue, and so disguised we'll go to the contest
whatever happens."

"Good, good!" cried the leader; "we will follow thy plan, Little John."

So, on the day of the great shooting match, Robin Hood and his best archers set out for Nottingham. They did not march in a company, for that would have drawn attention to them, but in twos and threes scattered through the great throng of countryfolk going to witness the day's sport. Not one man wore his dress of Lincoln green, but Little John wore a blue jacket and hood, Much the Miller's Son was in brown, Will Scarlet in white, Will Stutely in yellow, and marching alone was a man in a ragged red coat and hood, and that was Robin Hood himself. When Robin came to the gate of the town he marched straight in, his bow over his shoulder. Beside the gate stood some of the sheriff's men who knew the outlaws. They were watching carefully to see if they could recognize their enemies amid the crowd which trooped into the place.

When the fellow in the tattered red coat strode through the gate they glanced at him, but never dreamed it was their archenemy. Robin had a patch over his left eye, and he had let his beard grow rough and ragged for the occasion, and he plodded along in stupid fashion.

"Look at yon fellow in red," laughed a forester. "I verily believe every ragged rascal within a hundred miles is tramping hither this day in hope of gaining the golden arrow."

Robin heard these words, but he only laughed to himself and pushed forward to the place where the butts were set up for the match. Here sat the sheriff on horseback, surrounded by a strong guard of his men, and, as the competitors gathered in a great crowd, the sheriff peered and pried on every hand for some sign of the outlaws whom he hated. But, though his wily eyes searched the throng through and through, he could not see a single man who had the look of one of Robin Hood's band.

Presently the shooting began, and soon it was seen that one of the finest bowmen there was a famous archer called William of York. But, though William shot very finely, yet he could not get ahead of a band of country fellows in jackets of different colors.

The people were delighted to see these poorly dressed men holding their own with the famous archer, and shouted their joy.

One man cried, "Well done, Blue Jacket!" another shouted, "Brown is the best!" A third cried "Bravo! Yellow Coat!" and a fourth declared "There is no one who can compare with the man in red!" The man in red was, of course, Robin Hood who was in the lead at every shot.

In the end the match lay between William of York and the archer in the ragged red jacket. A fresh butt was set up at a much greater distance than any had yet been placed, and the two archers took their places ready to shoot. They were to loose three shafts each, and many good bowmen shook their heads when they saw how distant was the butt from the shooting point.

"'Twere a feat to reach the butt at that distance," they said, "without getting anywhere near the center"; and the crowd waited in silence to see the champions finish the contest. Behind the two competitors sat the sheriff and some of his friends on their horses. "We have seen some rare shooting already," said one of the sheriff's friends. "We could scarce have seen better if Robin Hood and his men had come to the match."

"Ay," quoth the sheriff, scratching his head. "I thought he would be here, but with all his boldness he did not dare."

Almost at the nose of the sheriff's horse stood the archer in the red coat, leaning awkwardly on his bow, his mouth open and in a rustic gape, and his one eye staring at the distant butt. But lumpish and clownish as Robin made himself look, he had hard work to keep himself in hand when he heard the sheriff's jeer. He longed to turn and beard the sheriff to his face, but it was too dangerous at that moment, and he kept quite still, but said to himself, "'Ere long thou shalt see, proud sheriff, that here is Robin Hood."

William of York shot first, and shot very slowly and very well. He put two arrows in the white spot in the center of the target, and one a little outside.

"Give up, Red Jacket!" shouted William's friends. "Thou canst not surpass that shooting. Give up, and yield the prize!"

But Red Jacket only grinned and shook his head.

"I'll e'en try my luck," he growled aloud in a broad North-Countree accent, and to himself he said, "Now, Robin, do thy best for the honor of Merry Sherwood."

So Red Jacket took three shafts in hand and discharged them so fast that the second was in the air before the first had reached the target, and so with the third. But, to the wonder and delight of the spectators, the first and second arrows struck out from the center of the target the arrows which William of York had placed there, and the third arrow lighted in the exact center of the white spot.

"Red Jacket! Red Jacket!" roared the multitude. "He is the very prince of archers. Red Jacket has won the prize."

So brave Robin Hood won the silver arrow with the golden feathers.

When the arrow was presented, the sheriff said to Red Jacket, "Prithee, good fellow, join my band of foresters. I would like to see so stout a bowman as thou art in my service.

But Robin shook his head, and said he must go home to his own master. Then the sheriff thought that he was the serf of some lord who had obtained permission to come to the match, and pressed him no further.

As the outlaws had come into the town, so they went out, in twos and threes, and returned every one in safety to the greenwood. There they laughed and jested merrily over the day's sport, and admired the golden arrow—all, that is, but the winner himself, who seemed rather vexed.

"You seem sad, master!" cried Little John, "and you should be the merriest of all since you have won the arrow and tricked the sheriff."

"Ay, that's just where it is," replied Robin Hood. "The sheriff knows not how well we have caught him in his own trap. I like it not that he should not know that I carried off his arrow."

"Why, that is easily done," cried Little John. "I advised

you before, and I will advise you again. Write a letter to
him and I'll deliver it."

"You, Little John!" said Robin. "Nay. I'll not have you
venture back into that town."

"I've a better plan than that," said Little John, laughing
gaily, "I'll stick it on the head of an arrow and shoot it into
the sheriff's window!"

This capital plan was at once carried out. The letter
was written, and back went Little John, without changing
his blue jacket, to the town. Near the wall was a lofty
building, the house of the sheriff, and Little John marked
that a window of the great hall was standing open; the
shutter which closed it at night was hanging back. The
giant had already fixed the letter to the head of a shaft,
and now he drew his bow, shot the arrow clean through
the window, and trotted back to the forest.

As it happened the sheriff had just sat down to supper
after a busy day, and he was raising a brimming horn of
ale to his lips as the shaft hummed in at the window and
struck into the table before him and stood there quivering.

"What is this?" he cried. "An arrow shot into my hall?
What does it mean?"

"There is a billet at the head!" cried a servant. "It is a
message."

"Unroll the paper from the shaft and give it to me,"
commanded the sheriff. This was done, and the paper
was handed to the great man. He ran his eyes over it,
still holding the horn of ale in the other hand, and all the
company looked eagerly to see what this strange affair
meant. To their surprise, the sheriff dashed down his

horn of ale on the table with such force that the horn split
and the ale flew in streams.

"What is it? What is it?" cried half-a-dozen voices. "Is
it ill news?"

"Ay," roared the sheriff, trembling with rage, "ill news
indeed! I had that arch rogue and strong thief at my very
side today and he hath slipped through my fingers. Who,
think ye, that Red Jacket was? None other than that rascal Robin Hood himself!"

Every face was turned to the sheriff in wonder. That
the famous Robin Hood! The rude, clownish fellow in
the red jacket? Yet it must have been, for he had shot in
so marvelous a fashion.

"By my faith, sheriff," said one of his friends, "but we
ought to have known it. Such archery did I never see in
all my life before! None but Robin Hood could bend
such a bow."

But the sheriff took no heed of his friend's words. He
was in such a rage that he knew not what to do. As the
old ballad says:

> "The sheriff that letter had,
>   Which when he read, he scratched his head,
>   And raved like one that's mad."

"I'll lay plans for the knave no longer," roared the sheriff. "I'll take him by the strong hand. Not another day
will I live before I have marched upon the rogue. Trust
me, I'll dust his red jacket for him and then hang him on
the highest gallows ever raised in the good town of Nottingham."

*The shaft hummed in at the window and struck
into the table before him*

Guy of Gisborne ∿
Seeks Robin Hood

THE next day the sheriff gathered a strong force of soldiers and archers to march into Sherwood to seek the outlaws. But the first thing of all that he did was to set up a notice proclaiming that three hundred pounds would be given for the head of Robin Hood.

Now among the sheriff's friends there was a knight whose name was Guy of Gisborne. Guy was a fine swordsman, but a man of wild and evil life. He had brought himself deeply into debt and was ready to do anything to gain money.

When he heard of this great reward he resolved to try to win it, and he thought he had a good chance. He knew the forest well and believed he could find the part which Robin Hood haunted. So he laid his plans with the sheriff and then went ahead by himself in disguise.

"It is of no use for a strong force to march into the

forest in the first place," said Guy to the sheriff, "for the
outlaws can easily avoid them. I will go in advance as a
spy to seek out the hiding-place of Robin Hood." So Guy
of Gisborne set off to the forest.

Now it happened that morning that Robin Hood had
been aroused from his woodland couch by the loud song
of a thrush.

"By my faith, I've had an odd dream this night," said
Robin, rubbing his eyes. "I thought I was fighting with
two stout fellows, and they beat me and took my bow
from me."

Little John laughed. "Dreams are nothing, master," he
said. "They are of no more weight than the wind."

"Nevertheless, we will go through the greenwood this
day," said Robin, "and haply we may meet the stout yeoman of whom I dreamed."

After breakfast Robin Hood and Little John set off into
the forest together. At the same time Will Scarlet and
two bowmen of the band went away in another direction.
"We will beat up some game," said Will, "and a fat buck
or two will not come amiss. The larder hath a lean look
at present."

So the two parties went their way and, after a time,
Robin and Little John entered a glade of great oaks. Almost at once they saw a very strange figure at the other
end of the glade.

"Is it man or beast?" cried Little John in wonder, "or is
it an evil fiend, But stand you still, master. I will soon
find out."

Robin at once bade his follower not to go, declaring that he would undertake the adventure himself. Little John was somewhat offended, and, after a few sharp words had passed, he swung away in a huff and left Robin to himself.

"I will seek Scarlet and his companions," said Little John. "I know the glade which they mean to beat for game."

So away went Little John through the forest and came to the glade where he expected to find his friends. He saw them, indeed, but it was a heavy sight. The three yeomen were flying along the glade as fast as they could set foot to ground, and there behind them came the proud sheriff and seven score of his bowmen and spearmen in full pursuit. This was the terrible game which had been beaten up by the unlucky outlaws.

Presently a great shower of shafts whistled after the fugitives. Little John gave a great moan as he saw two of his friends pitch headlong on their faces, each man with three arrows through his body. But Scarlet was yet untouched, and he fled on faster and faster still, as the sheriff roared, "Take him, too, my lads! Dead or alive, seize the rogue!"

But Scarlet was so swift of foot that it was plain he would escape save for one man. The latter was far ahead of the rest of the sheriff's band, and he could run with wonderful swiftness; he was rapidly coming up with Will Scarlet.

"'Tis William-a-Trent!" muttered Little John, for he knew the speedy runner well. "He must not close with Scarlet, or Will is sure to be taken."

So Little John bent his bow and loosed an arrow straight at William-a-Trent, and the runner let out a great cry and went to earth with the arrow through his heart. As the old ballad says:—

"It had been better if William-a-Trent
  To have been abed with sorrow,
Than to be that day in the greensward glade
  To meet with Little John's arrow."

Will Scarlet ran on and disappeared among the trees, and Little John gave a cry of vexation. For his bow, his yew bow, had failed him. It had snapped across under the strain of the last arrow and was now worthless.

"Bad luck to ye, most worthless branch that ever grew on a tree!" groaned Little John and tried to fly also, for he could fight no longer. But there burst through the bushes five or six spearmen and bid him stand. It was a scouting party of the sheriff's troops hastening back to their fellows on hearing the uproar of the pursuit.

Little John made a great leap for freedom, and would have burst away had not a fellow thrust out the tough ashen shaft of his spear and tripped up the mighty outlaw. Down sprawled Little John, and at the next instant the spearmen were all over him, clutching at arm and leg and body, and striving to hold him down. Five they were to one, but their numbers would not have brought them victory had not more help speedily arrived. Twice the giant fought his way to his feet with the spearmen hanging to him like dogs upon a lion, and twice they dragged him down. Then he worked one huge fist free, and two tremendous blows laid two assailants senseless at his feet.

But at that moment up raced a dozen or more of the sheriff's men and hurled themselves upon him. To these tremendous odds even Little John was forced to succumb, and soon he was bound hand and foot, and lay helpless and at their mercy.

Up came the sheriff and laughed a cruel laugh. "One for the gallows, at any rate," he said, "and a big one, too. Up with him, lads, and bind him fast to that tree. There he will be safe until we have some others to hang beside him. As for thee, thou false knave," went on the sheriff to his prisoner, "thou shalt be drawn by dale and down and hanged high on a hill."

But, though death stared him in the face, Little John was no craven. He laughed and looked the sheriff boldly in the eye. "If it be the will of Heaven," cried Little John, "thou shalt fail of thy purpose yet, proud sheriff, for all that's come and gone."

But now we must leave Little John, a helpless prisoner in the hands of his cruel enemies, while we see how his master had been faring.

Robin Hood went up the glade, and, as he advanced towards the strange figure, he soon made out that it was a tall, strong man leaning against a tree and wrapped in the oddest mantle that Robin had ever seen. For it was no more nor less than a capull hide, the dried skin of a horse upon which the head, tail, and mane had been left. The stranger's face looked out under the horse's head, the mane flowed over his shoulders, and the tail dangled between his legs. A queerer figure Robin had never seen before. But the fellow seemed a man of his hands, for he bore a strong bow, and a sword and dagger hung at his side.

"Good morning, good fellow," said Robin. "I see you have a stout bow of your own there, and I should judge you to be a good archer."

"'Tis a strong bow," replied the other; "but I am not out after deer today. I have lost my way in this thick wood. Who art thou?"

"I am a yeoman of Locksley," replied Robin. "'Tis a village on the other side of the forest."

"And do you know the forest ways?"

"I dare swear that none knows them better," replied Robin. "I will be your guide if you wish."

"Well, hark ye, good yeoman," said the stranger. "I am in search of Robin Hood. Take me to the haunts of that proud outlaw, for I would rather meet with him than have paid into my hand forty pound good money down."

Robin looked at him more closely and knew him. "It is Sir Guy of Gisborne," said Robin to himself. "He hath ever had the name of a traitor and an ill-liver. Oh, ho! I see why he had rather meet me than have forty pound. Belike, if he could cut me off by treachery, my head would be worth much more than forty pounds to him."

"Why," said Robin aloud, "if you are in such anxiety to see Robin Hood, I daresay I could guide you to a place where he can be met with. But I am not one who would be guide to a man who can carry a bow but mayhap cannot draw it."

"Can I not?" cried Guy of Gisborne. "Set up thy mark, fellow, and I will soon show thee whether I can shoot or no."

This was what Robin was aiming at, for he met no stranger in the greenwood but he ever loved to have a bout of archery with him.

Well, a mark was set up, and soon the stranger found that he was no match at all for the yeoman of Locksley.

"A blessing upon thy heart, yeoman!" cried Sir Guy, clapping Robin on the shoulder. "Thy shooting is beyond common. Were thy heart as good as thy hand, thou wert a stouter fellow than Robin Hood himself. What is thy name? I would fain know more of thee."

"By my faith," cried Robin, "that will I not do till thou hast told me thine." Robin thought the stranger would give a false name, but he did not.

"I live near the hills and valleys," quoth the stranger, "and when I am called by my right name I'm Guy of Gisborne."

"Ay, ay," said Robin Hood. "I thought as much. I knew that no peasant wrapped in a horse hide would carry a knight's bugle horn under his cloak."

"True, yeoman," laughed Sir Guy, "and when I have seized the rogue, Robin Hood, I have but to sound this horn, and my friend, the sheriff, who is in the forest, will know that I have won the day, and the great reward is mine."

The outlaw's face flushed, and his eyes shone.

"Then seize him, Sir Guy of Gisborne," cried Robin, "for here he stands. I am Robin Hood!"

Sir Guy must have been suspecting something of this and making himself ready, for scarce were the words out of Robin Hood's mouth, and ere the outlaw had made a single movement towards his weapons, Guy of Gisborne whipped out his dagger and struck at Robin's heart. Nothing but Robin's matchless dexterity saved him. He sprang aside with wonderful quickness, and the keen blade flashed within an inch of his breast.

"A foul stroke, Sir Knight!" cried Robin, "but a worthy stroke, indeed, for a traitor as thou art. To strike at a man who had not offered to touch his weapon! But now we will try it hand to hand."

Robin Hood had drawn his good broad-sword, and Sir Guy of Gisborne was already hilt in hand. Without word or sound the treacherous knight attacked Robin Hood with the utmost fury and with the greatest confidence of an easy victory. He was no match for Robin with the bow, but he did not dream that a yeoman could stand two minutes before his sword. He was one of the best swords-men in the shire, and had been long trained in the use of this knightly weapon.

But two minutes passed, and five, and ten, and Sir Guy of Gisborne began to see that here would be no easy victory. Robin had been content to stand on the defense at first, for the knight's attack was so furious that the yeoman had all his work cut out to keep his head and body safe from that whistling blade. But soon the fury of attack failed, for Sir Guy could not keep up such a rain of blows, and, more than that, he knew too much of sword play to waste all his strength while his opponent remained almost fresh. But still the swords clashed together briskly, and the fight went savagely on until Robin tripped over a root of the oak beneath which they fought and stumbled and fell.

Then Sir Guy showed to the full how brutal and un-knightly was his nature. A true knight would have held his sword, in courtesy, and allowed his opponent to rise, but Guy of Gisborne leapt forward and struck a fierce blow at the prostrate man. Luckily, in his eagerness, he struck a little too soon, and Robin did not receive the full force of the stroke, yet was he wounded.

Up went Sir Guy's sword to deal a last murderous blow when Robin cried, "Ah! by our Lady, it was never a man's destiny to die before his day."

And with that, he sprang like a wildcat straight at Guy of Gisborne's throat, leapt inside the knight's guard with his sword shortened, then drove the bright blade home through Guy of Gisborne's body. So he who already thought himself to be the victor, became in that instant the vanquished and the slain.

For a few moments Robin Hood stood looking down on the body of his prostrate foe, then the smart of his wound recalled him to his own needs. He stripped off his doublet and examined the injury. It was more painful than serious, a mere flesh wound, and he bound it up as well as he could and took no more heed of it, for his mind was full of fear for the safety of his men.

"The sheriff with a strong band is in the forest," thought Robin. "Well, those tidings must be conveyed to my stout lads at once, lest some roving parties fall into the hands of

Robin Hood stood looking down on the body of
his prostrate foe

that old hangman. Ah! and I must look out for myself,
too."

Robin thought for a moment, then stripped off his doublet again and seized the capull hide of Sir Guy. In two
minutes he had disguised himself so that he had the very
look of Guy of Gisborne. "Now the sheriff's men will not
stop me if I meet a band of them," thought he. "They
will take me for Guy of Gisborne in search of Robin
Hood." And away he went, carrying with him the bow
and arrows and bugle of the fallen man.

Robin was marching along the side of a hill when he
heard in the distance shouts and cries, a confused uproar
of voices; it was the sheriff and his men in pursuit of Will
Scarlet. Robin ran to the top of the hill and looked out.
From this point of vantage he saw everything: there was
Will flying in the distance, and there was a tall man being
bound to a tree trunk.

Just at that moment Robin saw a spearman lift his spear
as if he were about to drive it through Little John's body.
It was done in cruel sport to try to make the prisoner
change color, but Robin thought it was meant for a stroke
of death. To draw the attention of the captors from their
captive, he raised the horn of Sir Guy and blew a loud
blast. His plan succeeded. Robin saw that all heads were
turned at once toward the hill on which he stood.

The sheriff heard the note and clapped his hands for
joy. "There is Sir Guy's horn!" he cried. "It means the
best of tidings, for he said he would never blow his horn
unless he had slain Robin Hood. And there he comes
himself, clad in the capull hide."

The sheriff hastened to meet the strange figure, whose

face was hidden under the head of the horse, and whose
body was covered by the great skin and the dangling,
waving mane and tail.

"What cheer—what cheer, Sir Guy?" cried the sheriff as
they met. "Did you meet Robin Hood?"

"Ay, ay, Sir Sheriff," returned the man in the capull
hide. "Guy of Gisborne and Robin Hood met sure enough.
And if you will but go to a great oak two miles south of
this, you will find one wrapped in Robin Hood's mantle,
dead, across the roots of the tree."

"Good news—brave news!" cried the sheriff, clapping
his hands. "Then this day will rid the forest of the two
knaves whom most I feared. For if thou hast slain the
master, I have seized the man. See, yonder great fellow
tied to a tree is none other than Little John himself."

"Little John," said the man in the capull hide; "is that
Little John?"

"Aye, it is," chuckled the sheriff. "Oh, happy day!
'Twill be the destruction of the band. Master and man
gone at a stroke; the outlaws will fly from the forest, I
warrant ye. But come, Sir Guy, thou wilt ask the reward
of me, I trow?"

"Ay, Sir Sheriff," said the man in the capull hide. "I
will ask a reward of thee, and it is this: I have slain the
master; let me slay the man."

"But what of the four hundred pounds I offered?"
gasped the sheriff.

"I want no penny of it," was the reply.

For a moment the sheriff stared in purest wonder, then
a cunning twinkle came into his eye.

"Assuredly Sir Guy has gone mad, or is possessed," he

thought. "I will grant him this wild freak and pocket the reward myself," for the sheriff loved only one thing beside himself, and that was his great treasure chest. So he made haste to grant the request.

Then the man in the capull hide strode forward and stood in front of the prisoner. "He is a stout knave," said the man in the capull hide, and Little John could not help giving a slight start, for he knew that voice. Then the head of the capull hide was raised as if Guy of Gisborne wished to have a good look at the famous Little John, and the prisoner stared calmly into a well-known face, and murmured to himself, "I see it is the will of Heaven that I should go free this day."

"I slew the master with the sword," said the man in the capull hide, "but to the man I will take a knife," and he drew out a long Irish knife with a broad, keen blade.

The sheriff and his men crowded closely around the man whom they thought to be Sir Guy, but he waved them all back.

"Stand back—stand back!" he said. "If a man is about to die, I will go forward alone to hear his last words and wishes."

So he went forward alone with the great knife in his hand. And when he came to the side of the prisoner the knife flashed across the bonds, and the prisoner was free. Then Robin gave Sir Guy's bow and arrows into the hand of Little John and drew his own from under the hide, and before the sheriff and his men could move a finger the outlaws had shaft on string and were loosing their arrows among them. And Little John's mightly voice burst forth,

"A Hood! A Hood! Robin Hood!" And the head of the capull hide was thrown back, and a face was seen that was not the face of Guy of Gisborne, and one of the sheriff's men cried, "'Tis Robin Hood himself! An ambush! An ambush! Fly, comrades, we are undone!" For in his fear he thought the whole of the outlaw band was upon them, and his fellows thought so, too, and before the two mighty archers the great crowd of bowmen and spearmen turned and fled. And where was their master, the sheriff? Why, spurring his horse to full gallop over the forest turf.

For, when he saw that Little John had possession of Guy of Gisborne's bow and arrows, he fled followed by his men at full speed towards his home in Nottingham. But he did not escape altogether scot-free. For Little John sent a broad arrow humming after him. And the arrow took him through the right shoulder, so that the sheriff fled back to Nottingham, groaning in pain and ruing the day that ever he started forth to seize Robin Hood.

Robin Hood Meets a Tanner

I N NOTTINGHAM town there was not the least doubt about their champion player at quarterstaff. If ever a stranger came there and challenged the players to a bout, the townsmen grinned and sent for Arthur-a-Bland. Arthur at once came out of his tanpit with the best will in the world, took his great staff, and was ready for the bout. After it, the stranger went away with sore bones, and Arthur-a-Bland, having tanned the stranger's hide, went back to the tanning of cow hides.

So great was his fame that only men from a distance could be induced to play a bout with him. All the local champions knew the terrible power of his great cudgel and gave him best man at once.

Now, although Arthur-a-Bland was a capital tanner, his heart was not altogether in his work. He loved the merry greenwood, and often, as he scraped a hide or was soaking his bark, his thoughts fled from the dirty tanpit to the pleasant depths of the forest, where the sun shone along the glades, and the dappled deer fled silently and swiftly under the shade of the mighty trees.

One lovely summer's morning he threw his work by and resolved, come what would, he would spend this glorious day in the greenwood and catch a glimpse of the wild red deer and of the free open-air life for which he longed. So he took his bow and arrows and great quarterstaff, without which he never moved, and set off to Sherwood to spend a day in the depths of the woodland.

The day was very warm, and after Arthur-a-Bland had spent three hours or more walking deeper and deeper into the forest, he was hot and a trifle tired, and he threw himself down to rest on a mossy bank under a hazel thicket. As he lay there he caught a glimpse of the sight which gave more pleasure to his eyes than anything else on earth; a herd of the graceful dappled deer moving slowly along a distant glade.

Arthur watched them some time and saw that the deer were coming towards him, and, as the wind blew from them to him, they were not likely to discover his presence. A lordly stag led the herd, and Arthur's fingers itched for a shot at the splendid deer. So he strung his bow and fitted an arrow on the string and began to creep up-wind towards the herd.

Now Arthur did not know it, but a tall, well-built man, clad in Lincoln green, was watching his every movement. And the man was Robin Hood himself!

At first Robin had thought it was one of his own men, but the tanner's leathern doublet and hood soon put that idea out of his mind.

"By our Lady, this is passing strange," murmured Robin. "This fellow is neither one of mine nor is he a forester. What doth he make in the greenwood? Marry, but the impudent knave is coolly marking down one of our finest deer."

When Robin said "our" deer, he meant himself and the king. For Robin was by now so much a lord of the greenwood that he reckoned that he had equal rights in the deer with the king himself. So Robin was up in arms at once at the idea of some fellow in leathern coat and hood letting an arrow fly at one of his noble stags. So he stepped forward and called to the stranger:

"Harkee, bold fellow, who are you who dares to poach so boldly? In sooth, to be brief, thou lookest like a common thief come to steal the king's deer!"

Arthur-a-Bland looked hard at the newcomer.

"This is no forester," thought Arthur. "I know them one and all. I care not for anyone else." So he spoke up boldly. "And who are you to bid me stand with such clamor that my shot has been spoiled?"

"I am one who keeps this forest," replied Robin Hood, "and I watch the deer for the king and for myself! Therefore, I must stay you from going deeper into the forest."

"Where are the others?" asked Arthur-a-Bland.

"What others, fellow?" demanded Robin.

"The others you will need at your back before you can stay me," replied Arthur-a-Bland with a grin.

Rob's quick temper rose at once at the hint that he could not stop the stranger by himself.

"Nay," said he, "I have none at my back, nor do I need them. Tempt me not, fellow, to crack thy crown for thy insolence!"

But Arthur-a-Bland, instead of looking frightened, only grinned the more.

"Marry, my fine keeper," said he, "you have a sword and a bow, but I care not for fighting with them. Did I not see you lay a quarterstaff on the grass yonder when you stepped forward to speak to me? That is the weapon with which I should wish to meet you."

"It will serve as well as another to teach you a lesson not to come meddling in the greenwood," said Robin, and went to fetch it.

The outlaw unbuckled his belt and laid down his sword and his bow beside it, then took his stout, oaken quarterstaff in hand and faced the tanner. Arthur-a-Bland had his staff ready poised, and held it in such fashion that Robin Hood knew at a glance that here was a good player.

"Wait a moment," said Robin. "Fair play and Old England forever! My staff is longer than thine, I think. Let us measure, and I will cut mine shorter, or it were foul play."

"Let the length pass," said Arthur-a-Bland with a careless laugh. "Mine is long enough to drub you soundly.

> "It is of oak so free;
>   Eight foot and a half,
>   It will knock down a calf,
> And I hope it will knock down thee."

At this Robin's quick temper was up again in an instant, and he let fly at the tanner with his quarterstaff, a stroke sudden as lightning. Arthur-a-Bland only partly checked it, and the heavy cudgel rang one o'clock on his pate and drew blood. But his return stroke was instant, and was so cleverly delivered that Robin failed to parry, and got a return knock on the head, so that the blood trickled down freely, and they were square, with a broken head apiece.

That shrewd stroke and counter-stroke had taught both men that each had a tough opponent, and now they faced each other warily and made feint and counterfeint, blow and counter-blow, their tough oak staves ringing and rattling as they clashed together.

Arthur-a-Bland had been expecting to gain another of his easy victories, for no common man could stand before him for five minutes; but he soon began to think this keeper the finest fellow who had ever crossed quarterstaff with him.

On his side, Robin was of opinion that this fellow in leathern coat and hood was the toughest blade he had ever met. Robin tried every trick he knew, but the other knew a trick worth two of it, and the outlaw got more than one or two shred bangs, while his staff hardly ever got home on the leathern coat. But Robin put everything he knew, and strove with all his strength and skill to gain the victory.

Around and around they fought, striving like two wild boars to injure each other. For more than two hours they struggled, making the wood ring with the fury of their blows.

At last these two well-matched champions fell apart from sheer weariness, and each leaned on his staff, gasping for breath, with the sweat pouring in streams down his face.

"Hold thy hand, good fellow," said Robin. "We'll let this quarrel fall. We shall but bang each other about in vain. I make thee free of Sherwood Forest."

"Thank you for nothing," chuckled Arthur-a-Bland. "If freedom I've bought, I may thank my staff, and not thee."

"What are you, and where do you come from?" cried Robin. "Let us know more of each other, I pray thee."

"I am a tanner," replied Arthur. "I have plied my trade for many a year in Nottingham and if thou wilt come there I'll tan thy hide for nothing."

"Come, then, leave your tanner's trade," cried Robin. "Come, live in the greenwood with me. I vow thou art the stoutest man of thy hands that ever I met since I gained brave Little John to my band."

"Little John, sayest thou?" cried Arthur-a-Bland. "Methinks I begin to suspect who hath played so stout a staff with me. And what is thy name?"

"I am Robin Hood!" replied the outlaw.

"Body o' me!" cried the tanner, "and are you, indeed, the prince of the outlaws who roam the merry greenwood? My heart has been with you many a day, so here's my hand. My name's Arthur-a-Bland; we two will never depart."

"Welcome, Arthur-a-Bland, to our company," said Robin Hood, as they shook hands, "for you play as stout a staff as our own Little John."

Then Arthur said, "Prithee, tell me where is Little John? We are kinsmen and I love him dearly."

"What, you wish to see Little John?" said Robin. "That is soon done, for my faithful follower is never at any great distance from his master."

And with that Robin put his horn to his lips and blew a long, shrill blast. In a short time a tall man came running through the trees and hurrying up to them.

"What is the matter, master?" cried Little John. "Pray, tell me. You have cast aside your sword and bow and stand with staff in hand against this fellow. I fear all is not well with thee." Little John might well say that, for the blood had run over Robin's face and dried on it till he looked a strange and sorry figure.

But Robin laughed, and said, "Indeed I have good fortune to be standing! This bonny blade beside thee is a master of his trade for he hath soundly tanned my hide."

"He is to be praised for being so clever as to do that!" cried Little John; "but he shall never dress down my master and think I will not take the matter up. If he be so stout, we will have a bout, and he shall tan my hide, too."

"No, no," cried Robin Hood. "There has been fighting enough. Besides 'twere shame for kinsmen to meet in battle, for, as I do understand, he's a yeoman good, of thine own blood, and his name is Arthur-a-Bland."

"What, my cousin, Arthur-a-Bland, the best quarterstaff in Nottingham town!" cried Little John.

"Ay, Little John, I am here," said the tanner, stepping forward and throwing back his leathern hood.

"Welcome, cousin, to the forest!" called Little John joyously, and the kinsmen gripped each other's hands, and Arthur said, "From this day a forest man am I, to live and die with you."

Robin Hood was delighted to get so bold a recruit, and Little John and Arthur-a-Bland were full of joy to meet again. And so happy were all three of them at this joyous ending of the matter that "Robin Hood took them both by the hands, and danced round about the oak-tree."

As they danced Little John struck up a jolly catch, and they made the greenwood ring with their voices as they sang:

> "For three merry men, and three merry men,
> And three merry men we be."

How the Sheriff Gained *cD*
a Queer Servant

ONE day, a few weeks after Arthur-a-Bland joined the outlaws, a rumor came to the forest that the sheriff was forming new plans and raising a great power of troops against his old enemies.

"I wonder what the sheriff is planning this time?" said Robin Hood. "We have had no word at all from Lobb the cobbler."

"But we'll soon learn for all that, master," said Little John. "This very day will I go myself in disguise to Nottingham and bring you all the news that may be gained in the market place and the alehouse, and in one place or the other I shall learn what is in the wind."

"Have a heed, Little John—have a heed," said his master. "I would not lose thee to gain all the news in Christendom."

"Never fear, master," said the great fellow, "I will look after myself."

That afternoon there entered the gate of Nottingham a huge, tattered, crippled beggarman. He walked with a great limp, one shoulder was half a foot higher than the other, his face was drawn on one side, and he had a patch over one eye. The warders at the gate called some rude jokes after the ragged figure, but the beggarman took no notice, only limped humbly forward as if seeking a place of rest. He crossed the market place, turned down a side street, and made his way into a little alley. Here he paused before a small shop, a mere booth, closed at night by a wooden shutter. It was the cobbler's shop, and, as a rule, Lobb the cobbler could be found there, busily stitching and hammering, but no sign of him was to be seen now.

The beggarman went through the shop and entered a small room behind. Here lay Lobb on a rude pallet.

"What Lobb, art ill, man?" said the beggarman in a low voice. Lobb knew the voice, and saw through the disguise.

"Ay, Little John," he replied. "I have been ill some three or four weeks, but I am slowly mending now."

"Why, that is good," replied the great fellow. "We wondered that we had heard nothing of you, so I came into the town to see what was amiss."

"You do well to come in disguise," replied Lobb. "I have heard of the fashion in which you sent the sheriff padding home with an arrow through his shoulder. It would be a short shrift and a long rope for you, my friend, if you fell into his hands."

"I believe you, Lobb," said Little John laughing, "and it

is to learn something of the sheriff's movements that I have now come in."

"If he is planning aught against you, it is being kept very secret," said Lobb. "There is nothing spoken of an excursion against Robin Hood's band in the gossip of the town."

"Well, I will move hither and thither and see if aught fresh hath arisen," said Little John, "so farewell, and take care of thyself, good Lobb."

The beggarman went back into the market place and sat down on the steps of the market cross, with his ragged cap in his hand. No one gave him the smallest coin, but he did not trouble about that, for he was more eager to listen to the gossip of the market people than to carry on his beggar's trade. After sitting for an hour in the market place, he got up and sought an alehouse, where he knew the sheriff's men went often to drink.

He was about to enter the door when the fat landlord stopped him and bade him go about his business.

"Get hence, beggarman!" said the host. "I'll not have thee in here pestering my customers for alms."

"Nay, nay," said the beggarman. "Good mine host, I come as a customer myself. What, do you think I have not the price of a pot of ale about me? Look here"—and the beggarman fumbled in the wallet at his leathern girdle and drew out a handful of small coins.

Seeing the beggarman had money to pay for his ale, the landlord permitted him to go in, but would not let him enter the chief room.

"Go in yonder," said the landlord. "That place is good

enough for such as thou art," and the beggarman went meekly into a rude chamber beside the chief room, a place where two or three stools stood about an old broken table. Here the beggarman sat and drank his ale in great content, for, through an open door he could hear every word that was spoken among the customers. Two of the sheriff's men were there, but nothing was said of any raid upon the outlaws. Instead, the talk ran upon a great shooting match that was to be shot at the town butts the next day. In those days shooting matches were the dearest sport of the people, and no fair day passed without a contest among the champions of the longbow.

The beggarman pricked his ears at the mention of the match, and murmured to himself, "A great match in the wind, eh? Then I'll be there if I can come at a bow by any means, for that's the place where tongues will wag freely of what is in the wind."

It was growing dusk by the time that he had finished his ale, and the beggarman left the alehouse and crept back to the cobbler's shop. Here Lobb made him a bed in the corner on a truss of hay and the beggarman lay down to sleep.

The next day, at noon, there was a grand fanfare of trumpets in the market place. There stood three heralds in shining new tabards, blowing till their cheeks were as round as apples. Since early morning, the market folk and the country people had been buying and selling, bargaining and chaffering; but now the serious business of the day was over, and the afternoon was to be given to sport. So there was a great crowd to listen to the proclamation of the games. They heard that the prize was to be a fine new horn filled with twenty silver pennies, and all agreed it was a noble reward which would stir the best archers of the town and countryside to give in their names.

Beside the market cross sat a clerk with a sheet of paper, pen, and inkhorn, and to him went the yeomen, one after another, to give in their names for the match. Among them marched the big, ugly, limping beggarman, a bow over his shoulder and a sheaf of arrows by his side. They had been lent to him by a friend of Lobb the cobbler.

As he went up to the clerk a roar of laughter rose from the onlookers, and a yeoman who was about to put down his name hustled the beggar back roughly.

"Stand back," said the yeoman, a tall, stout, red-faced man in the dress of a forester. "How dare ye thrust forward in face of your betters? And what dost mean in coming forward at all? Begone, and finish plundering the scarecrows amid the corn!"

The crowd laughed at this jest cut upon the beggarman's sorry clothes, but the laugh was checked when they saw the beggarman thrust out an arm strong as the bough of a great oak, and seize the forester by the neck and twitch him aside as if he had been a three-year-old-child.

"First come, first served," quoth the beggarman. "Let me tell you, my fine forester, that I was the nearer the clerk, and, therefore, had the better right to be entered first for this merry play."

The forester went red as fire with rage, and leapt at the beggarman and launched a tremendous blow at his face.

"Right, right, Hal o' the Croft!" shouted his friends. "Give the rogue a forester's knock!"

But the forester's knock was delivered in vain. The limping beggarman dodged aside, and Hal o' the Croft's fist missed him by inches.

"Run, beggarman—run!" cried a friendly bystander. "Hal will beat thee to a jelly with his fists an thou dost not escape."

"Nay, run will I not," grunted the beggarman. "Form a ring, and Hal shall beat me as much as he pleases."

"A ring! A ring!" yelled the crowd in high delight. "Hal o' the Croft is to fight with a big beggarman."

Nothing could have given greater pleasure to the onlookers than this unexpected encounter. A ring was formed at once, and Hal o' the Croft stripped off his jerkin, handed his bow to a companion, spat in his fists, and promised to give that impudent beggarman the biggest thrashing a man could receive. In all Nottingham town none could use his fists like Hal o' the Croft, and many a victory had he won on this very spot.

For his part the beggarman neither stripped nor straightened himself. He handed his bow to an honest country yeoman, and made no other preparation, only limped up and down his side of the ring in so comical a fashion that the spectators shrieked with laughter at his queer actions and queerer figure.

When the fight began, the yells and shouts of delight rose from the crowd like smoke from a furnace. Hal o' the Croft let out sledge-hammer blows again and again at the big beggarman's head, and not one blow got home. For the beggarman had such a limp that his head shot up and down a foot or more as he moved, and when Hal struck out for his opponent's face it went down like lightning, and Hal hit the air, and at the next instant felt the beggarman's big fist play tattoo on his ribs. And, lame as he seemed, the beggarman dodged about the ring in so quick a fashion, and withal, in so comical a style, his rags and bags fluttering as he hopped and limped, that the crowd shouted itself hoarse for joy at sight of this strange combat. Suddenly it was ended. Hal, spluttering with rage, had chased the beggarman into an angle from which there was no escape.

"Cornered! Cornered!" shouted the forester's friends. "Now you have him, Hal. Now give him the forester's knock."

But at this instant when all looked to see the famous boxer punish his opponent, that terrible beggarman uprose and, for the first time, his huge fist struck home. Crash! Every man in the crowd heard three of the forester's ribs splinter as if they had been dried sticks, and Hal o' the Croft was hurled clean across the ring and dashed senseless to the ground. For a moment all stood silent in surprise at the strength which had dealt that tremendous blow.

Then several foresters pressed forward, cudgels in hand, to beat the beggarman who had overthrown their champion so easily. But this roused the temper of the crowd, and a loud cry of "Fair play! Fair play!" arose.

"'Twas an honest blow and honestly dealt!" cried a

townsman. "Hal only got what he intended to give. Fair
play for the beggar!" and the speaker flourished a great
quarterstaff round his head.

This honest fellow was so strongly backed up by his ac-
quaintances that the foresters had to give up their purpose
of beating the beggarman, and they drew off with sullen
faces, bearing their defeated champion with them.

"Beggarman," cried the townsman who had stood up for
him, "canst thou shoot as well as thou canst strike?"

"Ay, master, that I can," replied Little John boldly.

"Well, then, neighbors," said the good-natured fellow,
looking round on his friends, "we'll e'en attend the beggar
to the butts, for we shall see shooting beyond common this
day, I think."

His friends agreed, and a strong band of them marched
with the beggarman to the scene of the shooting match
lest he should be meddled with by the angry foresters. So
Little John entered his name and went to the shooting.
And he had his name put down as Reynaud Greenleaf,
which is as much as to say "Fox of the Greenwood," and
he chuckled to think how well the name fitted him.

When the shooting match began there was first a contest at the butts, and here the beggarman shot best of all.
The three best men at the butts were now set to shoot at
the hardest mark of all—a willow wand set upright in the
ground. Of the three only the beggarman could accom-
plish the feat. His arrow split the willow wand as cleanly
as if a sharp knife had been run through the center.

"This is the best archer that ever I saw in all my life!"
cried the sheriff, who was watching the archery closely.

It was the first time he had been abroad since the wound in his shoulder had healed and he was enjoying the day's sport very keenly.

"Come hither, beggarman!" he cried, and Little John came forward and bent his knee humbly before the proud sheriff.

"What is thy name, and where dost thou come from?" cried the sheriff.

"My name, your honor, is Reynaud Greenelaf, and I was born at Holderness," replied Little John.

"Thou canst draw a good bow, Reynaud Greenleaf of Holderness," said the sheriff.

"Ay," said Little John to himself, "or I would never have put a shaft through thy shoulder, proud sheriff"; but he made no answer aloud, only bent his knee again in respect.

"'Tis a shame to see so bold a bowman as thou art in rags and tatters," quoth the sheriff. "Come, good fellow, enter my service, and every year I will give thee twenty marks to thy fee."

Little John agreed at once, for in the sheriff's service he felt sure he could find out all the things he wished to know. So he went to the sheriff's house and entered his service; and the sheriff thought he had secured a fine archer for his bodyguard. Little John grinned to himself, and said softly, "Gramercy, proud sheriff, Reynaud Greenleaf is your man, as you think. Marry, I shall be the worst servant to him that ever yet had he!"

For some days Little John, or Reynaud Greenleaf, spent a fine time at the sheriff's house. He ate and drank of the best; he sat by the fire or in the sun, and never did a hand's turn of work of any sort. This vexed the steward, a self-important fellow, who expected every servant to run before him. But when he gave Reynaud Greenleaf a job, that big, lazy fellow would not touch it, and merely said, "I am an archer, Master Steward. Fetch me when there is shooting to be done, and I'm your man. Till then, leave me alone."

One morning Little John lay in bed very late, and when he got up he found the sheriff had gone hunting.

"So," thought Little John, "the sheriff has gone to hunt in Merry Sherwood, has he? Well, upon my faith, I, too, am longing to be back in the greenwood, and I may as well go!" For Little John had listened when many thought him asleep, and looked when many had thought his eyes closed, and he had neither heard nor seen anything to show that the sheriff was plotting mischief against Robin Hood and the outlaw band. He began to see that it was but a false rumor which had reached them in the forest.

"I'll make a good meal," thought Little John, "and then I'll betake myself to my master." So Little John rose and went in search of bread, meat, and ale.

Little John went to the buttery, and in the passage leading to it he met the steward. "Good Master Steward," said he, "Give me a hearty breakfast, I pray thee, for I am as hungry as a wolf in midwinter."

"As so you may be, for me!" cried the steward. "The hour of breakfast is long since past, Reynaud Greenleaf, and the food is put away. Why, 'tis more like the time to dine!"

"Call it dinnertime then, as you please," replied Little John, "so that I get the food. I am careless of the name of the meal."

"Neither bite nor sup shall you have!" cried the steward, "till my lord, the sheriff, has come back from hunting."

"What!" cried the hungry giant, "and I am to fast till then? Master Steward, be wary and rouse not my anger, or I may crack your crown."

The other said never a word, but slammed the buttery door to, turned the key in the lock, and laughed in triumph. But the fat steward, who was also butler, laughed too soon.

Little John dealt him such a blow that it seemed as though his back would break in two.

Over went the steward in a heap in the corner, and Little John stepped forward and gave the buttery door such a terrific kick that he burst it clean off its hinges. He stepped in, and licked his lips when he saw the well-laden shelves. A great venison pasty, with the crust well browned, caught his eye first, and he cut a huge slice of it with his knife and washed it down with a great black jack of humming brown ale from a barrel in the corner. Then he took a dozen or so slices from a cold haunch of vension and washed these down with a flagon of rich Canary wine, and so he tried this and that of all the daintiest, and made the finest meal he had ever stood up to, for there was no seat in the place, and he ate off a tall shelf for table.

Now, while Little John was thus eating and drinking merrily, the cook came to the buttery in search of the steward. For a moment the cook stared in wonder at the scene. There was the steward groaning in the corner where Little John had flung him, and there was the big archer making havoc of the buttery shelves. This havoc went to the cook's very soul, for the archer was disposing of the dainties which the cook had prepared for the return of the hunting train. The cook's anger arose at once, and, as he was a stout and bold man, he sprang straight at the archer and fetched him three heavy blows across the shoulders with a stick that he held in his hand.

"I make my vow," cried the cook, "you are the sturdiest knave that ever dwelt in a household, to ask to dine in this fashion!"

"I make my vow," said Little John, as he swallowed a last mouthful, "that you are a bold man to disturb another at his meal. And before I leave the place I will make trial of you."

Little John and the cook thereupon drew their swords, and, neither dreaming of retreat, they set to.

For a good hour Little John and the cook fought sore together and neither had harmed the other, so well matched were they at every trick of fence.

"Hold your hand!" cried Little John at last. "I make my vow, Master Cook, that you are the best swordsman that ever I met. 'Tis a waste of a stout blade that such a man as you should hang over pots and pans cooking fine things for other men's stomachs."

"I like my task little enough," replied the cook; "but what am I to do?"

"Say you so?" cried Little John. "Why, if you can but shoot with the bow as you can play with the sword, I

*For a good hour Little John and the cook
fought sore together*

could take you to the greenwood and find you a good master, whose service would fill you with delight."

"And who might he be?" asked the cook.

Little John bent forward and whispered in his ear, "Robin Hood!"

The cook gave a great start of astonishment, and for a moment stared at the archer in surprise. Well might he be filled with wonder at finding one of the outlaws in the service of the sheriff. Then he raised his left hand.

"Put up your sword," said the cook. "I am your fellow from this day."

"Then join me in this pasty," laughed Little John. "I had returned to it just as your stick fell across my shoulders, and our little bout hath made me hungry again."

So the cook laid aside his sword and attacked the good victuals instead, and fetched fresh dainties, and they ate and drank together, and resolved to fly together to the greenwood.

"Nor will we go empty-handed," quoth the cook. "I can show you the way to the sheriff's treasure room."

"Would that I could get into it," said Little John, "for they say it is full of fine silver vessels that the sheriff hath purchased with the fines he wrings from poor people."

"The saying is truth," said the cook; "but come now with me and I will show you the place."

They went to the treasure room, and found it guarded by a thick iron-banded door, the latter held in place by hasps of steel with strong steel padlocks.

"Fetch me the heaviest hammer you can lay your hands

on," said Little John to the cook, and the cook ran and fetched a great sledge hammer.

High in the air Little John swung the great hammer and dashed the padlocks off the fastenings with a few tremendous blows. Then into the treasure chamber they went.

"Fetch me the biggest sack you can lay your hands on," said Little John to the cook; and the cook fetched a sack which would have held a man. Then Little John put the sheriff's silver vessels and his money into the big sack and swung the sack on to his shoulders.

"Now for the greenwood," said Little John; and, following the cook along a secret path to a little postern door, gleefully off they went.

The Sheriff Spends a ∾ Night In the Greenwood

ROBIN HOOD, Much, Will, Scarlet, and Friar Tuck were standing near their cave in deep talk. "I am uneasy about Little John," said Robin. "It is some days since he went, and we have heard no word of him."

"No news is good news, master," said Much. "If the sheriff's men had caught our bold comrade there would soon have been a noise through the countryside."

"I am willing to go into the town and see if aught can be heard of him," said Will Scarlet.

"Nay, nay, I will go," said Friar Tuck. "I can take on the guise of a wandering pilgrim, and in those garments I can come and go in safety anywhere." Then he started and raised his hand. "But, look yonder!" he cried. "Look yonder! Talk of the stag and you see his horns. By my gown and beads, if yonder great fellow bearing a sack be not Little John I am no true churchman."

His companions turned quickly and set up a shout of joy as the huge archer strode up to the spot.

"Brave lad!" cried Robin Hood. "By our Lady, Little

113

John, but I am glad to see thee back. And what tidings dost thou bring from Nottingham?"

"I bring, master, the sheriff's greetings," said Little John, bowing. "I also bring the sheriff's cook," and he pointed to his companion and bowed again. "And, moreover," he went on, "I also bring the sheriff's treasure."

He bowed once more, swung down the sack to earth, and its contents tinkled and jangled cheerfully. His comrades shouted applause and laughed aloud to see the beautiful silver vessels and the store of money which were drawn from the sack.

"I fear thou hast brought none of these with the sheriff's good will," chuckled Robin Hood, and at that moment up ran Will Stutely with news.

"Master!" cried Will, "as I live, the sheriff himself is hunting in Holly Chase. I have seen the train sweeping along under the trees and have run to warn you."

"Say you so, Will?" cried Little John. "Then on the faith of an archer, I say that we have the sheriff's cook, we have the sheriff's treasure, and now we will have the sheriff himself;" and away went Little John into the forest as fast as he could run.

Little John never stayed his flying feet until he came to Holly Chase, and here he found the sheriff riding slowly along in deep dudgeon. Hounds were baying and horns were blowing, but there was no sign that the huntsmen had met with any success. Little John hastened up to the sheriff, and bent low before him.

"Save you, my lord, save you!" cried Little John.

"Ha, Reynaud Greenleaf," said the sheriff, "where hast thou come from?"

"I have followed you to the forest, my lord!" cried Little John. "What sport? What sport, Sir Sheriff?"

"None, none, good Greenleaf," replied the sheriff. "We have spent the day with hound and horn, and yet never a deer have we brought to bay."

"Why then, my lord, let me show you game!" cried Little John. "I have been in this forest, and there did I see a fair sight, surely a fairer my eyes never beheld. It was a mighty hart, of a green color, and with him seven score in a herd. His horns were so keen, master, that I dared not shoot at him for fear that he should set on me and slay me."

"A wondrous sight, indeed, Reynaud Greenleaf," quoth the sheriff, "and one that I fain would see. Lead me to that spot."

"That will I at once, master," said Little John; "wend with me and I will give you a fair sight of that great hart."

Little John ran back at so smart a pace that the sheriff was forced to put his horse to a gallop, and so master and man outstripped the rest of the company. Presently they came to a break in the trees, and there stood Robin Hood in Lincoln green, his bugle in his hand.

"Lo, master!" cried Little John, "here be the mighty hart!"

And now Robin Hood sounded a note on the bugle and at once seven score archers sprang from the cover of the trees and hailed the sheriff with a great shout which made the woods ring. The sheriff's men heard that shout and fled, but the sheriff was in the midst of the outlaws and knew that he was a captive.

The sheriff glanced about him in consternation. "Woe

betide thee, Reynaud Greenleaf!" he muttered. "Thou
hast betrayed me, but thou shall'st suffer for it!"

"I vow, master," said Little John, "that you are to blame.
For if you had ordered your household better, I should
have had my dinner at the proper time, and this would
not have happened."

"Welcome to the greenwood, sheriff!" said Robin, but
the sheriff still pulled a very sour face and looked as if he
feared what kind of welcome he would get. But he could
not escape, and now Little John seized the bridle of his
horse and marched forward, and the outlaws followed behind. A march of three miles brought them to an open
space in the very heart of the forest. Here a great fire
blazed in the center of the clearing, and a merry frizzling
sound smote on the ears. The sheriff's mouth watered, for
he was very hungry, and his eyes opened wide with surprise when he saw that his own cook was busy frying the
good venison collops.

"You shall have supper with us, sheriff!" cried Robin
Hood. "Our fare is but plain, but hunger will be a kingly
sauce to this kingly feast, for such it must be when we sup
on the king's deer."

The sheriff sat down on the foot of an oak, and looked
round with a harassed air. He had made many attempts
to seize these fellows, and now they had seized him. He
knew their deaths would have been certain had they fallen
into his hands, and he felt his head sit very uneasily on his
shoulders now that he was in their power. Presently Robin
Hood came up to him.

"To supper, to supper, Sir Sheriff!" he cried. "Come,
the good venison awaits us."

The sheriff went at once, for he was very hungry, and besides he began to hope that the outlaws might spare his life; it seemed unlikely that they meant great harm to him if they began by offering him a good supper.

The meal was laid on the turf, and at first sight of the dishes the sheriff gasped in surprise: the venison collops were being served on dishes of solid silver.

"Marry," quoth the sheriff; "here be splendor for the greenwood. I vow that these outlaws eat off plates of silver; the king himself could not be more finely served!"

But when the sheriff looked closer and saw that it was his own silver service, his jaw dropped in such a fashion that all the outlaws burst into a great roar of laughter, so comical was the swift change of his face.

"What is this?" he roared, purple with fury. "Mine own silver treasure! I thought it safe in my treasure chamber, and it is here in the hands of runagate knaves. Ah, Reynaud Greenleaf, Reynaud Greenleaf, I doubt me thou art at the bottom of this."

The great fellow grinned at the sheriff, and said, "Call me Little John, Sir Sheriff. I have done with the other name as a man casts off an old cloak."

Little John! The sheriff's eye glittered savagely to think how he had been deceived and cheated. His servant, Reynaud Greenleaf, had been the redoutable Little John in disguise, and he had not known it. He flung himself down on the turf and, for a time, could not eat for pure sorrow and vexation. But Robin Hood pressed him so courteously, and his hunger returned to urge him still more strongly, until, in the end, the sheriff made a good supper.

Now, as a rule, when the sheriff had made a good supper he was in the habit of retiring to a very soft feather bed and taking a good night's sleep; but there were no feather beds in the greenwood.

"You shall stay with us, sheriff," said Robin Hood, "and this night you shall enjoy a woodland couch. That is but fair since your oppression hath driven many a poor fellow to the forest where he must lie on the bare ground, with scarce a cloak to cover him."

So Robin Hood gave orders to Little John, and Little John stripped the sheriff of his hosen and shoon and of his fur-lined cloak and of his thick doublet. Then a mantle of Lincoln green was given to the sheriff, and he gladly took it and wrapped himself in it.

"And now good night, sheriff," said Robin Hood.

"Good night is it?" quoth the sheriff. "But where am I to lie? Where is my bed?"

"Your bed!" laughed Robin Hood. "It is e'en the same couch as my men will occupy. Look upon them and do the same."

He pointed with his hand, and the sheriff saw that the hardy outlaws were flinging themselves upon the earth to sleep, and knew that he must do the same. Wrapped in their cloaks of Lincoln green, the followers of Robin Hood stretched themselves upon the turf, took an outstanding root for a pillow, and fell at once into the deep sleep of tired men who live in the open air.

The sheriff had to lie down on the same bed, but to him it was a bed of misery. He tried to sleep, but a sharp-pointed root stuck in his side, and he rolled over.

Now a big stone caught him in the back, and he tried a
new place. Here there was nothing to rest his head upon,
and he moved to a place where a raised turf made a sort
of pillow. But now he could not sleep, for he shivered
with cold till he shook again. Altogether, he passed a
most dreadful night, with never a wink of sleep, and he
was very glad to see the gray light of dawn show in the
east. He now got up and walked to and fro to warm himself until Robin Hood came to his side.

"Did you ever sleep on a finer bed in your life, Sir Sheriff?" cried the outlaw. "What think you of our order of
life under the greenwood tree?"

"This is a harder life," said the sheriff, "than that of a
hermit or friar. I would not live here for all the gold in
merry England."

"For twelve months," replied Robin, "thou shalt dwell
with me; I shall teach thee, proud sheriff, to be an
outlaw!"

When the sheriff heard Robin say that he should be a
prisoner in the greenwood for twelve months, he lost heart
entirely, and gave a great moan.

"Robin Hood!" he cried; "I tell thee that sooner than
spend another night like the last, I would give up my
life. Strike my head off, and I will forgive thee. But
keep me here to live an outlaw's life! No, no, never!"

Robin Hood laughed. "It is clear you would make a
poor scholar in my school," he said; "but what then am I
to do with you?"

Upon this the sheriff begged hard for his life and freedom, and promised over and over again that in the future

Robin Hood should have a strong friend in him if only he might go this time.

Robin Hood listened; then lifted his hand to check the captive's flow of entreaties.

"Hark ye, Sir Sheriff!" cried the outlaw, and his bright eye was fixed on the sheriff's face with a piercing glance. "Your life has never been for a moment in danger with me. But do not think it is because I have respect for you. I have none. But I have respect for your office. I will not lay violent hands on the representative of the king. Were you not set in authority by him I would string you upon the highest oak in the greenwood. And now I must have a promise before you go." And as the old ballad says:

> "Thou shalt swear me an oath," said Robin,
>   "On my bright brand,
> Thou shalt never do me harm,
>   By water nor by land;
> And if thou find any of my men
>   By night or by day
> Upon thine oath thou shalt swear
>   To help them as thou may."

The sheriff was only too glad to make these promises, and we shall see how he kept them. But Robin took his word, and gave him his horse, and led him out of the forest, and set him on his way to Nottingham.

So home went the sheriff, sore and aching in every bone and brooding bitterly on the thought of his empty treasure house.

Robin Hood Meets ❧
George-a-Green and Then a Beggarman

O<small>NE</small> day Robin Hood, Will Scarlet, and Little John were out along the highroad. They had gone beyond the forest and were in the open country, when they heard a merry voice singing. They stood still to listen and heard these words:

> "There is neither knight, nor squire, said the pinder,
> Nor baron that is so bold,
> Nor baron that is so bold,
> Dare make a trespass to the town of Wakefield,
> But his pledge goes to the pinfold."

The three outlaws went a little farther along the way, and then saw a stout, jolly-looking fellow seated on the ground, with his back against a thorn, carolling like a blackbird.

"I know him," said Little John. "'Tis George-a-Green, the pinder of Wakefield."

A pinder was a man who kept the pinfold, or pound, and it was his duty to lock up all stray beasts.

"He seems a merry fellow, said Robin Hood; "but he is not of the sort we seek. We will go this way," and he turned aside from the road. But they had not made a dozen steps when the pinder ceased his song, and shouted to them to halt.

"Turn back," said the pinder, "you have forsaken the king's highway and made a path through the corn."

"Here's a bold fellow," said Robin Hood, quietly, to his followers. "We are three, and he is one, yet he commands us not to leave the highway."

"I believe he is as stout a blade as can be found in the North Countree," quoth Little John. "He hath fought many a good wager with sword and buckler to my knowledge."

"We will try him," said Robin. "I love a bold heart, and will add him to our band if his metal rings true."

"How will you try him, master?" asked Will Scarlet.

"By our Lady, a sharp trial will I devise," replied Robin Hood. "We will all three rush upon him as if in anger at his bold challenge, and if he stands against such odds he is a man worth having."

"Now, now!" roared the pinder at this moment. "Do not stand talking there among yourselves, but get out of the corn and back to the highway."

"What!" shouted Robin; "dost thou think, rude varlet, that we will submit to be ordered about by thee? By our Lady, but we will crop thy ears from thy head." And he drew his sword and made a rush at the pinder, and Little John and Scarlet followed, waving their bright brands above their heads, and shouting, "Ay, ay, master! Crop the knave's ears with your hunting knife!"

The pinder turned, and made one tremendous leap. But it was not in flight; it was to gain a broad old thorn tree, and here he set his back against the trunk and his foot against a stone. Out flashed his sword, up swung his buckler, and he was ready for his assailants. They dashed upon him, and their swords clattered on his buckler, for as swiftly as they struck at him, he caught the blows with wonderful deftness on his shield of steel. Nor did he fail to get in such swinging cuts in return that the outlaws came very near to being paid back in their own coin. It was not long before Robin Hood was satisfied that George-a-Green was indeed a stout man.

"Hold thy hand!" cried Robin Hood, "and my men will do the same. Verily, this is one of the best pinders I ever tested by the sword!"

So the contest came to a pause, and the pinder was glad to have a chance to fetch a few breaths and lean on his sword. Nevertheless he kept a wary eye on the three out-laws, and was ready at any instant to take to blade and buckler again.

"Come!" said Robin Hood, "you are a man after my own heart, pinder. Will you follow me?"

"Whither?" cried the pinder.

"To the merry greenwood," replied Robin, "where my lusty fellows chase the deer through the forest glades and live a life of jolly freedom."

"And who are you?" cried the pinder.

"I am Robin Hood," said the outlaw.

The pinder thrust his sword into the scabbard, flung aside his buckler, stepped forward, and put his hand into Robin's.

"I am your man," he said, at once; "I have wished for many a day to meet you, and I love a wild free life. Enroll me in your band."

"I will, good fellow," cried Robin Hood, gladly. "And these shall be your companions; they are Little John and Will Scarlet."

"Ay, Little John, I thought it was you," said the pinder, taking the giant's hand. "I have seen you in Wakefield in the old days before you took to the greenwood."

Little John and Will Scarlet shook hands with their new comrade, and then all four sat down under the thorn and ate from a bag of food with which the pinder was provided. When the bread and beef and ale had been dispatched, Robin Hood said to his three followers, "Stay you here, and watch the road. I shall walk a little farther, and if I meet with no adventure, I shall be back anon."

"And if we meet with no adventure, master," said Little John, "what then?"

"Oh, you may follow me," said Robin Hood.

So the three men remained chatting under the thorn, and Robin went on his way along the road. Within two miles, the road he was following ran into another, and at the meeting of the ways Robin stood for a good while. At length he saw a beggar come marching, with long, even stride. The beggar was coming toward Robin and the latter stood and watched him.

"By my faith," thought the outlaw, "yonder fellow goes with sturdy step, and he has a stiff heavy crabstick in his hand. I have heard that a strong rogue such as yon will often pick up valuable things, and that a dirty bag may

often have a load worth lightening. I will have a few
words with him."

So Robin placed himself in the path, and waited for the
beggar. The latter had seen the outlaw, but he came on
with the same long, even stride, neither faster nor slower.
The nearer he got, the plainer it was to be seen that he
might prove a very awkward customer to tackle. His rags
flew in the wind, and through the rents his brown arms
and legs showed thick and muscular. His ragged cloak
was patched in every color of the rainbow, and on his
head were three old hats jammed down one on top of the
other. Round his neck hung a great bag, buckled to a
stout strap of leather.

"Tarry, my friend," said Robin; "tarry, and speak with
me."

The beggar made no sign that he had heard a word,
and pushed straight ahead, without slackening his stride.
Then Robin sprang straight in front of the beggar, and
said, "Nay, but tarry thou must."

"By my troth," said the beggar, "but I have no fancy to
obey you. Let me tell you that I have far to go today,
and I have no mind to reach my lodging house late, for
then, look you, the supper would be all eaten, and I
should look wondrous foolish to be too late for the last
meal."

"All very fine," said Robin. "You are very careful about
your own supper, but what of mine? Come, lend me
some money, and I'll betake myself at once to the nearest
tavern."

"Money!" cried the beggar; "I've no money to lend, and,

if I had, not a penny would I lend to you. You are as young a man as I am, and just as active. Be off with you and get money for yourself. If you wait to buy bread with aught I lend you, you'll eat nothing this twelve-month, that I warrant you."

Robin's temper rose, and he spoke out sharply.

"Now, by my faith, thou art a saucy rogue. Down with your wallet, beggarman, and let me see what it may contain. Loose the strings, or I will tear the bag open with my own hand. If thou hast but a small farthing, I will see it ere I go."

"It takes two to make a bargain," jeered the beggar; "how if I will not obey you?"

"Why then!" cried Robin, "if thou darest to make any din, I will try if the head of a broad arrow may not pierce a beggar's skin."

"Far better let me be," said the beggar, with a grim smile; "I care not a rap for thy bow and broad arrow. You will get nothing but ill from me, I warn you."

Robin was now so angry that he swung up his bow, and set a broad arrow on the string. But quick as he was, the beggar was quicker. The latter fetched so swift and heavy a stroke with his great pikestaff that "bow and broad arrow in flinders flew about."

Seeing that his bow and arrow were useless, Robin clapped his hand on his sword hilt. Down whistled the pikestaff again, and dropped across Robin's knuckles, so that his hand was numbed, and he could not draw his blade. Then, with a third tremendous blow came the great crab-stick, crash! on Robin's head, and laid him flat

*The doughty beggar leaned on his staff, and now
began to laugh and jeer at poor Robin*

on the ground. The doughty beggar leaned on his staff
and now began to laugh and jeer at poor Robin.

"Stand up, man!" he chuckled; "'tis early yet to go to
rest. Get up and count the money you have taken from
me, and then you may go to the tavern and have a merry
bout with your friends, drinking wine and ale at the beggar's expense. Get up, I say!"

But Robin Hood had had too shrewd a crack on the
head to get up in a hurry, and, after crowing over his fallen enemy again, the beggar marched on his way.

Scarce five minutes later Little John, Will Scarlet, and
George-a-Green, the jolly pinder, came along the road.
They had met no adventure and so were seeking their
master. When they saw him lying at full length in the
road they began to run as fast as they could and soon were
at his side.

"What's wrong, master?" cried Little John; "what's
wrong? Your bow and arrow and eke* your head are
broken. How comes this about?"

"Marry, my good lads," replied Robin Hood, sitting up;
"I have met with a beggar who can wield his pikestaff in
such fashion that there be few to match him," and he told
the story of the encounter.

"Gramercy!" cried Little John, "no beggar shall so evilly
use my master and escape with a whole skin. You, Will
Scarlet, stop by our leader while George-a-Green and I
follow up this scurvy rogue and deal with him."

So it was arranged, and Will Scarlet began to bind up

---

*Even.

Robin's head, while Little John and the pinder ran after the beggar.

"Take care of his pikestaff," called Robin after them, but Little John replied:

"You shall soon see that his staff will stand him in poor stead. He shall be bound and led back to see if ye will have him slain or hanged on a tree."

"I know a sure way of having him," said Little John to George-a-Green as they hurried along. "There is a short cut through a wood near at hand which is nearer by three miles than following the highway." So the two men went through the wood and ran up hill and down dale in their eagerness to get in front of the man who had given their master such a beating. At last they came to a little wood in a glen, and through this wood the highway ran. Little John stooped down and looked in the dust of the road.

"There is no new footmark of man or beast," said he, "so the beggar has not passed yet."

"We have him," said George-a-Green, "and we will make his hide pay for what he has done this day."

At one point of the way the road was narrow, and ran between two great oaks. The two companions hid themselves, one behind each oak, and waited for their prey. Presently the beggar came marching along, his step neither faster nor slower than his usual pace, and whistling softly as if he had naught to fear from anyone. But as he strode between the oaks Little John and George were upon him at a bound. Little John mastered his formidable staff, and George-a-Green whipped out a dagger and held it at his breast.

"False rascal!" cried George; "give up your staff or this dagger will be thy portion."

The beggar loosed his staff, and Little John took it and stuck it in the turf by its iron-shod point.

"Grant me my life!" cried the beggar, finding himself helpless in the grip of these two powerful men. "Hold away that ugly knife, or I shall die of fear. What harm have I ever done to you that you should slay me?"

"Harm!" cried Little John; "harm enough, thou ragged rogue! Thou hast come near to slaying the gentlest man and best master that ever was born. So thou shalt be led back, fast bound, to see if he will have thee slain with a dagger or hanged to a tree."

But the beggar continued to plead for his life. "Brave gentlemen," he said, "what good will it do to you to take a poor beggar's life? Let me go, and I will give you the hundred pounds and some odd silver which is hidden at the bottom of my bag. It is the savings of many years, but 'tis better for a man to part with his money than his life."

"Hearken to the rogue!" cried George-a-Green. "He hath a hundred pound and more in his beggar's bag. Well, never judge a man by his looks, say I."

"'Tis no surprise to me," said Little John, "for I have often known a ragged cloak to cover riches in these unsafe days. But come, man, turn out thy store, and let us see this money."

"Gladly will I do that!" cried the beggar, and unstrapped his great leathern wallet and let it down on the ground with care as though it was very heavy. Now, there was a strong wind blowing through the glen, a breeze which flapped the beggar's rags about him, and he turned his back to it as if to avoid the keen blast. Little John and George-a-Green were facing their prisoner, eager to see what was in the bag and watching his every movement as he unfastened the straps from the buckles.

The beggar plunged both hands into the great wallet and raised them. But they were not filled with money, but meal, which he dashed right into the faces of the waiting outlaws. In an instant Little John and George were blind and gasping. The fine meal filled their eyes, noses, and mouths, till they could neither see nor breathe. The strong wind helped the beggar, and raised a blinding whirl of meal, in which all sight of the cunning fellow was lost.

Handful upon handful of the meal the beggar hurled upon them, and finished by shaking his great bag in their faces. The two outlaws tried to shout in their rage, but the meal choked them, and they could only splutter and gasp. They drove their knuckles into their eyes to clear the fine particles away, but that only made matters worse, for the more they rubbed the blinder they became.

Then the beggar made one jump, and seized his great pikestaff which stood where Little John had placed it.

"How now, my masters?" he shouted. "It seems I have done ye wrong in mealing your clothes. The least I can do is to dust your jackets for you," and with that he began to lay on them fast and heavy with his big stick. Whack! thump! bang! down came the great stick across the shoulders of the outlaws, and the meal rose again in clouds under the swinging blows. Little John and George groped hither and thither, trying to seize the beggar, but he dodged them easily, and hit them again and again, where and how he liked, his staff falling on their heads and backs as a flail falls on a sheaf.

At last there was nothing for it but flight, and the outlaws hurried away down the glen, blinded and smarting.

"Why this hurry?" cried the beggar, following them up, as they stumbled over the roots and fallen branches. "Tarry a little; you are not paid in full yet; do not fear that I shall prove a niggard."

But the outlaws had had enough of the coin with which the beggar paid his debts, and they fled faster still.

"Well, if you must go!" cried the cunning rogue, "here's one for luck!" and he gave each of the outlaws a last tremendous buffet, turned back, and went his way merrily.

When Little John and George-a-Green found that they were really free of this terrible beggar, they stopped at a spring and washed the meal from their eyes. But when at last they could see, there was no sign of their assailant. He had taken to the woods and vanished completely. So there was nothing for them to do but to return to their master and Will Scarlet.

"Why," said Robin Hood, "how is this? Ye went after a beggar, but I think ye have been at the mill, for your clothes are full of meal."

Little John grinned for, though he had come off with the worst end of the stick, he could see the fun of the thing.

"We seized the beggar, sure enough, master," said he, "and he offered to ransom himself from his great bag," and he went on to tell the story of the meal and the big pike-staff.

Robin Hood and Will Scarlet could not help laughing at this droll story, and Will Scarlet laughed loudest of all, for he had never felt the beggar's stick.

"Well, the beggar is the best man this time," said Robin, who could respect a bold foeman. "We must go back to the forest with naught but bruises to show for our gains this day, and, by our Lady, I think he hath banged you two worse than he banged me."

"I shall be sore for a week," grumbled Little John.

"And I am black and blue all over," said George-a-Green.

"I think we had better say naught about this matter," said Robin Hood, "or we shall be shamed forevermore, thus to be overcome by a sly beggar."

Little John and George were quite willing to say nothing, but it is very likely that Will Scarlet thought the joke too good not to be told, for the tale got abroad. And a ballad was made about it and sung for many a day of Robin Hood and his men and the beggar with a meal pack.

Friar Tuck and the ❧
Bishop of Hereford

A FEW days after his meeting with the beggar, Robin Hood was seated, one sunny morning, on a log outside the cave where he and his band lived. Robin was mending a bow, and, looking up from his work, he saw Lobb the cobbler coming up to him. Lobb was now quite well again and had come from the town with tidings.

"News, master, news!" cried the cobbler.

"News of whom, good Lobb?" asked Robin.

"Of the Bishop of Hereford," replied Lobb.

Robin Hood's brow darkened, for the bishop had been a bitter enemy of his since the wedding of Alan-a-Dale, and, more than that, Robin hated the bishop because the latter was greedy and cruel.

"Say on, Lobb!" cried the outlaw.

"The bishop is now in Nottingham town," said Lobb, "and tomorrow he rides through Barnesdale Forest. He has been collecting the rent of church lands, and his wal-

134

lets will be stuffed with gold and silver, for he hath forced everyone to pay in full, though times be hard and money be scarce. He hath taken the last penny of the widow and orphan sooner than bate one coin of the heavy and unjust dues laid upon his tenants."

"Ah!" said Robin, "I think it is time this proud prelate was taught a lesson. I will ask him to dinner."

Lobb grinned, for he knew what that meant. The rich oppressor who dined with Robin Hood had to pay stiffly for his meal.

The next day Robin and a strong band of his men betook themselves to that part of the forest through which the bishop must pass.

"Come, kill me a good fat deer," quoth bold Robin Hood, "for the Bishop of Hereford is to dine with me to-day, and he shall pay well for his cheer."

The deer was killed and laid on an open grassy space beside the way, and around it gathered Robin Hood and six of his men; the rest of the band were posted in hiding.

Now, Robin and the men who stayed with him were dressed like poor shepherds. They had laid aside their garb of Lincoln green, their bows, and swords, and had clothed themselves in old torn cloaks of gray duffle,* with long sheepcrooks in their hands. Thus they looked as innocent as possible, and when the Bishop of Hereford came riding along the road, with a strong train of attendants, he thought them some shepherds making holiday: for they had made a fire on the green, and were dancing round it.

---

*Woolen.

But when the bishop came nearer and saw that they had a fine fat deer to roast at their fire, he felt very angry. In his opinion no one save a noble or a wealthy churchman had a right to eat rich venison, and he felt sure he had discovered a nest of poaching rogues.

"What is the matter?" said the bishop. "For whom are you making all this ado? Why do you kill the king's venison for such a small company?"

"We are shepherds," replied Robin Hood, "and we keep sheep all the year. We feel disposed to be merry today, so we have killed a fat deer for our feast."

When the bishop heard this cool answer he was ready to burst with rage. He was accustomed to see poor shepherds kneel before him in most humble fashion, and here was one giving him a careless and insolent reply.

"You thieving rogues!" he cried, "as sure as I am Bishop of Hereford, you shall hang for this. The king shall know of your doings, and he will send you at once to the gallows."

"Oh pardon, oh pardon," said Robin Hood, "a bishop should show mercy. It would be a stain on your lordship's cloth if you were to take so many lives away for the killing of a single deer."

"No pardon for you this day," said the bishop; "you must come with me, and go before the king."

He made a sign to the train of armed attendants who followed him, and several of them came forward to seize the shepherds. But Robin sprang away, and set his back against a tree, and drew his horn from beneath his cloak of gray duffle. He set the horn to his lips, and blew such a piercing blast that, for a moment, the bishop and his men were silent in wonder. And at the next moment they were silent in terror; for every bush, every tree, every thicket, gave up its man. Seventy bold bowmen sprang into sight, each with shaft on string, and waiting but the word of their master to loose their arrows.

The bishop's men saw at once that they had fallen into an ambush, and fled for their lives. The bishop would have fled with them, but he pulled his palfrey round so hastily that it stumbled and fell on its nose, pitching the bishop clean out of the saddle. Little John picked up the churchman, who was more frightened than hurt, and now found that he was in the power of the men whom he had intended to see hanged.

"This is the Bishop of Hereford," laughed Robin to Little John, "and no pardon shall we have from him. Luckily, we do not need it now."

"Cut off his head, master!" growled Little John.

Upon hearing this the bishop was dreadfully frightened, and his fat face went as white as paper. It was now his turn to beg for mercy.

"Pardon! Pardon!" cried the terrified bishop. "If I had known that it was you I'd have gone another way."

"I dare say you would," replied Robin; "but no pardon do I owe you. You must come with me and go to the forest."

So, willy-nilly, the bishop had to go with Robin Hood, and they went by glade and forest path until they reached a secret nook among the woods where the outlaws had made a camp.

A great fire was already burning there, and two or three

men were busy cooking, while Friar Tuck overlooked
them and gave directions.

When the bishop saw Friar Tuck he thought that he
would surely find a friend in a fellow churchman, and he
spoke to him, and called him brother. But Tuck took no
notice—he only spoke in a louder voice to the cooks, and
rated one of them who was allowing a panful of venison
collops to burn, so the bishop had to turn away.

Before long the meal was ready, and so delicious did
the vension smell that the bishop's mouth watered. He
had made a long ride that morning, and the forest air was
keen.

Friar Tuck said grace, and they all fell to, and the bishop
cleared his dish as promptly as any hungry outlaw of the
company. He had a tankard at his elbow, and first it was
filled with brown ale and then with red wine, and the
bishop ate and drank as if he would never stop. At last
he could eat and drink no more, and the day was waning.

"I must be going," said the bishop. "Call in a reckoning! What have I to pay for this good dinner?"

"Ah, yes," said Robin; "your lordship speaks well and
truly. After a guest has eaten and drunken he does well
to call for the bill. But who shall count the reckoning, my
Lord Bishop?"

The bishop looked round and thought for a moment.

"I will choose this worthy friar to do so," said the fat
bishop, pursing his mouth in a very important manner. "I
am certain that a good son of the church will do right by
me and by you, Robin Hood."

The bishop thought to save his purse by these flattering

allusions to Friar Tuck, but he did not know the jovial priest. Tuck's face was hidden for the moment behind a great leather black jack from which he was drinking ale, and when it came to view his little merry eyes were twinkling.

"Is it even so?" said the friar, in his deepest voice. "Am I then to say what payment the bishop shall make for this good cheer?"

"Yes, good Tuck," said Robin, "the bishop has chosen well. I will abide by your decision."

"Then," said the friar, "his lordship shall empty his purse—"

"That will I gladly do!" cried the bishop, and whipped out his purse from the bag which hung at his girdle. "Here it is. Eleven silver pennies are in it, and I will give them all—"

"Let me finish!" cried Tuck, interrupting the bishop in turn. "His lordship shall empty his purse, and also that large wallet of leather fastened at his saddlebow."

"No, no!" screamed the bishop; "let that be. Touch not that, I pray you. It is not money that profane hands should meddle with. It belongs to the church, and consists of the poor dues owing to her by tenants of her lands."

"Poor dues!" cried Robin Hood. "Say poor tenants, rather, my Lord Bishop, for much of this money hath been wrung from the needy, as I am well advised. Little John, let us see what wealth the bishop carries."

Up rose the giant, seized the bishop's own cloak, and spread it on the turf. Then away he went and fetched the big leathern wallet, so carefully and tightly strapped at the bishop's saddlebow.

All eyes were fixed on the heavy bag, and a general Murmur arose when Little John opened the mouth of it and poured a great stream of pieces of gold onto the cloak.

"Here's money enough, master!" said Little John, "and a comely sight is it to see."

"How much is there?" asked Robin.

"Three hundred pounds," replied Little John.

"We will take it," said Robin Hood. "First we will give back to the poorest tenants the money they have paid; the rest we will keep in memory of the pleasant dinner at which my Lord of Hereford has joined us."

The bishop's face was black with rage at this free disposal of the money he loved so much, and he broke into a storm of angry words, but Robin only laughed.

"A man ought to be in a better temper than that, after a good dinner," said the chief outlaw. "This is a time for music and dance, not for evil words and bitter speeches. Strike up a merry tune, Alan-a-Dale, and my Lord of Hereford shall dance to it."

"Ay, that he shall!" roared Little John, as Robin Hood seized the fat bishop by the hand; "I will help you, and dance he shall."

So, to the great delight of the outlaws, Robin Hood and Little John seized the Bishop of Hereford and made him dance to the sweet music of Alan-a-Dale's harp. The bishop danced with a very ill grace, and looked very sour as he hopped up and down. But he was too frightened to disobey. He had lost his money, but he did not want to lose his life. So he danced until he was very tired, when Robin Hood bade him get on his palfrey and be off. The bishop did not need to be told twice. He scrambled into the saddle and was off in a moment, making for Nottingham as hard as he could go.

Robin Hood Meets with ⟡
a Tinker by the Way

WHEN the poor old bishop got back to Nottingham without a penny of his dearly loved money, he took counsel with the sheriff whose treasure chamber was empty. Both were filled with the most furious rage against Robin Hood and issued a proclamation that a warrant would be given, in the name of the king, to any man who would go against the famous outlaw to seize him and that a reward of one hundred pounds would be paid for the capture of Robin Hood.

Now when this proclamation was made at the market cross, the crowd of townsmen who heard it looked at each other and smiled. They knew how easy it was offer a hundred pounds for Robin Hood and how hard it would be to earn the money, and not one of them came forward to offer to take up the quest. But, on the outskirts of the crowd, stood one who was not a townsman. This was a short, thick, sturdy fellow, with a very dirty face and a turned-up nose. On his back was a leathern bag of tools hanging from the handle of a large hammer which he carried on his shoulder and held with his left hand. In his right hand was a long, stout, crab-tree staff, upon which he leaned as he listened with the deepest interest to the proclamation. He was a wandering tinker, and his name was John Sly.

"A hundred pounds," thought Sly to himself, "why, 'tis a noble sum of money. And all for seizing some outlaw rogue in the forest near at hand. I might mend pots and pans all my life and never see so much money. I' faith, I'll have a try at that."

He tapped a man near by on the shoulder. "Is it difficult, friend, to come at the place this Robin Hood haunts?" asked Sly.

"Nothing easier," said the townsman, with a grin; "but when you're there, then 'tis likely your troubles will begin."

Sly the tinker nodded loftily, for the day was hot and his last silver penny had gone in ale to quench his thirst.

"I'll warrant you he will not slip through my fingers so easily," said the tinker, and went forthwith to obtain the warrant which should give him authority to arrest the notorious outlaw, Robin Hood.

Not only did he obtain the warrant, but full information as to the place where he might meet the person named in it, and he set out of town by break of day next morning to make his fortune by seizing Robin Hood.

"I'll show these North-Countree thick-heads a trick or two," said Sly the tinker, twirling his great quarterstaff round his head. "They have no idea of the cunning and wit on South-Countree people. I'm a Banbury man, and we don't breed dullards in Oxfordshire."

By the time he had been walking for a couple of hours, the day was hot. He sat down under a great oak at a turning of the way to mop his forehead and to glance over the warrant, the possession of which made him very proud.

He had returned the paper to his wallet and was about to go on his road, when he saw a tall man in a suit of scarlet cloth, a sword at his side, walking gently towards him.

"Good," said Sly to himself, "here comes a fellow who looks like a respectable yeoman. I'll warrant he can put me on the right track for finding the haunt of this rogue of an outlaw."

So Sly went at once towards the yeoman in the scarlet suit. The latter had been walking with his eyes on the ground, and when he looked up and saw the tinker, with his bag of tools over his shoulder, he greeted the newcomer with a pleasant smile, and a courteous wave.

"The seal of the day to you," said the tinker, "and I'll go bail you're a native of these parts."

"True; I live near at hand," said the polite stranger. "And where do you live?"

"I am a tinker, my name is Sly, and I come from Banbury," replied the man of pots and pans. "And what is the news with you?"

"Why I fear me it will not be pleasant for a man of your

trade," said the stranger, laughing softly. "It is that two tinkers were set yesterday in the stocks for drinking too freely of ale and beer."

"Marry, come up!" growled Sly, who was rather a short-tempered fellow, "practice none of your jokes upon me, friend, or you may have reason to know that I carry a heavy stick."

"You asked for the news," returned the stranger, mildly, "and I obliged you. But, come, you are a man who goes from town to town and village to village. You have the news of half a shire at your finger ends. What have you to tell?"

"My news!" cried Sly, "is that there is a hundred pounds of good money to had for the picking up."

"Say you so?" said the stranger. "How may that be?"

"Why, in these woods there is a bold outlaw they call Robin Hood, and I have a warrant to seize him. And as sure as I can get my hands on him and drag him to Nottingham, there is a hundred pounds reward to clink in my pocket. Now, if you'll help me in this matter, I'll give you a good share of the reward."

The stranger scratched his forehead, and seemed to be in deep thought for a time.

"'Tis a fine sum of money," said he, at last, "and I believe I could show you where he is to be found."

"Good, good!" chuckled Sly the tinker, "let us go together, for I have a warrant from the king to take this outlaw wherever I find him. Point him out to me, and I'll make a rich man of you.

"Let me see the warrant," said the friendly stranger; "if it is all right, I will do the best I can to bring about a meeting between you and him."

But Sly only grinned, and winked the other eye. "No, no!" he said, "I'll not show my warrant to anyone. I'll trust no one with it. Help me to find him, and you shall share the reward. Refuse to help me, and 'tis all one; I'll find him myself."

"I see you are a cautious fellow," said the stranger; "well, I do not blame you for it. We meet with strange companions on the road in these days. But the reward is great, and I tell you frankly that I should like to share in it. Suppose we go together as far as the 'Royal Hart' and talk it over with a can of cool ale."

"With all my heart!" cried the tinker, licking his lips at the idea of a tankard of ale and hastening to follow the stranger along the way.

They went a mile or more, came to an inn, and met the landlord at the door. The landlord was very respectful to the stranger and bustled off at once to fetch a great jug of ale and a flagon of Canary wine. The tinker's little eyes glittered again at sight of such provision, and he tossed off cup after cup with heartiest good will and many expressions of delight at such splendid entertainment. He did most of the drinking, for the stranger only sipped at his cup and explained that he was deep in thought, planning the best and surest way in which to seize Robin Hood.

By the time the jug and flagon had been emptied, the tinker's head began to nod, and soon he was snoring peacefully in a corner of the settle.

The stranger smiled and opened Sly's wallet

The stranger smiled and opened Sly's wallet. From this he took out the warrant and read it with a broader smile still upon his face. When he had read the paper, he slipped it into his pocket. Then he rose and marched softly from the place.

Ten minutes later the landlord came into the room. The host started when he saw that the man in scarlet had gone, leaving the dirty and rather ragged tinker all alone, and began to feel uneasy about his bill. He stepped across to the settle and seized Sly by the collar.

"Wake up!" he said, and shook the sleeping tinker.

"No more, friend, no more," said the half-aroused tinker. "I have drunken well already at your expense."

"I'll take care it isn't at my expense!" cried the landlord. "Wake up, and settle the reckoning."

"Settled the reckoning, have you?" said Sly, who still thought he was talking to the stranger in scarlet. "Why, that's noble of you, but, trust me, I shall not forget it when we come to sharing up the reward."

"I want no reward!" shouted the landlord; "give me my me my just dues, and I am content," and with this he gave the tinker such a shake that Sly was fully awakened.

"Why? What? How? Where?" said the tinker, in confused fashion. "Where is my comrade, the bold yeoman who was to lead me to my journey's end, who was to pay the shot of this day's reckoning?"

The tinker's eye fell upon his unstrapped wallet. He caught it up and looked in. Now he began to bellow like a bull with a ring in his nose.

"Help! help!" he roared. "I am ruined! I am undone!

I have been robbed, plundered, and betrayed! Where is my warrant, my warrant from the king? It is lost and stolen."

"Warrant!" cried the landlord; "who would trust such a fellow as thou art with a warrant? And against whom was it drawn?"

"Marry, good host, but I had the warrant from the sheriff of Nottingham himself, and it was a warrant from the king 'which might have done me good—that is to take a bold outlaw, some call him Robin Hood.'"

"Robin Hood!" cried the landlord; "why this affair becomes stranger and stranger. That was Robin Hood with whom you came here and were drinking. 'Twas Robin in a dress of scarlet, instead of green such as he commonly wears."

When the tinker heard this he opened his mouth and eyes till he could open them no wider, and his uproar was stopped dead in pure surprise and astonishment. At last, he gasped, "That Robin Hood! Men told me he was a fierce-looking fellow, with a savage face, a true outlaw. Why that man looked like a worthy yeoman."

"Robin carries many faces under one hood," replied the landlord; "but it was he, as sure as I stand here and as sure as you have drunk a great jug of my best ale and a flagon of my best Canary.

"But he was going to pay the shot!" cried Sly. "He asked me to come hither to drink with him."

"I know naught about that," said the landlord, in a dry tone. "I only know that my drink has gone and you must meet the reckoning."

"How much?" asked the tinker, sadly.

"Ten shillings," was the reply.

"Ten shillings!" cried the tinker. "I have not ten farthings in the world."

"Then you must hand over your hammer and your bag of tools," said the landlord.

"What!" cried Sly, "my hammer and tools! How am I to earn my living?"

"You should have thought of that before running into debt," returned the other.

The tinker raved and stormed and shouted. He raged against the quiet stranger in scarlet; he denounced the landlord; he swore he would have the law of them all.

"Very good," said the landlord, "but the law will be on my side, I think. Here you sit drinking with an outlaw, and when he slips off you try to cheat me of the reckoning. I fancy the law will have something to say to you about that."

The tinker saw that the landlord spoke truth, and that he must e'en make the best of a very bad bargain. So he gave up his hammer and tools, took up his great crabstick, and left the "Royal Hart" in as sad case as ever a tinker found himself.

"If only I could come across that rogue in scarlet!" he said to himself, and swung his great stick vengefully about his head; "would I not thrash his jacket for him, a murrain* on the knave."

When the tinker came out of the inn he dashed away

---

*Plague.

along the road and, by sheer good luck, took the very
track which Robin was following. For, before Sly had
gone a mile, he caught a bright flash of color at a bend of
the path and next saw the stranger in scarlet standing to
watch a herd of deer. Up rushed Sly as fast as he could
go, shouting threats and calling on the man in scarlet to
turn and face him.

Robin Hood turned at once, and smiled when he saw
the angry tinker.

"What knave is this," quoth he, "that draws to me so
near?"

"No knave, no knave!" roared Sly; "the boot's on the
other leg this time. It seems I've found Robin Hood after
all, and now I'll show him with my crab-tree staff who has
done wrong and is to be paid for it."

And saying that, he ran in with wonderful nimbleness,
and fetched Robin a stunning crack with the great stick.
So quick was the tinker that down came the staff upon his
head, whack! before Robin could draw his sword.

Robin reeled under the shrewd stroke, but managed to
draw his blade, and face his foe. For two or three
moments he was compelled to dodge hither and thither to
escape the sweeping blows; then in he dashed, for his
blood was up, and the tinker was forced to act on the defensive. But Sly proved as good a man in defense as
in attack. Time and again he caught Robin's blade on his
hard crab-stick, and metal rang on wood till the forest
echoed again. Then with a swift twirl of his huge cudgel
Sly followed up a parry with a stroke at Robin's sword
arm, and caught him so smart a rap on the elbow that the

arm became numbed from finger tip to shoulder, and the outlaw could hold his sword no longer.

"Let us cry halt for a moment, tinker," said Robin; "I would e'en beg a boon of thee."

"A boon, indeed!" cried the tinker. "Before I grant that, I'll hang you on this tree. Marry, come up, but it seems I've taken the great Robin Hood, and the reward is mine."

Upon thought of this, Sly was so merry that he cut a caper and then looked about to see which road ran towards Nottingham. When Robin saw that the tinker's head was turned for a moment, he seized his horn and blew the forest call.

"Nay, nay!" roared the tinker, "here is no time to be blowing calls and winding horns. You must come along with me, or I must e'en give you a gentle love taps with this little persuader of mine," and he made his mighty crab-tree whistle through the air.

But at that instant up bounded Little John and Will Scarlet, running to the aid of their master.

The tinker stared in surprise at Little John, for he had never seen such a giant of a man before.

"By my faith!" cried Sly; "but here comes the stoutest knave I ever set eyes on. But if ye think that I will fly, ye know not Jack Sly," and he set his back against an oak and placed himself in guard, his quarterstaff held in readiness either to strike or to parry. Robin Hood sat down on a bank, for he was too stiff to stand so sharply had the tinker's staff played tattoo on him.

"What is wrong, master?" cried Little John; "and why do you sit so wearily beside the highway?"

"By our Lady," said Robin Hood, "here is a tinker that stands by that hath paid well my hide."

"Say you so, master!" cried Little John, "then I would fain try a turn with him. We'll see if he can do as much for me."

The huge outlaw sprang forward and swung up his heavy staff, and the tinker faced him as boldly as possible. But before the sticks clashed together Robin Hood called upon his lieutenant to hold.

"I do not blame the man," said the leader. "He had good reason to pay me a few knocks. I had marred his fortune by taking the warrant for my arrest, by which he set much store. But if I have spoiled his fortune one way I will make it in another. Tinker, how dost thou fare on the road?"

"So, so, master!" replied Sly; "sometimes a few jobs and a supper, sometimes a day's march without a penny taken. Then, if a pot of ale should come my way, I am like to find myself fast in the stocks."

"Not a very gay life," laughed Robin.

"A dog's life, master," replied the tinker; "a dog's life."

"Change it then for ours in the merry greenwood!" cried the outlaw. "By day we hunt the deer; at night we feast high on venison around our blazing fire, and wash down the feast with nut-brown ale. Come, join us!"

"Ay, master, that I will!" cried the tinker. "Such a life will fit me like hand and glove. I am with you to live or to die," and Robin and he clasped hands upon the bargain.

So John Sly, the tinker, turned from hunting Robin

Hood to become Robin's sworn man, and he made as
stanch a servant as he had been stout as an enemy. The
old ballad which tells us how Robin won this recruit ends
with Robin Hood's commendation of his new henchman.

> "In manhood he is a mettled man,
>   And a mettle (metal) man by trade,
> Never thought I that any man
>   Should have made me so afraid.
> And if he will be one of us,
>   We will all take one fare,
> And whatsoever we do get,
>   He shall have his full share.
> So the tinker was content
>   With them to go along,
> And with them a part to take,
>   And so I end my song."

The Bishop Tries His Own Hand ౿

FOR some time the Bishop of Hereford stayed with the Sheriff of Nottingham, and every morning they asked eagerly if there was yet any news of the capture of Robin Hood. The bishop was in hopes that he could get back his three hundred pounds if the famous outlaw should be seized, and the sheriff's thoughts were filled night and day with the vision of his empty treasure house.

But day after day passed, and those who had gone to search for the outlaws came back to the town and said there was no sign of them in the forest. It was true that John Sly, the tinker, did not come back, but no one noticed that he did not turn up again, and no one cared.

Then one day there marched into the town a strong company of men-at-arms on their way from the north to London. The captain who commanded this company was a foreign mercenary, who was at any time ready to sell the services of his men to the highest bidder. The bishop saw

the troops march into the town, and an idea came into his
mind: These were the very fellows to aid him in catching
Robin Hood; he would employ them for a few days, pay
them out of the store of wealth to be captured from the
outlaws, and avenge himself on the outlaw leader.

It was quite easy to make a bargain with the captain of
the band, and so confident was the bishop that these
trained troops would make short work of the bowmen of
the forest that he rode with them to aid them in finding
the retreat of the outlaws.

As luck would have it, Robin Hood himself was out
alone along the highway at the very moment that the
bishop and his company rode up to the forest. At a sharp
turn of the way Robin came full upon two of the bishop's
servants who were riding a little ahead as scouts. Both of
these men had been with the bishop when he was seized,
and they knew Robin Hood again at once.

"Here he is!" they shouted. "Here's Robin Hood,
himself!"

At a glance, Robin knew that he was in the midst of his
enemies, and there was the bishop riding hastily upon
hearing the shout.

"What shall I do?" thought Robin Hood. "If the bishop
takes me he'll show me no mercy and I shall be
hanged."

But he was in no mind to give up and be easily taken.
He turned and flew at his utmost speed for a wood near
by. Then what a running and racing there was! The
bishop and his men rode hard after the fugitive, but he got
among the trees and was lost to sight for the moment.

"Ride round the wood!" roared the bishop. "It is not a

very great wood. We can surround it on every side, and then there will be no chance for the rogue to slip through out hands."

This was done, and soon a circle was drawn around the wood, and Robin was inside the circle. Then the company began to search the wood, but they went to work slowly and warily, for they knew not how many of Robin's men might be at hand, and they feared an ambush.

As it happened, there was no need for fear. Not a single follower was within hail, and Robin Hood had nothing to depend on save his own wit and courage. The bold outlaw knew that he was in the greatest danger of his life, and he ran to the very heart of the wood, where he hoped to find a refuge. Here stood a tiny cottage of two rooms, where lived a poor old widow who earned a living at her spinning wheel. Robin had often helped the old woman, and he felt sure she would now help him in turn. And, besides that, her three sons were members of Robin's band.

He ran into the cottage, and the old woman looked up from her spinning wheel.

"I am Robin Hood!" cried the outlaw; "and the bishop and his men are at my heels. If they take me I am a dead man, for the bishop has sworn he will hang me on the highest oak in the forest."

"Never fear, Robin Hood!" cried the quick-witted old woman; "that shall never be. I'll cheat the bishop and his company yet. What, shall you be taken, who have so often helped me in my need! Marry, never, say I. Come, go into the inner room and put on the old skirt and mantle of mine which you will find there, and leave me your suit of Lincoln green."

"A noble plan!" cried Robin Hood; "we'll see if the bishop's eyes are sharp enough to find Robin Hood in an old woman's dress."

In a trice Robin Hood was clothed like a poor old woman, and his disguise was finished by a big old hat, with a broken brim, which fell over his face. He left the cottage, hobbling along and leaning on a stick, while he carried spindle and twine, like an old cottage woman who intends to work while she rests on her way.

In a short time Robin heard the trampling of hoofs, and now he bent lower still and hobbled more lamely than ever. Then he heard a voice, and knew it.

"Who is this?" cried some one, in pompous tones, and Robin knew that the bishop was before him. "Seize that old woman and bring her to me."

One of the bishop's men caught hold of the trembling old crone, and led her to the spot where the bishop sat on his dapple gray palfrey.

"Whence dost thou come, old woman?" demanded the churchman.

"From my cottage in the wood, noble lord," croaked the old woman, from under her bent hat. She did not raise her eyes from the ground, but the bishop did not wonder at that. He thought it showed no more than a proper humility in his presence.

"And hast thou seen anyone in the wood this day?"

"None save a man in a green dress, who entered my cottage a short time back."

"Ah, ha!" cried the bishop; "a man in a green dress, sayest thou?"

"Yea, my lord, and he was bearing a long bow and a sheaf of arrows, and on his head he wore a green hood. He entered my inner room to rest."

"On, on!" cried the bishop. "We have him! We have him! Haste to the cottage and drag him out."

In their eagerness to seize the outlaw the bishop and his men rode forward at once, while the old woman hobbled on her way. But no sooner was she hidden by the bushes than a most wonderful change took place in her movements. She straightened herself, she became nimble and swift, her hobble became a stride which covered the ground like a running deer, and away she flew at top speed for a certain glade in the great forest where a number of outlaws were in waiting. As she hurried into the glade, Little John saw her, and broke out in wonder:

"Who is that yonder coming over the lea? She looks so like a witch I'll let fly an arrow at her!"

Little John said this, for when he saw the figure of an old cottage woman moving at such wonderful speed he thought it could be nothing short of witchcraft.

"Hold thy hand! Hold thy hand!" shouted Robin Hood. "Do not shoot your keen arrows at me for I am thy good master, Robin Hood."

"And is it you, master?" cried Little John, in amazement. "What brings you here in the guise of an old woman?"

"I have had a narrow escape of falling into the hands of the bishop," replied Robin, and told Little John of his adventure.

"By my faith!" cried Little John; "I think, master, we

ought to show the bishop that it is no safe sport to come into the forest to hunt us."

"I think so, too," replied the chief; "wind your horn, Little John, and call our brave fellows together."

Little John wound his horn, and the outlaws trooped up, till a hundred of them stood before Robin Hood, ready to obey his smallest command. They stared in wonder at the figure of a poor old woman among them till they recognized their leader's face under the broken hat; and when the story was known, there was much laughter at the disguise and the clever escape which Robin had made.

But we must now return to see how the bishop had got on at the cottage.

When he came to the old woman's hut, the bishop called out furiously, "Bring out that traitor Robin Hood and let me see him."

"Burst in the door!" roared the bishop, and the door was broken open, and soldiers rushed in.

"Here he is!" cried the man. "Here he is! I know him again. This is the very fellow, in a green hood, who flew from us into the wood but just now."

"Drag him out!" commanded the bishop, and three or four soldiers darted on the figure clad in Lincoln green, and dragged it from the corner where it was hiding.

"Put him on that white horse, and guard him closely!" cried the bishop; "and now back to the town at once to put him in gaol. I'll never rest till I have him under lock and key, and tomorrow shall be the hanging day."

The old woman, who wore the clothes of Robin Hood,

said nothing at all, and they thought the prisoner was silent from fear. Nor did anyone lift the hood to look at the captive's face; all were full of eagerness to get away from the forest with the captured outlaw. As for the bishop, he was as proud as a peacock to think of this clever seizure.

He placed the old woman on a milk-white steed and bestrode a dapple gray himself. As he rode along through the forest, he laughed for joy because he had captured Robin Hood.

The bishop laughed till he came to the edge of the wood, and then his face became as long as a fiddle and his jaw dropped. For what did he see before him but five score archers, each with his bow bent and shaft on string. And the bishop knew that they were outlaws and that each of them was the match of four common bowmen such as he led.

"Archers!" gasped the bishop; "and see who appears to command them! By my gown, it is the old hag who met us in the wood. Who is she?"

"Marry," said the captive, "I think it is one they call Robin Hood."

"Robin Hood!" cried the bishop. "Then who art thou?"

"Hee, hee! Ho, ho!" chuckled the captive, and she threw back the hood, and the bishop saw the skinny face and the toothless gums, bared in laughter, of the old woman. "Thou canst see who I am, my Lord Bishop!" she cried in shrill tones. "What a clever Lord Bishop art thou to be carrying off an old woman for the King of Sherwood, Robin Hood!" and she laughed and clapped her hands.

"Woe is me," said the bishop, "that ever I saw this day!" for he saw that he was in a trap, and at the next moment a shower of shafts came whistling among his followers, who at once took to flight.

The bishop wheeled his dapple gray, and drove the spurs home, thinking to escape, but the outlaws were too quick for him. Much and Will Stutley ran like hares and seized the bridle of the dapple gray, and next came Robin, striding along in his disguise, and tied the bishop's horse to a tree and made the bishop alight.

"What, my Lord Bishop, "he laughed, "and have you come again to visit us in the greenwood? I fear we cannot invite you to another merry feast, for we may not stay to prepare it."

"We have time to see what is in his port-mantle," said Little John, and he searched the saddle bags and took all the bishop's money—the very money which the bishop had bought to give the men-at-arms if they should seize Robin Hood.

"Give fifty silver pennies to the old woman," said Robin Hood, "for she has saved my life this day," and it was done.

The bishop looked on with a very sour face while a division was made of his money, but he could not help himself and was only too glad to hear Robin Hood say, "Now, let him go."

"Bishop, Bishop!" cried Little John, laughing, "you have made a sorry business of your hunting this day, and you know how a rogue is made to ride through the town in penance. In that way shall you return to Nottingham."

So the bishop was made to mount the dapple gray, with his face to the horse's tail, and thus he was led through the wood, and the dapple gray sent at a canter along the road towards Nottingham. And thus, riding backwards in disgrace, the bishop went back to town, with neither money nor prisoner.

Robin Hood Becomes a Butcher

O NE morning Robin Hood woke with a restless feeling at his heart. This quiet time was irking him; he felt that he must undertake some adventure, and he made up his mind to go to Nottingham and see how things were faring in the town. He said nothing of his intention to Little John, for he knew that his faithful follower would urge him not to venture into such a nest of enemies, but slipped away by himself.

He took care that he should not be easily recognized, for to be known for Robin Hood inside the walls of Nottingham town would be a dangerous business. So he put off his dress of Lincoln green, donned a plain russet suit, and went his way, looking like a worthy yeoman or tradesman.

Within two or three miles of the town Robin came to a place where two roads met, and here he saw a butcher going to market with a fine mare; over the back of the mare were slung panniers full of meat.

"Good morrow, good fellow!" cried Robin. "Where do you dwell and whither are you going?"

"No matter where I dwell," replied the other; "I am a butcher, and I am going to Nottingham to sell my meat."

"Say you so?" cried jolly Robin, into whose mind a plan had just come. "Why, now, it is my great fancy to become a butcher. Will you sell?"

"Sell what?" said the butcher.

"The mare, the panniers, and the load of meat," replied Robin. "Come, put your own price on them."

"The price of my meat and the mare," replied the butcher, "is four marks, and that is cheap enough."

"Four marks I will give at once," answered Robin, and drew out his purse. The money was counted into the hand of the butcher, and the bargain was completed on the spot. The butcher turned home, and Robin Hood drove the mare on towards Nottingham.

"Now," thought Robin, "I shall enter the town with as innocent an air as one could wish. Who will look twice at a tradesman coming to market with his load?"

He drove the mare through the gates without looking to right or left, and no man challenged him; he went into the market, found the stall which the butcher used, and set his meat on it. Soon the butchers' row became busy with people who had come marketing, and the butchers began to shout, "Come, buy! buy! buy! Fine and prime meat, come buy! buy! buy!"

When Robin heard the other butchers crying their wares he began to cry his, too, and when customers came he gave them, in his ignorance, as much meat for a penny

*He gave them as much meat for a penny as
other butchers were giving for three*

as other butchers were giving for three. The news of this soon got abroad, and Robin's stall was crowded with buyers, while his rivals sold nothing at all.

The butchers began to scratch their heads, and stare at each other.

"Who is the newcomer?" they said. "He will ruin us. He sells as much for one penny as we do for three. We shall get no custom at all."

Some of them began to sell a little cheaper, but still the buyers thronged about Robin.

"This is some prodigal fellow," said one of the butchers. "He has sold his father's land, and is wasting the money is this stupid fashion."

"Ay," said another, "or he hath stolen his beasts, and so can sell very cheap."

"Listen to me," said a third; "he is, mayhap, some gallant in disguise, who is selling cheap meat to win a wager."

"Let us become acquainted with him," said a fourth. "I will go up to him and ask him to join us at the butchers' feast today."

So he stepped up to Robin, who was just handing over the last joint on the stall, and said, "Come, brother, we be all of one trade and should know each other better. Will you dine with us today, for it is the day of the butchers' feast?"

"Indeed, yes," said jolly Robin, "I will go to feast with you, my true brethren, as fast as I can."

"Good," said the other; "the feast is to be held at the house of the sheriff. We will go there together."

So when the market was over the butchers trooped off

to the sheriff's house. Robin grinned to himself as he went into the hall and saw the mean, miserly looking, old sheriff sitting pompously there at the head of the board.

"If yonder old hunks but knew who I was, there would be a fine to-do," thought bold Robin.

The feast was set on the long table, and Robin, as the youngest butcher there, was asked to say grace, and he did so. Then he called upon the company to drink as deeply as they pleased at his expense.

"Come, brothers, be merry," said jolly Robin. "Let's drink and never give over, for I'll pay the shot ere I go if it cost me more than five pounds."

"This is a mad blade," said one of the butchers in the sheriff's ear, and he told the story of Robin and the cheap meat. The sheriff pursed his lips and shook his head.

"He is some wild prodigal," said the sheriff, "who has sold his land and is getting rid of the money as fast as he can."

"That's just what we thought," replied the butcher. "We said the very same thing."

During the rest of the feast the sheriff ate and drank but little. He was deep in thought, and ever and anon he cast a sly and wily glance at Robin.

"That careless spendthrift is casting his money from him with both hands, I know," said the sheriff to himself. "Why should not I get some of it?" And the sheriff sighed as he thought of his empty treasure house, which so sorely needed refilling.

"I may get a little from him," reflected the sheriff, "and

I am thankful for even small gains since I was stripped so completely by that arch-rogue Robin Hood and his knaves of followers."

So, when the feast was over, the sheriff took a seat beside the young butcher, and began to talk pleasantly with him.

"I have heard of the joke you played this morning," said the sheriff, wrinkling his nutcracker face into a harsh grin, as if he loved a joke as well as anyone. "You put the curb on our butchers with your splendid pennysworth of meat."

"I fear me I made but a lame hand of it," replied Robin; "the truth is I am new at the trade, and I scarce know the value of beasts as yet."

"Have you many?" asked the sheriff, smoothly.

"Hundreds," replied Robin, "and they pasture on a hundred acres of good free land."

"Why, that is a very pretty little estate," returned the sheriff.

"Well enough," replied Robin carelessly, "but I would gladly change it for ready money."

"Ay, ay," thought the sheriff to himself; "here is your true spendthrift—always eager to get money to spend on his pleasures. Beshrew me if I turn not this to great advantage." Then he spoke aloud. "Why, then, have you not already sold your beasts and land?"

"I have found no purchaser," said Robin, yawning, and stretching his arm, "though, to be sure, I am willing to sell at an easy rate. But none seems to have money to buy."

"True, true," said the sheriff; "times are hard, and money is scarce. But sooner than see you lack a purchaser, I would make a bid myself."

"How much would you give?" asked Robin.

The sheriff named a sum about one-tenth of the value of the estate which Robin had described, and Robin agreed instantly to take it. They shook hands on the bargain, and the sheriff secretly chuckled to himself to think how neatly he was stripping this wild spendthrift.

"The day is not far spent," said Robin. "What say you to an hour's ride to see the beasts and the land?"

"With all my heart," said the sheriff, "and I will bring the money, pay you on the spot, and take possession at once."

"Good," said Robin. "Short bargains make long friends. And I protest and vow that I will make over the beasts and land you as freely as ever my father made them over to me." Then he smiled to himself as the sheriff hurried away to get the money and order a horse for the ride.

In a short time they set out, Robin riding the mare he had bought from the butcher and the sheriff riding his own nag. Robin took the road which skirted the Sherwood Forest, and soon they were deep among the outlying woodlands.

"I had rather your estate lay in some other direction," said the sheriff uneasily. "I like not this forest. God bless us this day, Master Butcher, and keep us from that rogue, Robin Hood."

"Pooh!" said the butcher. "I care not a snap of my finger for aught that Robin Hood could do to me. Best let us ride on. We may come in sight of the beasts at any moment now."

They rode on and turned a bend in the way; the butcher reined in his horse and laid his hand on the bridle of the other.

"Stop you, Sir Sheriff—stop!" he said. "Here be my horned beasts. What think you of them? Are they not fat and fair to see?"

The sheriff gasped in wonder, and his heart began to beat thickly in alarm. Before him a herd of a hundred of the king's deer were calmly feeding in a grassy glade of the forest.

"What is this trick, fellow?" blustered the sheriff. "We came hither to see the cattle."

"Nay, nay, Sir Sheriff," laughed the other. "I never promised you aught but horned beasts, and yonder they stand."

The sheriff began to feel more and more uneasy. "I tell thee, fellow," he said, "I would I were gone, for I like not thy company."

"Why, Sir Sheriff," said Robin, "be not in such haste. Here is the bargain I promised you, and I should like you to see some of my friends, who will gladly witness it."

Thereupon, Robin set his horn to his mouth and blew three blasts. In a few moments Little John and the whole company of outlaws appeared.

When the sheriff saw the outlaws troop out of the wood and surround him he cried out in fear. He saw that he had been completely trapped, and he turned to the butcher.

"I know you now," he cried. "You are Robin Hood himself?"

"That am I," laughed Robin, "and these are my merry men whom you do not love, Sir Sheriff. Natheless the bargain must be made. Put down the money, sheriff."

And the sheriff was forced to pay down every piece of the money which he had brought in order to buy the prodigal's estate. Then his horse was turned round, and he was started back to Nottingham a sadder and a wiser man, sadder because his treasure house was now more empty than ever, and wiser because he had learned to his cost who the butcher was.

How Robin Hood ❧
Saved the Widow's Sons

Now it happened one day that Robin Hood went on a journey and left the band in charge of Little John. Six days was he absent, and on the seventh he crossed a ridge, and his heart leapt for joy when he saw far off a great mass of purple woodland, and he knew that he was drawing near once more to his beloved forest haunts.

He was on the edge of the trees when he paused and raised his head to listen. Someone was coming along the way and making sounds as of one in deep distress, crying and moaning. He waited a moment and then saw an old woman moving towards him. She seemed to be in great grief, and the tears were streaming down her face. Robin knew her at once. It was the widow who lived in the wood, the old woman who had helped him to escape from the clutches of the bishop.

"Hey day, Gammer Green!" he cried. "What is to do

now? Has anyone wronged thee, old friend? If so, by our Lady, he shall learn that thou hast a friend and protector in Robin Hood."

"Oh, Robin, Robin!" cried the old woman. "My sons! My sons!"

"Why, what is amiss with them?" said the outlaw.

"They have been seized by the sheriff," she replied. "They lie this day in Nottingham jail, and tomorrow they die."

"What, Hal, and Hob, and Dickon!" roared Robin. "Three as brave lads as ever twanged a long bow. This is heavy news, Gammer. How know you that their fate is so near?"

"I am just returning from Nottingham town, and I have had the news from Lobb the cobbler," she replied. "Oh, save them, Robin Hood!"

"Trust me, dame!" cried Robin, his merry face suddenly grim and his eyes sparkling. "I am bound to do my utmost for any members of the band, and your sons have a special claim on me. I will give instant orders in the matter."

He hurried on at once, and never slacked his speed till he had gained the camp in the heart of the forest. Little John saw his master coming and stepped forward to meet him.

"This is a bad business about Hal, and Hob, and Dickon!" cried Robin.

"Ay, master, it is," replied Little John, gravely. "How heard ye the news so soon?"

"I met their mother," replied Robin Hood. "And how were the poor lads seized?"

"Pure ill-luck," returned Little John. "They were in hot chase of a great hart and ran fairly into the arms of a strong body of the sheriff's men. They were prisoners before they knew that they were in danger."

"They must be saved," said Robin. "I can never face their mother again if I let the sheriff put a noose round their necks;" and he sat down with Little John to make plans for cheating the sheriff and winning the freedom of the widow's sons.

The next morning Robin Hood set off by himself towards Nottingham town. The sun was up, and when it stood at the height of noon the widow's sons were to die, so Robin stepped briskly along the road, for he knew he had no time to lose. But suddenly he stopped, for a foot passenger was coming towards him, and Robin scanned him, as he scanned everybody, in wary fashion. Then he marched on again, for this was a quiet palmer, a poor, ragged old fellow, who begged his way as he went through the land on pilgrimage. As they drew near each other, the palmer paused, and leaning on his pilgrim's staff, awaited Robin's approach.

"What news—what news?" cried the outlaw. "What news, I do thee pray?"

"News enough," replied the palmer, "for in Nottingham town yonder three squires are to die this very day. I have seen the gallows a-building and have seen the countryfolk flocking to the town in crowds to witness the execution, for it is not every day that three brothers are hung side by side."

Robin said nothing, and did not appear to pay any heed to this great piece of news. His forehead was wrinkled in thought, and his eye was running over the palmer's dusty and tattered dress. Then he snapped his fingers briskly as one who has found what he sought.

"Come, change thy apparel with me, old man," laughed Robin. "Come, change thy apparel for mine, and here is forty shillings in good silver. Go drink it in beer or wine."

The palmer looked down in wonder at his travel-stained old clothes and then at the money in Robin's hand, and then at Robin's handsome dress of forest green.

"Though thine apparel is good and mine is ragged and dirty," he said, "thou shouldst not laugh in scorn at an old man."

"I do not laugh you to scorn!" cried Robin. "I am as serious as man ever was. Come, change clothes with me, and take the money to feast thy brethren."

So they changed clothes, and when Robin had put on the old man's hat, which stood full high on the crown, and the old man's tattered cloak, patched with scraps of every color—black, and blue, and red, and the old man's torn and patched breeches, and hose full of holes, and shoes which scarcely hung together, he was so transformed that Little John himself would not have known his master. And, as Robin put on the palmer's rags, he made a score of merry jokes and cried, as he ended and surveyed his sorry figure, "Well, it's good habit that makes the man!" But he had now what he wanted, a splendid disguise, and away he strode for Nottingham town.

Two hours later the sheriff was walking along the town streets, his brow knitted in vexation, for he had not yet found a hangman for his three prisoners. "But they shall hang, the rascals!" cried the sheriff, "even if I have to swing them off the gallows with my own hands."

At this moment his path was blocked by a queer, little, bent, ragged old man, who called out in a shrill voice, "Heaven save ye, noble sheriff! Heaven guard ye, my good lord!"

"Well, old palmer, what d'ye want with me?" demanded the sheriff in surly tones, thinking that the pilgrim meant to beg of him and at the same time resolving that he would not give the smallest coin.

"Why, Sir Sheriff!" cried the tattered palmer, "I am told that today you need a hangman."

"Ay, that I do, badly," replied the sheriff, his tones a little more pleasant as the palmer had not started to beg of him. "Ay, that I do, for I have had the great luck to get hold of three of Robin Hood's rogues, and I will string them up by the head on the stroke of noon. Would that I had their leader to hang beside them!"

"Ay, my Lord Sheriff," said the palmer, wagging his head piously. "I can understand your feelings. I have heard that Robin Hood hath done you great despite."

"He is the biggest rogue unhung," growled the sheriff; "but the day will come when we shall stand face to face, and then let him escape from my clutch if he can."

"Ah!" bleated the palmer, "it will be a sorry day for Robin Hood, I warrant you. But now, here is the matter of hanging these three fellows of his band. I am, I know, but a silly old man, yet I would fain hear what reward you would give me if I became the hangman today."

"A good fee—a good fee, old man," said the sheriff eagerly. "Thirteen pence in money and the suits of clothes from the bodies of the prisoners, and, by my faith, old palmer, a suit of clothes, I think, would not come amiss to thee."

"It is enough," said the palmer. "I am your man, and I will take these fellows in hand."

At ten minutes before the stroke of noon a procession started from the doors of the jail and moved towards the market place. It was formed of a strong band of Norman soldiery with the three prisoners in their midst. In front of the prisoners hobbled the old palmer who was to hang them. The procession entered the market place, which was so packed with a vast throng that the soldiers had to force a way for themselves towards the grim gallows, where three noosed ropes hung from a beam. Around the foot of the gallows a space had been cleared, and here the sheriff was awaiting them.

"Up with them—up with them, old man!" said the sheriff. "Let me see thee prove thyself a good hangman this day."

"All in good time, my Lord Sheriff," said the palmer; "but first I must hear the last confessions of these men who are about to ascend the gallows."

Then he whispered to the prisoners, and, while the sheriff thought that he was confessing them, he was really giving them his orders for the sharp piece of work now at hand.

"Hang them up, old man—hang them up!" cried the

sheriff impatiently. "And hast thou a bag with thee to
carry off their clothes?"

"Ay, Sir Sheriff. I have bags enough," laughed the
palmer, and then he began to sing:—

> "I've a bag for meal, and a bag for malt,
>   And a bag for barley corn;
>   A bag for bread, a bag for beef,
>   And a bag for my little small horn."

"Of what use is a horn to thee, ole fellow?" jeered the
sheriff. "I doubt if thou canst blow it."

"Can I not?" roared the palmer. "Nay, but thou thyself,
proud sheriff, shalt hear my blast and say if it be blown
truly."

And with these words a marvelous change came over
the figure of the palmer. The bent, crouching form
straightened itself and became a tall, commanding figure:
the thin quavering tones were changed for a full, ringing
voice, and, standing on the edge of the scaffold, Robin
Hood raised his horn to his lips and blew three ringing
blasts.

The sheriff knew him at once.

"Treason! Treason!" shrieked the sheriff. "Robin Hood!
'Tis Robin Hood himself! Seize him! Slay him!"

But the guard of soldiery had other work to do than to
seize Robin Hood: they were fighting for their own lives.
For at the very instant that those shrill blasts rang over
the heads of the crowd, scores of men, who had looked
like common peasants, threw aside their cloaks and

showed the Lincoln green of Robin's men. They rushed forward with sword and buckler in their hands.

"A Hood! A Hood!" roared a gigantic man at their head as they charged down upon the Norman soldiery. "A Hood to the rescue!" and the men in green followed Little John with an answering cry of "A Hood to the rescue! Robin Hood forever! Down with our Norman tryants!"

In an instant there was the greatest confusion and uproar. The peaceable portion of the crowd fled in every direction to escape the fray, women screamed, men shouted, swords clashed on bucklers, and the guard, assailed on all sides, had their work cut out to look after themselves without attending to the disguised palmer on the scaffold. Beneath the gallows tree Robin Hood was as busy as any that day. He whipped out a sharp knife and cut the ropes which bound Hal, and Hob, and Dickon, and shouted, "Follow me!" and leapt down from the scaffold. The three brothers sprang after their leader with a shout of joy, and in an instant were surrounded by a band of their friends.

"Draw together!" cried Robin Hood, and the outlaws formed in close order about their rescued comrades.

"March for the gates!" was the next order, and the forest band pressed steadily across the market place. Twice they were assailed by the sheriff's men, and twice they drove the soldiery off with showers of keen shafts and shrewd strokes of sword play. Soon the gates were reached, and these stood wide open, for Little John had left Much and Will Stutely and a dozen more to master the guard as soon as they heard the uproar break out in the square. This had been done, and the warders were already disarmed and bound when the outlaws came marching in triumph to the gates. Out they trooped to the open country, and then Little John banged the gates behind them, and locked them, and marched off with the key, so that no pursuit could be made. On the edge of the forest they met the poor old widow who had been waiting in trembling hope that Robin would make good his promise of rescuing her sons. When she saw Hal, and Hob, and Dickon safe and sound among their friends she wept again, but this time for pure joy, and she blessed Robin Hood a thousand times.

Robin Hood Meets Maid ✑
Marian In Sherwood Forest

Now, while Robin Hood was leading his men in Sherwood Forest and living the life of a bold outlaw, his thoughts were often full of someone whom he had left behind in his old home. This was Maid Marian, the beautiful daughter of a great man whose house had stood near Robin's home. Robin Hood and Maid Marian had been close friends since childhood. They had played together, hunting for birds' nests, fishing in the brook, climbing trees, or running races over the meadow grass, and when Robin was forced to go out into the world he bore a sore heart with him after parting with Marian.

Since Robin's departure, things had gone very hardly with Marian also. Her parents died, her friends proved unkind, and her heart often dwelt on the friend of her youth—bold, brave Robin. For a long time she did not know where he was, but at last his name began to ring through the North Countree, and she knew that her old friend had become the renowned outlaw of whose daring deeds minstrels sang and of whom men talked as they sat about the evening fire. At last, lonely and friendless as she was, Maid Marian resolved to seek Robin in Sherwood Forest and see if he still remembered the old happy days of their childhood. But she knew how unsafe it was for a woman to travel about the country alone, so she put on the dress of a page and took quiver and bow, sword and buckler, and thus armed and disguised she set out to seek Robin. At last she reached the skirts of the great forest and, as soon as she entered the dark shades of the mighty oaks, she looked eagerly forward to watch for the first sign of a forest dweller who could direct her to the haunts of her old friend.

As it happened, that very morning Robin had set out alone to make an expedition in search of news. He had taken great care to disguise himself, for his fate would be certain if he fell into the hands of the foresters. The sheriff, fuming with rage at the clever manner in which Robin had outwitted him and brought off the widow's sons, had given orders that every outlaw should be put to death upon capture, and no mercy whatever should be shown.

So Robin went out in a ragged suit of hodden-gray,* with a big hat down over his face, a huge patch over his left eye, and a tattered cloak huddled over his shoulders. He had been walking an hour or more when he saw the figure of a handsomely dressed stripling coming along the way towards him. Robin at once stepped out of sight be-

---

*A coarse gray cloth.

hind a bush until he could be sure that the youth was
alone. In these days it behoved him to be wary, so many
and so fierce were his enemies. He suspected some trap
or strategem at the sight of every stranger. But the
youth came on with a quick, even step, and seemed to
be entirely alone. Just as he was passing the bush behind
which Robin stood, the outlaw sprang out and commanded him to stand.

"Who art thou, and what dost thou want in Sherwood!"
demanded Robin Hood

The stranger was Maid Marian, and she looked at Robin
and never dreamed that her old friend stood before her in
the person of this wild, ragged man of the woods. She
thought it was some savage freebooter who would belike
plunder her, and she sprang back and laid her hand on her
sword.

"This is not one of Robin's men," thought Maid Marian.
"This is some footpad whom I must meet boldly or I am
undone. So she said, "Stand aside, fellow, and let me go
on my way. I have nought to do with thee."

"Ay, but I may have something to do with thee," replied
the tattered stranger. "Tell me whither and why thou
goest through the forest or I must turn thee back."

"Turn me back," said the page. "That wilt thou never
do, rude man. Put me not to the need of drawing sword
in my defense or thou mayst well rue the day."

"Why, this is a brave youth!" laughed Robin Hood.
"And what wouldst thou do with that pretty little bodkin
of thine, youngster?"

" 'Tis a bodkin that thou mayst find over sharp," said

the page, and drew the glittering blade from its sheath and waved it on high. "Give way, for I seek the heart of the forest and none shall check me."

When Robin heard that the newcomer was bound for the depths of Sherwood, his suspicions grew fast. It seemed to him that a bold, smart lad such as this was just the person the sheriff might send as a spy, and he became resolved to turn the page back. "Nay," said Robin, "I bid you return. Seek your own safety and leave the forest or I shall be compelled to draw also."

"Draw an thou wilt!" cried the other, "but go back I will not."

"The sight of my blade will frighten a mere lad like this," thought Robin, and he drew out his sword and sprang forward and made a lunge as if in fierce attack. But, to his surprise, the lunge was deftly turned aside, and the slender page met him as boldly with sword and buckler as ever Robin had been met in his life.

Clash-clash! went their swords as the keen blades grated together, but Robin did not put out the whole of his strength and skill against a mere lad like this, and so the combat lasted much longer than it would otherwise have done. Nor was the page at all unskilled in sword play, for on one occasion Robin's guard was passed and he received a small wound in the face. The outlaw became full of admiration for this brave young opponent and tried to make a peaceful ending to their fray.

"Hold thy hand," said Robin Hood, "and thou shalt range the forest with bold Robin Hood and hear the sweet song of the nightingale."

"What!" screamed the page. "Robin Hood! And are you indeed Robin Hood? And oh, Robin, I have hurt you! I knew you not, Robin."

The outlaw started in surprise at the figure before him.

"Why, who art thou?" he said. "And why should it trouble thee that I am hurt?"

"I came hither to seek you, Robin!" cried the page, "but never dreamed that I should meet you in this guise. And, Robin, don't you know me?"

Robin Hood stood for a few moments in greater wonder still at the fair, blushing face, then memory rose like a flood.

"I know you!" he cried—"I know you now! You are Maid Marian. Dearest Marian, how came you here?"

"I came to seek you, Robin," she replied, "for I have no friend in the world but you. And I knew you not and have wounded you."

"Tush! that is nothing," said Robin. "We get many shrewder cuts and knocks in the greenwood. And as for not knowing me, that is no wonder, for I am disguised lest my enemy, the Sheriff of Nottingham, should seize me."

The two friends now sat down on a mossy bank near at hand and fell into talk, telling each other how their lives had passed since their separation.

"And have you room for me in the greenwood, Robin?" asked Maid Marian.

"Ay, and proud to see you there, Marian," cried the outlaw. "Come, we will seek the wife of Alan-a-Dale; she will gladly take you under her care."

*Right welcome did the wife of Alan-a-Dale
make Maid Marian*

So they set off together and sought the hidden glade
where the band formed their camp. And right welcome
did the wife of Alan-a-Dale make Maid Marian, and right
merry was the feast which was held that evening. Little
John and Will Scarlet went off at once with their bows
and killed a brace of fat bucks, and a joyous feast was
held in honor of Maid Marian's coming to the greenwood.

The yeomen formed a jovial ring around a vast fire of
great oaken billets and ate their fill of the sweet vension
and washed it down with flagons of wine and brimming
bowls of nut-brown ale. And so Maid Marian came to
Sherwood and reigned as queen of the forest revels.

Sir Richard of the 🌀
Lea Pays His Debts

Y ou will all remember how Robin Hood helped the
poor knight who had no money to pay his debts
and so stood in danger of losing his lands. Well, Sir
Richard of the Lea did not forget his good friend in the
greenwood, and when he had saved four hundred pounds
he set off to repay Robin. He took with him also a hundred good bows and a hundred sheaves of fine arrows as
a present for the kindly outlaw.

This time Sir Richard rode through the forest in very
different case from his last journey. Then he was sorrowful and sad and looked the most wretched man in the
world; now he was gay and cheerful, riding a good horse,
and attended by a gallant band of men-at-arms. And all
this change was due to Robin Hood, for if the knight had
once lost his lands he would have been ruined forever. So
Sir Richard blessed the name of Robin Hood who had
saved him from the cruel, grasping hands of the covetous
Abbot of St. Mary's.

Now, as the knight rode along at the head of his men, he came to a broad meadow beside a river and near the head of a bridge. This meadow presented a very lively, bustling scene, for the whole countryside had gathered there for a great merrymaking. There were jugglers and tumblers with gaping crowds round them; there were Saxon gleemen and wandering harpers; there were rude booths where merchants and peddlers showed their wares; but the biggest crowd of all was gathered about a ring where the best wrestlers had gathered from far and near to hold a contest for some very rich prizes.

The winner of the wrestling match was to have a fine courser, whose saddle and bridle were burnished with gold—a splendid prize. To the second man would be given a white bull; while a pair of beautifully embroidered gloves, a gold ring, and a pipe of wine would fall to the next three in order of merit. With so many prizes it was no wonder that stout yeomen had thronged to the merrymaking from all parts: every man hoped that one prize would fall to him, if it were but one of the smaller rewards.

The crowd was so dense near the bridge that the knight and his men could not pass without forcing their way roughly. This Sir Richard was not willing to do, and, as the day was yet young and he had plenty of time, he sat his horse to watch the wrestling for an hour, while his men clustered about him, delighted to witness the keen contest which was expected.

To the astonishment of everyone, there was no keen contest at all. And this lay at the door of a big, clumsy-looking fellow who shambled into the ring and threw every man pitted against him with the utmost ease. It did not matter who opposed him, the champion of this village, the best wrestler of that hamlet, every man went down as soon as the big fellow put his arms about an opponent.

"Who can this be?" cried the people. "Such wrestling was never seen in England before. It is no match at all. The big fellow treats the others as if they were children coming against him."

Shouts of wonder and applause rose as the powerful stranger brought about fall after fall, but in a short time shouts of anger began to mingle with the outcries. The angry uproar burst from a band of foresters gathered at one corner of the ring. They had come there to support a comrade, Hubert o' the Strong Hand, a famous wrestler, and they had laid heavy wagers on their champion's success.

The foresters had jeered at wrestler after wrestler as he crept beaten from the ring. "Wait till Hubert faces yonder big fellow, they cried. "Then ye will see what wrestling should be. Big as he is, Strong Hand will toss him over one shoulder."

These taunts, jeers, and promises greatly raised the expectation of the crowd; and when Hubert stepped confidently into the ring, all were excited by the hope of at last seeing a great contest. But, though these hopes were at once dashed to the ground, yet the onlookers saw a wonderful piece of work. For the big wrestler seized Hubert of the Strong Hand and flung the forester clean

over his head. Arms and legs flying like the sails of a
windmill, the defeated champion whirled through the air
and dropped flat on his back on the turf.

"A foul catch!" roared the angry foresters. "A foul
catch! No throw! No throw!"

"Nay, nay," shouted Sir Richard, who loved fair play.
"The hold and catch were fair enough. 'Twas a true
throw."

The foresters knew that quite well; they were only raising a clamor and false accusations of foul play to cover the
defeat of their champion and to avoid paying the wagers
they had lain on his head. A great uproar now arose
around the ring. Some shouted against the big wrestler;
some for him. But the former were greatly in the major-
ity, for he had earned the enmity of many parties by
overthrowing the man in whom the party had put its
trust.

"I've seen that big fellow before," mused Sir Richard;
"but where was it?—where was it?"

He thought for awhile, then started in his saddle. "I
have it—I have it," he said to himself. " 'Tis the big man
who was with Robin Hood. Now I remember that he
fetched the bag with the four hundred pounds in it. Ay,
I am never likely to forget that."

Sir Richard was right. Yes, it was Little John himself.
He had been out on a scouting expedition, had heard of
the wrestling, and had been unable to keep away. He
had come intending only to look on at his favorite sport,
but, at sight of the ring and the prizes, he could not re-
strain himself and had entered his name as Will o' the
Glade and had swept all before him.

"Turn him from the ring!" roared the foresters. "Away with him! 'Twas a foul catch! Let the wrestling begin again!"

This cry was echoed by many who wished to see their men have another chance in a contest from which this terrible champion had been, excluded, but there were plenty of lovers of fair play who spoke up stoutly for Little John and said that he had wrestled fairly.

Suddenly Little John stood in great danger, for the angry foresters had burst into the ring and sprang at him, several with sword in hand, threatening him with death if he did not at once retire from the contest. But they were threatening the wrong man. The burly giant knew not what fear was and stood his ground resolutely defying them all. He would have been severely handled and, possibly, slain, had not Sir Richard interfered at once. Calling upon his men to close about him and follow, the good knight rode into the crowd and forced his way to the place where Little John stood in the midst of the angry mob.

"Stand back!" cried Sir Richard to the foresters. "Stand back, and offer no violence to the man!"

The sheriff's men would have paid but little notice to the knight's words had not the latter been seconded by the crowd. Great numbers present knew Sir Richard, and they called out:

"We will take Sir Richard for our judge. He is a good and honest knight. We know him and trust him. He shall decide the matter."

The foresters were overawed by the general voice, and the assembly became silent to listen to Sir Richard.

"Come, come, my masters," said the knight. "Is this

our English fair play that anger should be shown to a man who has proved himself the best wrestler I have seen for many and many a day? I have watched every fall, and each was fair and true, and I challenge any man to deny it. Why, then, try to shout down a man whom no one can beat honestly in the ring?"

These words went home, and caused a strong expression of feeling in favor of the big wrestler. Only the foresters still looked darkly upon him and murmured of what they would have done had not the knight and his men-at-arms interfered.

It was now agreed that the first prize should go to the great wrestler, and the others should wrestle again for the lesser prizes. When the latter were awarded Sir Richard bought the pipe of wine from the man who won it, for five marks, and gave orders that it should be broached at once that whoso wished might drink. This put the crowd in very good humor with the exception of the sheriff's men who had been compelled to pay the wagers and were in the worst of tempers.

They stood muttering among themselves and casting evil looks on Little John, who was now examining the noble courser he had won. Suddenly, in the strange way that a rumor springs up, there ran a whisper through the crowd that the famous wrestler was one of Robin Hood's men. Perhaps someone else besides Sir Richard had recognized Little John, for, although the great fellow had disguised himself as well as he could, yet it was impossible for him to hide his mighty frame, his broad shoulders, and brawny limbs.

The whisper ran around and came to the foresters' ears in an instant. They leapt at it: it was just the thing they would wish to believe, for it put the famous champion into their hands.

"An outlaw!" An outlaw! Seize him! Seize him!" they yelled and made a fierce rush at the winner. Then Little John knew that he must be quick to save his neck. He made one bound into the saddle, drove his heels into the flanks of his splendid steed, and was gone like an arrow from the bow. He had plenty of friends there, for the people loved the outlaws, and the crowd parted right and left to give him passage and then closed up once more to block the way of the pursuing foresters. In a trice Little John had galloped over the bridge and was out of sight round a bend of the road.

"By my faith, I am glad that the brave wrestler has escaped, both for his master's sake and his own," quoth Sir Richard, and he ordered his men to march on, and they followed the way which Little John had taken.

Little John rode fast and far, and the splendid courser did not pause in his wild gallop until his rider pulled him up in a glade where Robin and dozen or more of the outlaws were gathered.

"How now, Little John, what means this haste?" cried his leader. "And from what noble hast thou taken this fine horse?"

"He is mine, master, fairly won in fair struggle," replied Little John, and he told the story of the wrestling, and gave much praise to the kind stranger who had seen that he received fair play. Little John had not recognized the knight again, so changed were Sir Richard's dress and mien.

"And didst thou see aught on the road of the sad knight to whom we lent the four hundred pounds!" asked Robin Hood.

"Not a sign, master—not a sign," said Little John. "Do you expect him today?"

"Ay, that I do," returned Robin Hood, "for it is a twelve-month this day since the money was lent, and before this sun sets it should be returned."

"Content you, master," said the cheerful giant. "The sun is not at rest yet. I dare swear the knight will prove true and honest, for I remember that he had a trusty look in his eyes."

"Well," said Robin, "I will not go to dinner this day until I have some guest to sit at meat with me. So take your bow, Little John, and go with Much and Will Scarlet and walk the Watling Street till you meet with wayfarers. Bid them come to dine with me, whoever they may be. If they be rich, they shall pay for their dinner; if they be poor, I will share my goods with them; if they be minstrels or jugglers, they shall make mirth for us."

Away went the three yeomen at once and hurried up to the highroad. They looked east, and they looked west, and saw no man. Then they looked along the way that ran towards Barnsdale, and what should they see there but a great concourse of people marching along.

"By our Lady," said Little John, "but our master will have guests enough today. Who are these coming here?"

The yeomen looked closely at the train and saw that two monks in black habits rode at the head, each mounted on a handsome palfrey. Behind them came seven sumpter* horses, well laden, with a train of fifty-two spearmen guarding the party.

"Why," said Much, "a bishop could not ride more royally than these black monks. By my faith, there is treasure of great worth on yonder sumpter horses or the guard would not be so strong."

"Brethren," said Little John, "here are only the three of us, yet we must bring these men to dinner."

Much and Will Scarlet said not a word, only nodded to show their agreement with these words, and the three outlaws took their stand at a place where the road made a sharp turn between high banks. In this position they commanded the head of the column, and the two monks rode round the bend to find the three bowmen, shaft on string, standing full in their way.

"Bend your bows," commanded Little John, "and order that crowd to halt. I hold the life of the foremost monk in my hand."

When the black monks saw the outlaws with bent bows they drew rein, and the whole cavalcade was thrown into confusion.

"Abide, churl monk!" cried Little John to the leader, who seemed to be a man of greater importance than his companion. "Stand where thou art, and remember that thy death is in my hand. Evil thrift be upon thy head,"

---

*Pack.

went on the outlaw, "for thou hast angered my master greatly, causing him to fast so long."

The monk stared at Little John in surprise, and fear, and wonder: he did not understand the outlaw's words, and he said at once, "Who is your master?"

"He is Robin Hood!" cried Little John in a voice of thunder.

"He is a strong thief," replied the monk sourly, "and of him I never heard good."

"Thou liest!" cried Little John. "He is a worthy yeoman of the forest, and he hath bidden thee to dine, and thou shalt come."

Much and Will Scarlet had said nothing, but were ready with their bolts. Yet not one needed to be loosed. For the train of spearmen behind the monks melted away in a most wonderful fashion. Every man had heard the name of Robin Hood as Little John's clarion tones had rung along the hollow road, and the very sound of that dreaded name had been enough. Every man feared an ambush, and before the three resolute outlaws they turned and fled, leaving only those whose bodies were covered by the arrows.

"March on," said Little John to the monks, and they were compelled to ride forward, while Much and Will Scarlet followed, ready to shoot if either should make an attempt to escape. As for Little John, he drove the seven sumpter horses with the help of a page and a groom, all that remained faithful to the monks in their train of followers.

And so they came to the forest and to the door of the lodge where Robin was awaiting them.

Robin stepped forward and greeted the newcomers with the greatest courtesy, doffing his hood, but the leading monk made no return to this polite salutation, and Little John became angry.

"The fellow is a churl, master," said Little John; "but I'll soon make him doff his hood."

"No force," said Robin—"no force. If he will not doff his hood for courtesy sake, e'en let him be. How many men had this monk, John?"

"Fifty and two, master, when we met, but many of them be gone."

"Sound your horn," said Robin, "that our fellowship may know we have guests."

Little John sounded his horn, and in a trice seven score nimble yeoman ran up the spot, every man clad in scarlet mantle and well armed. The monks looked at this brave array and then uneasily at their sumpter horses as if they feared for their wealth.

Soon the dinner was served, and the monks sat down to it, and Robin Hood and Little John helped them to the best that was on the board.

"Dine well, monk," said Robin to the Superior.

"Gramercy, good yeoman," said the monk, "that will I, for your cheer is plentiful."

"Where is your abbey when you are at home?" went on Robin.

"St. Mary's Abbey," said the monk. Robin lifted his eyebrows and gave a little laugh.

"And what may your position be there?"

"I am the high cellarer," said the monk in a very important voice. Robin laughed again.

"Why do you laugh, yeoman?" demanded the high cellarer.

"I cannot help but laugh," replied Robin, "to think that the High Cellarer of St. Mary's Abby should be my guest on this day of all days in the year."

"Why this day in particular?" asked the monk.

"Because twelve months this day I lent four hundred pounds to be paid to the Abbot of St. Mary's, and now the repayment is due. Perhaps you have brought it, monk?"

"I?" cried the high cellarer. "I have brought nothing. To whom did you lend the money?"

"To a poor knight."

"Then let the poor knight pay his own debts," cried the monk.

"Well," said Robin carelessly, "I thought perhaps the abbot was sending the money back. It looks to me as if much treasure might be in yonder packs," and he nodded towards the loads which had been taken from the sumpter horses and piled in a heap.

"There is no money in there!" cried the high cellarer hastily, "only some clothes and baggage of little account."

"No money?" and Robin lifted his eyebrows in surprise. "And art thou setting out on a journey with no money for expenses by the way?"

"Ah! now, you remind me," said the monk quickly. "Yes, there is a little money, a small matter of twenty marks for spending silver on the road. Nothing to make it worth your while, good yeoman, to unloose the packs."

A glittering stream of gold poured on the mantle

"No," replied Robin thoughtfully, "and yet they must be opened. It may be that Saint Mary herself is returning the poor knight's money and has caused your twenty marks to increase miraculously. Open the packs, Little John."

The tall outlaw spread his cloak on the ground and seized the coffers which had been swung across the leading sumpter horse. He forced the lid of the first open and held it over the cloak. A glittering stream of gold poured on to the mantle.

"A miracle! A miracle!" cried Robin Hood. "Did I not say that mayhap the twenty marks would have increased?"

Little John forced another coffer open, and a second stream of gold tinkled on the shining heap below.

"A miracle! A miracle!" roared the outlaws in chorus, their sides shaking in laughter at their leader's jest, while the high cellarer looked on with a brow as black as night.

"Count the money, Little John," said Robin Hood. Little John did so, and found that it was eight hundred pounds and more.

"Give the monk his twenty marks, Little John," commanded the leader, and Little John counted out twenty marks.

"There you are, monk," said Robin Hood. "We have not robbed you of a single silver penny. From your own mouth we heard that twenty marks was every piece of money in your coffers, so our Lady hath wrought a miracle in bringing eight hundred pounds there, and it is clear that Saint Mary wishes to repay me double for the money I lent the knight to pay her abbot."

"Thieves and rogues you are!" burst out the high cellarer fiercely. "Render back my Lord Abbot's treasure or ye shall suffer under his heaviest curse. With bell, book, and candle he shall curse ye, and ye will be lost here and hereafter."

"Gadzooks!" cried Robin Hood. "Here is a change of tone, Master Cellarer. Now you talk of abbot's treasure and curses. But a fig for the curses of such a man. He is hard-hearted and covetous, one who grinds the poor, and will snatch the widow's mite to add to his store. Dost think we care a pin for the ill-wishes of such a man? Give the monk his palfrey, Little John, and let him begone, but the sumpter horses and the baggage are ours."

The outlaws welcomed this decision with a loud shout, and the high cellarer, on second thoughts, was only too glad to find that he was to get off in safety. He scrambled to the back of his palfrey with more haste than dignity and rode away, and his companion was allowed to follow him.

Hardly had the monks disappeared among the trees than Sir Richard of the Lea rode into sight, advancing from an opposite direction. He had spent a much greater time on the road from the wrestling than Little John, for, while the latter had covered the way on a swift horse, Sir Richard and his men had come at a slow pace, many of his followers being on foot.

"Heaven save you, good Robin Hood, and all your company!" said Sir Richard as he came up to the spot here the outlaw stood.

"Welcome, gentle knight!" cried Robin. "Right welcome are thou to the greenwood. And how didst thou fare at St. Mary's Abbey?"

"Oh! the abbot was very anxious to seize my land," replied Sir Richard; "but, thanks to thee, kind yeoman, I ransomed it, and am here today as I promised."

"I feared I should never see thee today," replied Robin. "It has gone so far towards the sunset."

"Do not blame me because I have been so long," said Sir Richard. "I was delayed on my way. I came by a wrestling, and there I saw a poor yeoman hard pressed by unfair men. Him did I stay to help, and the more gladly that I think he was a man of thine."

"Ay, Sir Knight, it was I, and I thank you heartily for your help," cried Little John, coming forward. "It would have gone hard with me at the hands of those rascally foresters had you not stepped forward to see that I had fair play. But I knew you not, so greatly have you changed from your former figure."

"I thank you also, Sir Knight," added Robin. "The man who helps one of my men helps me, and Little John is my right hand. I should be, indeed, lost in losing him."

"I am glad that I was of service," replied Sir Richard. "And here, good Robin, is your four hundred pounds in this bag. Count it and see that the sum is right. And here, again, is twenty marks, a small present for a great kindness to me.

"Put up your money, Sir Knight," laughed Robin. "The debt has already been paid."

"Paid!" cried Sir Richard. "What mean you, good Robin Hood? I have never a friend that would lay down so large a sum for me."

"By our Lady, but you have," chuckled Robin, "and his name will surprise you, for it is no other than the Abbot of St. Mary's."

"Never!" said Sir Richard. "Never can I believe that. What, can anyone think that a fat, greedy old rogue such he is would lay down willingly the sum required to clear my debt to you!"

Robin laughed again. "Willingly I do not say, Sir Knight," he replied; "but the sum has been received from his coffers, and I have given his high cellarer a full discharge for the money by letting the fellow go free."

Sir Richard now began to see how the matter stood, and when he learned of the miracle which had changed the black monk's twenty marks to eight hundred pounds and more, he laughed heartily.

"But, all the same, good yeoman," said he, "I must insist on paying this which I fully owe you."

"I will not take a penny," declared Robin. "I have had my money, and that from the right hands. Now, Sir Knight, what means that array of handsome bows and beautifully feathered arrows?"

He said this to turn the conversation, and Sir Richard replied, "In faith, they are meant as a poor present to thee."

Then Robin thanked him heartily, and the bows and arrows were given to the yeomen who received them with delight, for the weapons had been fashioned by the most skilful craftsman and were of the finest quality.

"Little John," said Robin, "go to the treasury and fetch the money which was paid me by the monk. Four hundred pounds were owing from St. Mary's Abbey, and the monk brought eight hundred."

Little John fetched the four hundred pounds over and above the debt, and Robin Hood put it into the hands of Sir Richard. The knight did not wish to take it, but Robin insisted.

"It costs much money to maintain the state of a knight," said Robin, "while I spend but little in the forest here. If you ever should be in sore straits again come to Robin Hood, and I will not fail to share with you while I have aught in my treasury. And now we will spread the board again, for you and your company must be hungry after your long march."

And so the feast was spread anew, and the grateful knight and his followers tasted of Robin Hood's cheer and blessed their noble host, who was the friend and helper of the oppressed and the unfortunate and the enemy of all proud tryants.

Robin Hood Sells Pots ❧
In Nottingham Town

FOR a long time after the widow's sons were rescued from the hands of the sheriff, Robin Hood and his men never went near Nottingham town. They moved to a distant part of the great forest and kept far out of the way of the strong force which the sheriff raised to search their old haunts. But one fine morning, when the birds were singing, and the sun was shining, and the green leaves fluttering in a pleasant breeze, Robin Hood, with a band of his followers, stood in a brake watching a road which ran through the forest. Robin was thinking of Nottingham town and how he would like to enter the walls and listen to the merry gossip of the market place, when a figure appeared in the distance. It was a potter, seated in his cart, and driving quietly along the way.

"This potter is a proud fellow," said Robin to his men. "He comes marching through our forest and yet has never paid a single penny of passage money."

"H'm!" said Little John. "He's rather an awkward fellow to deal with. I once had a turn with him, and he hit me three such blows that my sides ached for days. I'll wager forty shillings that there is not a man among us can stop him."

"I'll take your wager," said Robin. "Stand here, my lads, and I will soon stop this saucy potter."

On jogged the potter's cart, the pots clattering together, and the driver whistling a blithe strain, and out went Robin to meet the potter—a big, burly fellow with a red face.

Robin Hood seized the horse by the head and bade the potter stand.

"What is thy will, fellow?" cried the potter shortly, springing down from his seat.

"All these three years and more, potter," said Robin, "thou hast haunted this way, yet wert thou never so courteous a man one penny of toll to pay."

"What is your name?" said the potter. "And why, under the sun, should I pay toll to you?"

"I am Robin Hood," said the outlaw, "and thou shalt leave me a pledge this day."

"I will leave no pledge, and I will pay no toll," said the potter sturdily. "Let go my horse, I say,"

When the potter saw that Robin still kept his hold on the horse, he ran to the cart and fetched out a great quarterstaff. Robin whipped out his sword and raised his buckler, and the men in ambush looked out eagerly to watch the encounter.

"Yonder potter will make a stiff stand of it," said Little

John to his companions, and the words were scarce out of him mouth when they saw a very clever piece of cudgel play. The potter made a spring at Robin as if to deliver a swinging blow at his head, and when Robin raised his buckler to ward the stroke, the potter made the staff twirl in his hands like a mill wheel and delivered a back-handed blow which sent the outlaw's buckler clattering to the ground.

Robin bent to pick up his buckler, for he did not dream that the potter could fetch another blow before the buckler was safely in his hands, but the potter was as quick as lightning. Down whirled the staff again, caught Robin across the neck, and sent him headlong to the ground.

When the men in hiding saw this they ran forward, Little John shouting, "Let us help our master or else yonder potter will slay him."

When the potter saw the outlaws rushing forward he stepped back and poised his great staff ready to defend himself. Robin Hood sat up and began to rub his sore neck.

"Well, master," said Little John, "shall I have your forty shillings, or will you have mine?"

"If the wager had been for a hundred shillings," replied Robin, "they had been all thine."

"It is full little courtesy, as I have heard wise men say," cried the potter, "to hinder a poor yeoman on his journey when he comes driving over the way."

"You speak truth, potter," replied Robin, "and thou are a stout yeoman, and if thou shouldst drive forth every day

thou shalt never again be hindered by me. Come, join
our fellowship. Give me your clothing, and I will give
you mine, and will go to Nottingham in your place."

"Master, master!" cried Little John. "Have a care!
What are you thinking of! You know very well that
Nottingham is no place for you. Beware of the sheriff!
If he once knew you were in the town you were as good as
a dead man at once."

"For all that, my mind is made up to go," replied the
leader. "The sheriff shall never discover me, I warrant
you. I will sell my pots under his very nose. The boldest
way is always the safest."

When his followers saw that Robin was resolved to go,
they gave over dissuading him, and one ran to fetch Friar
Tuck, who was very clever at disguising a man. The Friar
came and made Robin look as different from his usual self
as if he had been transformed by a fairy. Robin's face
was stained with the juices of herbs till he was browner
than a gipsy; his hair and beard were dressed in a different fashion from his usual way of combing them, a big
patch was fastened over one eye. When Friar Tuck had
finished with him, Maid Marian herself would not have
known her Robin.

When he was ready to start, Robin took the reins and
drove the potter's cart down the road, and the potter
stayed with the yeomen, who took good care of him and
made him very comfortable among them.

Singing as he went, Robin soon came to Nottingham,
where he stabled his horse and gave him a feed of oats
and hay.

Next, Robin took his pots and marched boldly to a stand within sight of the sheriff's windows.

"Pots! Pots!" he cried in a loud, merry voice. "Pots and pans! Good and cheap! Who'll buy? Who'll buy?"

His ringing tones soon brought a group of women about him, and they asked the price of his pots. When he replied, they stared in wonder, for he asked threepence for a pot well worth fivepence, and in a few moments he was selling pots as fast as he could hand them out.

"This is a queer fellow," said the women of the town. "He is selling his pots at about half the usual price. It is plain he does not know much about his trade, but it is lucky chance for us, and we will buy while we may."

When the news spread that there was a strange potter selling pots at half-price a crowd of people gathered round the cart, and there was so much commotion that the sheriff's wife came to the window to see what the concourse meant.

Robin had been waiting for this, and had been keeping back some of the finest pots on purpose. There were only five left, and these he sent at once to the sheriff's wife asking her to accept them as a present from a potter on his first visit to the town over which her husband ruled.

The sheriff's wife was pleased with the fine pots, and came herself to thank Robin for them. And she was so pleased with Robin's politeness and good manners that she invited him to dine with herself and the sheriff, and Robin accepted the invitation at once.

In the hall Robin and the sheriff met, and the potter bowed low to the great man.

"Look what the potter has given you and me!" cried the
sheriff's wife. "Five fine pots, just the things I stood in
need of."

"He is full welcome," said the sheriff. "Let us wash
and go to meat."

Now, as they sat at dinner, there arose a talk of a great
shooting match that was to take place the same afternoon,
and the prize for the winner would be forty shillings.

"A good prize," said the potter, and to himself he said,
"As I am a true Christian man that shooting will I see."

When they had enjoyed a capital dinner, all the company went to the butts to see the sheriff's men shoot for
the forty shillings.

As the prize was a good one, the butts were set up at a
good distance from the shooting point in order to test the
mettle of the archers. One after another the sheriff's men
loosed their arrows at the mark, but the test was too severe, and not one of them got within half a bow's length
of the center of the target.

"What dost thou think of the shooting, potter?" cried
the sheriff.

The potter smiled. "I would I had a bow," he said; "I
would show you how we shoot where I come from."

"And a bow thou shalt have!" cried the sheriff. "Thou
dost look a stalwart fellow and shalt make trial of thy skill.
Three bows shall be brought that thou mayst choose the
best."

The sheriff commanded a yeoman to fetch some bows,
and when they were brought, the potter looked them
over.

"This is the best," said the potter, and bent a string to it and drew it. "But it is not of much account, after all," he added. "This is but right weak gear, Master Sheriff. Where I come from men can bend a bow twice as stiff as this one. Natheless, I will make trial of it."

The potter now chose an arrow with care and placed it on the string. Then he drew the bow and loosed the shaft without dwelling for an instant on his aim.

"I' the clout!—i' the clout!" shouted the bystanders. "Well shot! Good bow!" To the surprise of all, the potter's arrow stood quivering in the very center of the target.

"Shoot again, my men!" cried the sheriff. "What one has done, others should do an they call themselves good bowmen."

The sheriff's men shot round again, and the potter shot with them. Not one of the men hit the target, but when the potter's turn came he sent an arrow which lighted on the first arrow and cleft it into three.

The sheriff's men looked darkly and angrily on the potter, for they felt great shame at being beaten so thoroughly by a stranger; but the sheriff laughed loudly when he saw his guest bear away the mastery, and cried, "Potter, thou art a man, and art worthy to bear a bow in whatever place thou goest."

"I would shoot better still," said the potter, "if I had the bow which lies in my cart."

"Is it a bow of special worth?" asked the sheriff.

"I' faith it is," replied the potter. "Why, I had it from Robin Hood himself."

You may be sure that the sheriff pricked up his ears when he heard the potter mention his archenemy.

"Knowest thou Robin Hood?" demanded the sheriff. "Potter, art thou one of his followers?"

"That am I not, Sir Sheriff," replied the potter. "A follower of Robin Hood was I never in my life."

"How comest thou, then, to know him?"

"Why, I travel through his country, and he has a friendship for me, and I am safe from his men. He loves, too, to try my skill in archery, and a hundred times have I shot with him under the gnarled oaks of the forest."

"I would give a hundred pounds!" cried the sheriff— "yes, a hundred golden pounds if that false outlaw stood as near to me as thou dost this day."

"How now, Sir Sheriff?" said the potter. "Why this heat against Robin Hood? Surely he hath not dared to raise his hand against the power and dignity of the Sheriff of Nottingham?"

"Hath he not, the villain!" cried the sheriff. "But in sooth, he hath done me great despite. My silver, ring, and money hath he purloined, and my bones hath he made sore, sleeping as I was forced to do on the gnarled and knobby roots of trees."

The potter seemed astonished and grieved to hear of such enormities, and the sheriff poured the tale of his woes into these sympathetic ears.

"He ought to be seized and dragged into Nottingham by the ears," declared the potter. "And it is a strange thing, but I can tell you the very spot where you might lay hands on him tomorrow."

"Thou wouldst do me a great service, and rid the country of a stout rogue, if I could seize him by thy aid," said the sheriff.

"It could be done," said the potter, and looked craftily at the sheriff, "but for such a deed there should be good reward, Sir Sheriff."

"Fear naught for that," hastily replied the sheriff; "only put him in my hands and I will pay thee gladly the hundred pounds."

"It is a bargain!" cried the potter, and smacked his thigh. "Tomorrow, within three hours of prime, I will set you within full sight of Robin Hood."

"Ay, but not with a score of his rogues about him," put in the sheriff.

"With not one about him!" cried the potter; "I happen to have learned all his plans for tomorrow, and you shall meet him quite alone."

"Good," said the sheriff; "I will requite thee as I have promised, never fear," and home they went to supper.

The next morning the potter and the sheriff started early for the forest. The latter was attended only by a couple of strong fellows, for he did not wish to arouse attention by a display of great force, and he felt certain that the three of them would be an ample strength to deal with a man taken by surprise.

When the potter took leave of the sheriff's wife, he bowed low before her, and thanked her for the good cheer she had spread before him. "Dame," said he, "I pray you wear this in memory of me," and he gave her a beautiful gold ring.

"Gramercy, good sir," said the sheriff's wife; "I am much beholden to you for this handsome gift," and so the potter and the lady parted the best of friends.

For nearly two hours the potter drove his cart along the forest road, and the sheriff and his men trotted behind on horseback. Then they came to a place where four woodland paths met, and the potter drew rein.

"Here is the spot where ye may meet with Robin Hood," he said,

The sheriff and his men looked uneasily round. It had seemed simple enough in the city to think of going out and seizing Robin Hood, but here, amid the solemn silence of the mighty forest, the name of the great outlaw seemed to have a different ring about it and to become a name of dread and fear.

"I see no sign of Robin Hood," said the sheriff, and looked over each shoulder in turn, as if fearing that Robin Hood might spring out of the earth behind him.

"No, but you soon will," said the potter in a low, mysterious voice. "Hide yourselves in this brake, and take your swords in your hands. I will watch for him, and when he is close at hand I will sound my horn. Then do you rush boldly forward and seize him. After that I shall claim the promised reward."

"It is ready for thee," said the sheriff, and patted the bag of money tucked under his cloak.

The potter left the sheriff and his men hidden in the thicket and went a short distance farther to an open space, where a spring of water bubbled up at the foot of a rock and ran away down the glade. Here he washed the stain from his face and hands and cast away his disguise save for the potter's clothes. Then he raised his horn to his lips, blew three sharp blasts, and slipped behind a great oak which hid him completely.

In a moment two parties burst into the glade. From the one hand, the sheriff and his men dashed through the bushes, sword in hand, ready to spring upon Robin Hood. From the other, Little John, Much, Will Scarlet, and a dozen more burst into the glade to answer their master's call. Robin Hood watched the meeting from cover of the great trunk and smiled.

In truth, one might well smile to see the sheriff and his men when they came face to face with stout band of outlaws. Their mouths opened, their swords fell from their hands; they turned to flee, when a shout from Little John gave them pause.

"Stand!" shouted the giant, "or we will stick ye as full of shafts as a boar is of bristles."

This fearsome threat fixed the three to the earth and they looked upon Little John and his companions with faces full of dread.

"What make ye here?" cried the giant, "and who sounded Robin Hood's horn?"

"Robin Hood's horn!" faltered the sheriff. "Nay, good yeoman, I know naught of Robin Hood's horn. Ye mistake. 'Twas only a potter who was with us but now and sounded the blast."

"Tell me no tales of potters!" cried Little John, apparently in great anger, though he began to scent his leader's trick. "No potter blew those notes. 'Twas none but

the prince of outlaws, Robin Hood, himself. Hast thou
done aught wrong to him? If so, a hundred deaths were
all too little for ye to suffer."

The outlaws seconded Little John's threat with a wild
shout and shook their bows in the air. "Death to him
who molests Robin Hood!" they roared.

The sheriff trembled from head to foot.

"Potter! Potter!" he cried. "Where art thou? Show
thyself, potter!"

"Here am I, sheriff!" cried a well-known voice, and the
potter stepped from the thicket whence he had been
watching the play in high glee.

The sheriff stood stiff with terror. For naught was left
now of the potter but his garb. The face was the face of
Robin Hood, and the sheriff knew it and trembled more
than ever.

"Potter! Potter!" he stammered, "thou hast played me
false."

"Nay, nay, sheriff," laughed Robin, "Say not so. I have
kept my word like a true man and an Englishman. Did I
not promise thou shouldst meet Robin Hood, and I have
carried out that same promise!"

"Ah!" growled the sheriff. "Had I but known of this in
Nottingham, ye had never seen the fair forest again,
Master Potter."

"That I know very well," laughed Robin; "but fear not,
sheriff, I will not hurt a hair of your head, and all for the
sake of your good wife who was kind to me."

On hearing this the sheriff plucked up his spirit at once,
for he knew that Robin was a man of his word. At this
moment Little John broke in, "Well, master," said the big

fellow, "how did you fare in Nottingham? Did you sell your ware?"

"Every piece of it, Little John," replied Robin, "and five pots of it the sheriff had, and he has brought the money to pay for them in a bag under his cloak,"

"The bag—the bag, Sir Sheriff!" roared the giant and the sheriff, pulling a wry face, had to give up the hundred pounds he had thought to pay for the capture of Robin Hood.

"He came on a horse. He shall go back on foot," said Robin, and in a trice the sheriff and his men were stripped of all their gear. Then Robin commanded that a white palfrey should be brought to the place, and a yeoman ran and fetched the animal.

"Now sheriff," said Robin, "off with you at once, and you shall lead this white palfrey home and tell your wife that Robin Hood sends it to her with his respects. For her sake you shall go free. Had she not been so kind to me you should have had a worse time of it than this in the forest."

The sheriff slunk away, only too glad to find himself on the way with sound bones in his body, and trudged briskly along until he came to the town and his house. At the very door he met his wife who had been watching from the window and had run to meet him.

"How have you fared in the Green Forest?" she cried. "And have you brought Robin home? Where is he? Let me see him!"

"Dame!" roared the sheriff. "Never say that name again in my hearing. Ye have seen the rogue truly enough."

The sheriff slunk away, only too glad to find himself on the way with sound bones in his body

"I!" cried the sheriff's wife in wonder. "Never have I set eyes on him."

"Truly thou hast!" shouted the angry sheriff. "'Twas the potter! The rascal who pretended to sell pots was none other than Robin Hood himself. And when he had drawn me into the forest he robbed me of my gold, my horses, my gear, and hath sent me empty back save for this white palfrey that he hath given to thee."

She cried out in amazement to hear this strange news, and then she said, "Well, you have paid now for all the pots that Robin gave me."

"Ay, that I have, dame!" groaned the sheriff. "I have paid right heavily," and he dragged himself wearily into the house, full of anger to think that Robin had tricked him cleverly once more.

When Robin had started the sheriff back to Nottingham he summoned the true potter before him and said, "Potter, what were those pots worth that I took to Nottingham!"

"Two nobles!" cried the potter promptly. "That is what I would have made of them had I been there."

"Here is ten pounds in thy hand," said Robin. "I have sold them at a great price, and thou shalt have thy share, and whenever thou dost pass this way, potter, remember thou art always welcome in the greenwood."

"Thanks, noble Robin!" cried the potter. "Would that I could meet with such a sale for my pots every day of the year!"

Thus parted Robin, the sheriff, and the potter. As he left the scene the potter exclaimed, "Heaven have mercy on Robin Hood's soul and guard all good yeomen."

How Robin Hood Was Seized by the Sheriff

A MORE lovely May morning never dawned than this Sunday morning. The sun was hot and bright, and the young leaves shook in a sweet, gentle breeze which was loaded with fragrance as it swept softly through the forest. The grass was dotted with wild flowers, and the dappled deer had left the sunny heights to lie in the shade of the greenwood trees. It was the most delightful day of that delightful time of early summer. And it was Whitsunday.

"By my faith," said Little John to his master, "but this is a merry morning, and I feel in tune with it: a more merry man than I doth not live today in Christendom."

But Robin Hood made no answer, and Little John saw that there was a cloud on his master's brow.

"Pluck up thy heart, my dear master," said Little John, "and bethink thee it is a full fair time in a morning of May."

"It troubles me much," said Robin Hood, "that on so solemn a day as this I can go neither to Mass nor matins. It is long now since I stood in a church to worship."

"There is no church nearer than Nottingham," said Much the Miller's Son, who stood near at hand.

"And to Nottingham I will go!" cried Robin, taking one of his sudden determinations. "Yes, I will attend St. Mary's Church in Nottingham this very day."

Much and Little John tried to dissuade him, but all to no purpose.

"None will suspect me of entering the town on a Sunday," replied Robin, "and I will wear a gray suit with a large hood and pull the hood over my face. I shall go and come as safely as walking to and fro in the glade."

"Well, master," said Much, "then take a dozen stout fellows with you, each man with his weapons, so that help may be at hand if you should need it."

"Nay," said Robin. "Twelve men would draw attention at the gate, where only one or two would pass unnoticed. Of all merry men I will have none save Little John to bear my bow."

So Robin Hood and Little John set off together through the forest towards Nottingham. Now it happened that as they went they fell into a wrangle, and the dispute grew so high that Robin Hood quite lost his temper and struck Little John a blow with his hand.

The giant was very angry at this insult and whipped out his sword.

"Had any man but my master struck me!" cried Little John, "his blood should have stained this bright sword.

Now, thou mayest get a man where thou wilt, Robin Hood, but thou gettest me no more."

So they parted in wrath, and, while Robin went on towards Nottingham, Little John turned back to the forest. Robin's anger soon died away, and he felt very sorry to think he had vexed his faithful follower. "I will pray at St. Mary's altar that Little John may be reconciled to me again," he said as he came in sight of the town and saw the church tower rising high above the walls.

He passed through the gate easily, for the warders did not look twice at a single man in the gray clothes of a peasant, and Robin went straight to the church. The service was about to begin, and he knelt down before the altar and prayed that he might leave the town as safely as he came in.

Now about the middle of the service, a tall monk, in a black habit, entered the church and began to move softly up the aisle towards his place in the chancel. Suddenly he stopped in the shadow of a pillar and stared with all his eyes. Just beyond the pillar, a man was kneeling devoutly on the rushes spread over the floor of the church. The man was clad in gray, and his hood had fallen back, for he raised his head in eager attention to the priest who was reading the service.

The black monk looked again and again. Surely he knew that face. Yes, he was quite sure, and the monk's eyes were filled with the light of anger and hatred as he turned and glided swiftly down the church again.

Robin Hood knelt on, quite unconscious that he stood in

the greatest danger, quite unconscious that the High Cellarer of St. Mary's had recognized him and was now moving hot-foot to take measures for his capture.

The black monk came to the door of the church, and now he fairly ran, such was his haste, to warn the authorities. First, he hurried to the gates and spoke to the warders. "Close the gates. Lock and bar them!" he cried. There is a great felon in the town. Your heads will answer for it if ye let any man pass to or fro until the sheriff gives you leave."

The warders made haste to shut the gates and place themselves on guard.

"Now, I have Robin Hood, yea, Robin Hood himself!" cried the black monk exultantly as he sped to the sheriff's house. "He cannot leave the town, and he lies in our hands like a bird in a trap."

Into the sheriff's hall the black monk burst without ceremony and found the great man sitting idly in his chair.

"Up, Sir Sheriff!" cried the high cellarer. "Up, and order out your men! I bring great news. The kings's felon is in this town and may be seized! I have spied the false felon as he stood at Mass. 'Twere an ill day for you, Sir Sheriff, should he escape the king's justice."

"What's this pother about?" demanded the sheriff in surly tones, for he had been roused from a nap, and the black monk in his haste had not mentioned the felon's name. "Some petty rogue, I warrant, who hath but made free with the abbey hen roost."

"Petty rogue!" roared the black monk. "Did I not

name him? Petty rogue, indeed, Sir Sheriff! Why, 'tis
Robin Hood!"

Now, you may be sure, the sheriff was roused. He
leapt from his chair and faced the black monk, and glittering eyes looked into glittering eyes.

"Robin Hood!" gasped the sheriff. "And in Nottingham
again? Never!"

"'Tis simple truth!" cried the high cellarer. "I have
seen him even now at Mass in St. Mary's. What! Think
you I could be mistaken in the sturdy rogue who robbed
me of hundreds of pounds in the greenwood and brought
me into dreadful trouble with the abbot? Nay, Sir Sheriff,
but his face is never out of my mind—never. I would
know him among a thousand."

The sheriff could still scarce grasp the idea that Robin
Hood was inside the walls, but he raised a silver whistle
which hung at his girdle and blew a call. A servant came
in at once.

"Bid Dickon and Hal attend me with thirty of the foresters," ordered the sheriff, and took down his harness from
a stand in the hall and began to array himself. By the
time he had donned steel cap and a great leathern coat
covered with steel links and girded his sword about him,
his men were mustered, and they marched at once to the
church.

The entry of this armed force caused a great commotion
in the place, but the sheriff cried out, "Fear not, good
people, I wish ye no harm. I have but come to seize a
great rogue who hath but now crept in among you."

"There he is!" shouted the black monk. "Yonder fellow in gray kneeling by the great pillar. He is Robin Hood."

No one was more surprised than Robin himself to hear his name ringing through the church. He had no idea that he had been spied upon, and his hood was now drawn so closely down that his face was quite hidden. But what an uproar arose in the church when the people heard that the thrice-famous outlaw was in their midst! Some crowded to look upon him, some tried to push their way out of the place, and the sheriff's men blocked Robin's way to the door.

The outlaw saw that his only chance was to make one fierce dash upon his enemies in the confusion and hope to cut his way out. He breathed but one wish: "Would that my faithful Little John stood at my side. Alas! but I miss him this day." Then he drew out his broadsword and rushed like a charging lion upon the ranks of the sheriff's men. Up rose a score of swords in the hands of the foresters, and many a blow was launched at the daring outlaw. But more haste, less speed, and the foresters only jostled each other and clashed sword against sword and missed their aim, while Robin's bright blade flashed in air and struck down man after man. A tremendous fight did Robin Hood make for freedom that day. Thrice he cut his way through his foes, only to find new enemies in his path. To and fro leapt the outlaw, dodging blows and dealing strokes which felled forester after forester.

"Slay him not!" shrieked the sheriff. "Strike him down, but seize him alive. 'Tis the order of the king."

Robin heard the voice, and knew it was the sheriff who

spoke. He turned and made a swift rush at his ancient
enemy, swinging his blade on high. The sheriff shrank
before that fierce assault and raised his shield to ward off
the terrific blow which Robin aimed at him. Down fell
the heavy blade, clanged on the shield, and drove it from
the sheriff's hand. Scarce checked in its fall, the sword
clashed on the sheriff's steel cap and hurled him to the
pavement. Well was it for the sheriff that day that he
had put on a helmet of proof, a splendid piece of work of
a great armorer, for naught else saved him. Had it been
common steel Robin's sword would have gone through it
as if it had been a cap of paper. As it was, the helmet
stood the blow and the sword broke in two in Robin's
hand.

"I'll befall the smith that made thee!" cried Robin flinging down the broken sword, "for now I am weaponless in
the midst of my enemies."

And with that he leapt upon the nearest man and tried
to wrench away the stout quarterstaff which the fellow
had in his hand. But at the very moment he was tripped
up from behind and stumbled and fell to the ground. At
once a dozen men flung themselves upon him, and he was
pinned down by the sheer weight of numbers; nor did his
enemies loose their frenzied grip upon him until he was
fast in bonds.

By that time the sheriff had got to his feet again, rather
dizzy from that thunderbolt stroke, but very glad to find
his head safe inside his good steel cap and almost beside
himself with delight to think that he had Robin Hood in
his hands at last.

Robin Hood was shut up in a dungeon where only at high noon a little light came through a thick grating

"Away with him!" cried the sheriff. "Clap him into the deepest, strongest dungeon in the castle keep, and let a double watch mount guard over him night and day."

This was done, and Robin Hood was shut up in a dungeon where only at high noon a little light came through a thick grating. The walls were seven feet thick, and the door was fastened by three locks.

"Let him break out of that, if he can!" cried the sheriff. "I have put the strong thief in a stronger place, and there must he stay."

"Why trouble to shut him up in so strong a place?" said the black monk, who burned to see Robin on the gallows. "Why not hang him up out of hand? I have heard you often threaten that you would do so if you could but seize him."

"And so I would if the matter stood with me alone," snarled the sheriff. "I would have bidden my men to slay him on the spot had I dared."

"And why dared you not?" demanded the high cellarer. "Who is there to gainsay the authority of the sheriff?"

"One who is above us all," replied the sheriff in a low voice—"the king! He hath sent orders to me that should Robin Hood be seized, the rogue must await his pleasure. The King hath heard so much of this strong thief that he wishes to see him!"

The black monk said nothing for some time, but his brow was furrowed in thought. Then he spoke up, "Sir Sheriff, it was I who discovered the knave and delivered him into your hands."

"Ay, ay," said sheriff.

"Then I claim the right to bear the tidings of the capture to the king."

"Ay, ay," chuckled the sheriff. "And get some rich preferment from His Majesty?"

"If there be a reward it is fitting it should come to me!" cried the high cellarer.

"I do not deny it," replied the sheriff, "and I wish with all my heart that you may get a fat abbey at the least to rule over. You have done me a great service, and I will make handsome mention of you in the letter which I shall write this afternoon to the king."

"And I will start with it at break of day tomorrow!" cried the black monk, who went at once to prepare for his journey.

* * * * * *

All that Sunday there was great commotion in Nottingham town. People ran to and fro talking of the capture of Robin Hood, and everyone that had been in St. Mary's Church that morning had a crowd round him eagerly listening to his account of the great struggle the famous outlaw had made. Yet not a whisper of all this passed the walls to the country beyond, for the sheriff had doubled the guard at every gate and absolutely forbidden that any should go in or out until he had learned the king's pleasure with regard to Robin Hood.

"If no man goes out," said the sheriff, "then Robin Hood must stay with the rest of us. If no man comes in, then his rascals cannot sneak in from the forest to attempt a rescue." So Nottingham town lay like a beleaguered city and its gates were barred and bolted night and day. But

for all that, Robin's men soon learned the evil tidings
through Lobb the cobbler. Lobb was one of the first to
hear of Robin's capture, and, as soon as darkness fell on
the city, he went to the roof of his house, which was built
against the inner side of the wall. With him were two
men who were stanch friends of the outlaw, and these let
Lobb down over the wall by a rope. As soon as the cobbler's feet touched the ground, he unfastened the rope,
and it was drawn back; then Lobb hurried away to the
forest as fast as he could go.

Lobb found a very uneasy band of outlaws gathered
around the great fire in the glade where their camp was
pitched. Every man was afraid that his leader had met
with some mishap, since Robin had not returned; and
most unhappy of all was Little John. The good-tempered
giant had quite forgiven Robin's hasty blow, and now
blamed himself that he had not stayed by his master's
side.

It would be impossible to picture the wrath and grief of
the outlaws when they found that their worst fears were
all too true, and that their beloved captain lay fast in hold
in Nottingham town. But Little John stoutly refused to
believe that the worst would happen.

"He went to Nottingham to pray to our Lady," said Little John, "and our Lady will help him. Many a time,
brothers, hath our noble master been hard bestead, yet
hath given his enemies the go-by, and I'll warrant ye it
will happen again. Let us pluck up our hearts and quit
this mourning. Let us go and watch the town and devise
some plan for breaking in and freeing our leader."

Before dawn, Little John was lying in wait in a thicket

before the southern gate of Nottingham. With him was Much. Both had laid aside their forest green and wore plain leathern doublets. They had the guise of graziers and dealers who went from fair to fair buying and selling cattle. In this dress they would attract no notice and could move freely about the country and through the neighboring villages.

It was another lovely May morning, and when the sun came up in all his glory, their hearts ached to think that Robin Hood lay in a foul, dark dungeon where no sound of the song of birds or the soft whisper of the rustling leaves could reach him. Then all their attention was drawn to the gates, for they saw a postern door opened and a small train come forth. The train was formed of a black monk riding a strong horse and a little page mounted on a white palfrey; the postern door was closed behind them, and monk and page rode towards the thicket where Little John and Much lay in secure hiding.

"I know yonder black monk," whispered Little John to his comrade. "'Tis the high cellarer. Dost remember him, Much? We cleared his saddlebags of a round heap of gold."

Much nodded, and then obeyed Little John's uplifted finger which beckoned him to leave the thicket. The outlaws now took a sweep through the trees and came out on the road the black monk was following, and walked towards the town. At a bend they came upon monk and page, riding at a foot pace and keeping a sharp look out for any sign of danger.

The monk cast a glance at the newcomers, but, seeing two plain-looking fellows in dirty doublets trudging along staff in hand, he made no attempt to avoid them, and presently the two parties met.

"Give you good day," said Little John, and bowed before the black monk. "Do you come from Nottingham?"

"We do," said the monk.

"Tell us the tidings, I pray you," went on Little John. "There is a story beginning to spread in the country that a desperate outlaw called Robin Hood was taken yesterday."

"See now how these tidings take wing in a manner none may understand!" cried the black monk. "How the rumor came to thee I cannot say, but it is true, good yeomen. The strong rogue was seized yesterday in St. Mary's Church in Nottingham."

"I' faith, was he?" cried Little John. "Well, he hath had money both from me and from my comrade here. We are fain to learn the truth."

"He robbed me, too," said the black monk. "Hundreds of pounds did the false thief strip me of; but I had my revenge yesterday. It was I who discovered him and warned the sheriff. It was I who had the chief hand in his capture, and you may, therefore, thank me for it."

"May Heaven reward you as you deserve," said Little John, "and if ever we have a chance we will reward you also. And now, by your leave, we will go with you and bring you on your way, for Robin Hood has many a wild fellow in this forest, and if they knew that ye rode this way, i' faith, ye should be slain."

"I know it," said the black monk; "but we are well mounted and ready to flee at the first sign of danger."

"It is not easy always to mark the first sign of danger," said Little John, shaking his head solemnly, "therefore we will attend you through the forest."

So they went on their way chatting together, and the black monk was so proud of his exploit that he could not forbear from boasting of it again and again and of the letters which he bore to the king.

Presently they came to a place where the road ran through a deep dingle, and in the duskiest part of the way, Little John suddenly seized the monk's horse by the head. The black monk was at once filled with suspicion and drew his dagger from under his mantle and struck at Little John. Little John whipped a sword from under his leathern doublet and gave the black monk such a return stroke that the monk fell to the ground a dead man.

"He brought our master into this great trouble," said Little John to Much, "and now he shall never go to the king to tell his tale."

Much had seized the palfrey of the little page, and now he sounded his horn. Soon a troop of their comrades ran up, and Little John bade these bury the body of the black monk and take the little page into safe keeping till he and Much should come again.

Next Little John took the letters from the monk and mounted the horse. Much mounted the palfrey, and away they rode to London.

When they reached London, they asked their way to the king's palace, and at the door the porter asked their errand.

"We bear letters to our lord the king from the Sheriff of

Nottingham," replied Little John, "and we may not give
them into any hands but his own."

So they were shown into a hall where the king sat in a
great chair, and a group of his lords stood about him. Little John went down upon his knee and held out the letters.

"Heaven save you, my Liege Lord—Heaven save you,
my Liege King," said Little John. "I have brought Your
Majesty these letters from the Sheriff of Nottingham."

The king took the letters and opened them and read
them, and Little John knelt and stared in admiration at the
king. And, in sooth, Little John did well to admire that
noble figure, the figure of Richard Plantagenet, Richard of
the Lion Heart. The bold, handsome face, the bright blue
eyes, the stalwart, commanding form proclaimed Richard
every inch a king, and Little John fixed every feature in
his memory that he might describe the royal warrior to his
comrades on his return to Sherwood.

Suddenly Richard raised one hand, and dealt a resound-
ing slap to the arm of his throne-like chair.

"What think you, my lords?" he cried. "Here be welcome tidings, indeed, from the Sheriff of Nottingham.
He hath seized that mighty outlaw, Robin Hood of Sherwood Forest, and hath the knave safely in hold and waiting my pleasure."

"Good news—good news, my lord King!" cried the fat
Bishop of Hereford, who was one of the prelates standing
about the throne. "In truth, you are now master of the
greatest rogue in Christendom. Have I not told Your
Majesty how the rascal plundered me and hast used me

despitefully many a time? Glad I am to hear that Your Majesty hath him and will hang him at last."

The bishop ended his speech panting and out of breath, partly because in his excitement he had spoken so fast, and partly because the very sound of Robin Hood's name always put him into a furious temper.

The king smiled and looked at the letter again; he did not seem much disturbed at the relation of the bishop's wrongs and sufferings.

"There is never a yeoman in merry England I have longed so sore to see as this Robin Hood," said the king. "I must learn what kind of man is it who rules the forest as I, who am crowned king, rule this country."

For a few moments there was silence, then the king looked up sharply from the paper and fixed his bright blue eyes on Little John.

"Yeoman," said he. "I learn here that this letter was dispatched by a monk, the High Cellarer of St. Mary's. Where is he? And how is it that thou has brought it?"

But Little John was ready with his answer. "So please you, my Liege Lord," said the outlaw. "The monk died by the way, and the letters were entrusted to me to deliver to Your Majesty."

The king nodded carelessly, for he cared not how the news came so that it was true.

"Now, I will see this Robin Hood," said Richard; "And as thou, good yeoman, hast brought the tidings, so shalt thou fetch him before me."

In token of his royal pleasure King Richard gave the messengers a reward of twenty pounds, made them Yeo-

men of the Crown, and ordered that they should attend on
his royal person when they had made an end of their journey to fetch Robin Hood to London.

With his own royal hand he gave the king's seal to Little John, and bade him to show it to the Sheriff of Nottingham, and tell the sheriff to hand over the prisoner and
to provide a guard of forty archers to bring Robin Hood
before the king. So Little John took his leave of King
Richard and rode back to Nottingham with Much at his
side and the king's seal stored carefully in his bosom.

When they came to the gates of Nottingham they found
them fast, and Little John beat upon them loudly and
shouted for the warder. In a short time the warder
looked over the wall and demanded his business.

"What means this?" cried Little John, feigning great
surprise. "The gates locked and barred in broad day!
Hast thou slept late, warder?"

"Nay," replied the warder. "The gates are kept shut
night and day because we have Robin Hood fast in deep
prison, and we bar the gates lest his men should rush in.
As it is, they are ever shooting at the men on our walls."

"Well, thou must open to me!" cried Little John, "for I
bring a message to the sheriff from our lord the king."

When the warder heard that he let them in; but the
gate was at once closed and fastened behind them, and
Little John saw that the portal was guarded by a strong
band of men-at-arms.

"I must see the sheriff at once," said Little John, and he
was led to the sheriff's house and found the sheriff seated
in the hall.

"I have a message from the king," said Little John, and took the king's seal from his bosom and showed it to the sheriff. When the sheriff saw the seal he rose from his chair, slid off his hood, and bowed as to the king himself.

"What is the will of my lord the king?" asked the shcriff.

Little John delivered Richard's orders, and the sheriff promised that they should be obeyed.

"And what will be done with the traitor when you have carried him to London?" asked the sheriff.

"There was talk there of hanging him on the gallows," replied Little John.

"Good, good!" said the sheriff gleefully, "a fitting end for such a rogue. But where is the black monk that bore the letters from me? He looked for preferment from the king on conveying such welcome news."

"He hath had it," said Little John. "Preferment so high that he will never return to Nottingham. He received a fitting reward."

"Was it in money or land?" asked the sheriff.

"In land," replied Little John. "He received enough land to amply content him. But I must go to an inn, my Lord sheriff, and rest and refresh myself and my follower. We have to start tomorrow with the prisoner, and we are weary."

"Nay, nay!" cried the sheriff. "Ye shall go to no inn this day. Ye shall be my guests, and this night will I make ye a merry feast, and the king shall learn that I know well how to entertain his messengers."

So that night the sheriff made a great feast in honor of

the king's messengers. Wine flowed in streams, and ale in floods, and all drank to the health of the king and to the safe hanging of Robin Hood.

Little John was given a bed in a small room opening from the hall, and Much lay down on a pallet at Little John's feet. The two comrades waited till all was silent in the house, and they rose, wrapped their mantles about them, and took their swords in their hands. They stepped softly into the hall and went across to the room where they knew that the sheriff lay. They had to move very carefully, for the sheriff's men lay asleep before the fire and on the rushes spread over the floor of the hall. But every man was full of strong ale and slept heavily, and when they gained the sheriff's room they found that he also lay in a drunken sleep. This made it easy for Little John to draw the sheriff's ring from his finger, and that was all they needed.

Next, they went down to the door and there they found the porter as fast asleep as any, for he had been just as deep in the carouse. So Little John and Much opened the door and went through the dark and silent streets till they came to the prison where their master lay. Now they beat on the iron-banded door with the pommels of their swords until the passages within rang again. This noise called up the jailer, and he came to the door with a torch in his hand and demanded to know who was without.

"Robin Hood hath broken prison and fled!" cried Little John. "A careless jailer art thou."

"By my faith, but thou speakest falsehood," replied the jailer. "He is safe in the deepest, darkest dungeon. I have

So that night the sheriff made a great feast in honor of the king's messengers

seen him there but just now, and his bonds were upon him."

"Natheless, we must see him with our own eyes," said Little John. "And we must know for a surety that he lies securely in ward."

"And who are ye?" cried the jailer.

"We are the messengers who arrived today from the king," returned Little John, "and we bring a token from the sheriff that ye may know we are men of trust."

In the door was a small, strong grating, through which the jailer might see those who sought admittance. The light of the torch was now streaming through the grating, and Little John held up the sheriff's ring full in the red light. The jailer saw it and knew it, and hastened to unbar the door. In sprang Little John and seized the jailer by the throat so that he should not call out and raise an alarm. In sprang Much and bound the jailer's hands and feet with a length of cord he had carried under his cloak. Then the jailer's head was muffled in his own jerkin, and the huge bunch of keys at his girdle fell into the hands of Little John.

"Now will I be the jailer," said Little John; and, first of all, he locked up the true jailer in one of his own dungeons. Then, seizing the torch, he descended the steps towards the prison cells which lay deepest of all. Here he saw an iron door fastened with three great padlocks of steel, and forthwith he began to try the keys on the locks, for he felt sure his master was shut up there.

Six or seven keys he tried before he found the right one, but at last the third padlock was unfastened and the

curved bolt drawn from the heavy staple. Then Little
John opened the door and went into the dungeon. On a
heap of straw in the far corner lay a man fast bound, but,
as soon as the light of the torch fell upon him, Little John
knew the figure and sprang forward. Robin Hood, for it
was he, sat up and blinked at the new comer for the glare
of the torch blinded him, so many days had he lain in
dreadful darkness.

"Master, master, I am here! Up, master, and escape!"

"Little John!" breathed Robin in the utmost wonder, for,
though he knew his voice, he could scarce believe his own
ears.

"Ay, master, it is I." Little John whipped out a keen
knife and freed Robin from his bonds with a few swift
slashes. Then he drew a second sword from beneath his
cloak and placed it in Robin's hand. Up sprang Robin
Hood, wild with delight to find his bonds stripped from
him and a good sword in his hand to guard his head.

At this moment they heard a loud cry of warning from
Much, who had been left above to guard the way of escape. Robin Hood and Little John rushed up the stone
stairs, and as they went a clash of swords and an uproar of
voices broke out above them. They ran out into the up-
per passages, to find Much hard beset by five men-at-arms
who had rushed from the guard room, having been roused
to discover that something was wrong. With a mighty
shout Little John leapt into the fray, and Robin followed
suit, and in a twinkling the guards were driven back into
their room where they had been sleeping.

"Off! Off!" cried Little John. "This affray will rouse

the town, and that swiftly. Follow me!" and he led the way to the outer door, which had been left wide open.

"To the West Gate!" cried Robin Hood, as they sprang into the street. "The slackest watch is ever kept there."

But at that instant clash-clang-clang! went the heavy bell in the turret overhead. Someone had rushed to the alarm bell and was tolling it madly to arouse the town.

"There will be slack watch at no gate now, master!" cried Little John as the thunderous clang of the great bell pealed over the sleeping city. "Yon bell will put all on the alert and fill every street with enemies anon. This way! This way!" and he darted down a narrow lane, and his companions followed him.

The night was so dark that in the narrow passage the three comrades could not see each other. Little John halted for a moment and thrust the end of his cloak into Robin's hand. Much took the hem of Robin's jerkin, and so they kept together and followed Little John as he wound his way through two or three lanes, for he knew every corner of Nottingham by day or night. At last he paused under the shelter of a pent house, and the three fugitives stood still to listen to the uproar which was growing in the town. The bell still clanged furiously, lights began to flash at windows, and people hurried from their houses asking whether it was fire or thieves which assailed the town.

"Stand still until the throng thickens," whispered Little John. "Then we will join with them and hide amongst them." Soon a number of townsmen, with staves and halberds in their hands, and one or two with lanterns, came hurrying along, and in a short time numbers of people were running to and fro asking for news, and the three friends could leave their shelter and move amid the crowd without being remarked upon. Little John again led the way, and his friends soon understood that he was making for the house of Lobb the cobbler. Just as they gained the head of the close in which Lobb lived, they heard a man shouting to another, " 'Tis Robin Hood has escaped and fled, neighbor. He hath broken out of hold, and the gates are kept, and the town is to be searched house by house."

"I' faith, that piece of news concerns us," chuckled Little John, "and we must be out of Nottingham as soon as may be."

So he went quickly down the close and tapped lightly on the window shutter, and Lobb himself came to see who it was. The cobbler opened the shutter, and Little John thrust his head into the house, for the window was no more than a hole in the wall, and had no glass in it.

"Lobb," whispered Little John. "Art alone in the house?"

"Ay, John," whispered the cobbler in return, for he knew Little John by his voice, low as he spoke.

"Well, then, unbar the door and let us in," said the big fellow, and the door was unfastened, and in they went. Lobb closed the shutter and lighted a lamp. When he saw Robin Hood in his house he was full of delight to think that the great outlaw had escaped thus from his enemies.

"Now, haste thee, Lobb," said Little John. "Even as

thou camest to warn us that our master was taken, in like manner must we escape this night."

"Come along to the roof," said Lobb. "The rope is ready coiled at the head of the ladder."

So they went up the ladder which led to the roof of the cobbler's house and out onto the roof, and thence they climbed to the top of the wall. And the rope was put round Robin's waist and his friends let him down. Then Much was lowered, and, as for Little John, he hung by his hands from the top of the wall and then leaped to the ground, for Lobb alone could not have held the weight of his great body. Then Lobb quickly drew up the rope and went back into his house, while the three comrades hurried through the darkness. As they went, a cock crowed loudly, and Robin Hood looked to the east. "By my faith!" said he, "we have not escaped a moment too soon. Yonder dawns the day," for it was all gray in the east, and the dawn was near at hand, and they ran on faster.

In the town the sheriff was longing for the dawn. He felt certain that with the day he would once more seize Robin Hood. He had been aroused from his sleep by the clangor of the alarm bell, and his wrath was beyond all describing when he knew that his famous captive had broken prison. But on the heels of wrath came fear, and the sheriff trembled.

"I dare never look in the face of the king!" he cried, "for should I come before him without Robin Hood, in truth he will hang me out of hand. I know his temper." So the sheriff urged on the search with the utmost fury, not only with the hope of putting the rope round Robin's neck, but also with the desire of clearing it from his own.

When he heard that no one had passed through the gates, he felt a little easier in his mind. "The knave is hidden by some friend in the town," he said. "The day will soon break, and we will search house and shed and sty but we will seize him."

True to his word, the sheriff searched the town from end to end, from cellar to garret, but all in vain. He knew it not, but while he searched, Robin was in Merry Sherwood with a heart as light as the bird which sang on the bough in the May sunshine. Again and again he thanked the good friends who had brought him safe and sound from his great peril, and his yeomen waved their bows in air and shouted again and again to see the master safely among them. Then Little John said to Robin Hood, "Master, I have done you a good turn for evil, for I could not bear to think that you should lie in hold and suffer a shameful death. Now I have brought you under the greenwood tree and you are safe and sound, farewell, and good day to you."

"Nay, nay, Little John!" cried Robin. "Leave me not because of that hasty blow, of which I repented sorely within a short time. By my truth, thou art fitter to command than I. I make thee now master of all my men and me. Thou shalt be our leader."

Little John's kind heart was touched at this generous offer, and he sprang to Robin Hood's side. "Nay, master," he said, "by my faith, that shall never be so. I will be thy follower as of old, and no other place will I take than that of Robin Hood's man."

And so Robin Hood and Little John stood together under the greenwood tree as master and man once more. And the joyous outlaws celebrated this great day with a merry feast. As for the sheriff, he was in despair when the news came to him that Robin Hood was ranging the forest as gaily as ever. He wrote a most humble letter to the king, and begged that Richard would forgive him, and said that nothing would have beguiled him had not Little John brought the king's own privy seal.

Richard was so vexed to think how cleverly Little John had played with him that his bright blue eyes sparkled with anger and his fresh face flushed hotly. But anger never stayed long in the mind of the Lion Heart, and soon he took a loftier view of Little John's daring trick.

"By my halidom, my lords!" he said to his courtiers, "but that man was true to his master. I say, by sweet Saint John, he loves Robin Hood better than he loves his king. Would that I had followers as true and loyal. Robin Hood is ever bound to him for this brave rescue, but i' faith, the rogue beguiled us finely. Surely there are not three such yeomen in England. I would give a jewel from my crown to see this Robin Hood who wins such devotion from his men. But he slips through the fingers of everyone." And Richard smiled as he thought of the fine reward he had given to the two yeomen whose only object was to thwart him and set their master free.

As for the little page who had set out with the black

monk, he liked the life in the forest so much that he became a servant of Robin Hood and never went back or ever wished to go back to Nottingham again, and in time he became as good a yeoman as any.

Will Stutely Falls Into a Trap

Now it happened on the night that Robin Hood, Little John, and Much made their famous escape over the walls of Nottingham that they were seen. A neighbor of Lobb the cobbler had been aroused by the alarm bell and the shouting and had run out to see what was the cause of the uproar. He was going back into his house when he heard stealthy movements on the roof of Lobb's shop. He was a sly, creeping sort of fellow, this neighbor, whose name was Higg. So he hid himself and watched the cobbler's house. Soon he became certain that three men had been let down over the wall, and he wondered what it meant. The next day he felt quite certain who the men were when he heard the sheriff's man proclaim that a great reward would be given for the capture of Robin Hood and the two men who had pretended to be messengers from the king.

Higg went at once to the sheriff and told his story. At

first the sheriff had it in mind to seize Lobb; but just as he was about to give the order he paused.

"Nay," said the sheriff, "to seize a wretched cobbler is scarce worth the trouble. He shall be my decoy bird. If the outlaws make such use of him, surely they often visit him. So I will have his house watched, and perhaps it will be a trap in which to seize a prize worth taking."

So he gave Higg twelve silver pennies on the spot and promised him fifty more if he would watch his neighbor's house closely and give the word at once when Lobb had visitors who had the air of men from the greenwood.

Higg pocketed his silver pennies and went home and kept a sharp watch on Lobb's house. More than a week passed before he came hot-foot to the sheriff's house.

"There is a stranger now with Lobb," he said. "Not a townsman, but I believe, an outlaw."

The sheriff sent three of his men at once to seize the stranger they would find in the house of Lobb the cobbler and to bring him to the sheriff's hall.

Away went the three men, burst into the cobbler's house, and found him talking with a tall, strong man. The latter was Will Stutely, and he had actually come on Robin's behalf to see if Lobb had escaped all suspicion of being concerned in the flight of Robin and his friends. Now Robin's care for Lobb, who had helped him, was the cause of Will's downfall, for no one dreamed that the sly and cunning Higg was watching the house for the sheriff.

As it happened, one of the three men sent by the sheriff knew Will Stutely well.

"Ay, ay, 'tis an outlaw!" he cried. "Seize him, comrades! Away with him to the sheriff! Our master will be pleased with this. 'Tis one of the chief among the rogues who serve under Robin Hood."

Will drew his sword and made a dash at the door. There was a fierce fight, and Stutely cut down two of his opponents, and burst out into the street. But there he met with fresh enemies, and was taken.

The sheriff laughed a grim laugh when he knew that one of Robin's men had been seized.

"No need to appeal to the king about this one, at any rate!" he cried. "This fellow is in my hands entirely, and up he shall swing with the break of day tomorrow. Put him in jail and let a strong body of archers watch the place until he is safely hanged."

When Robin Hood heard this news he was deeply grieved and said to his men, "Let us swear that Will Stutely we will rescue, or, if we fail, many a gallant wight we will slay in revenge."

Robin at once gathered his men from every part of the forest, and the outlaws marched away to the rescue of their comrade.

Away they marched to Nottingham, and before the break of day, Robin placed his men in ambush before the walls. To their surprise the first light of dawn showed them a gallows erected before the gate. The sheriff was so confident that this swift hanging would be carried out with success that he had built the gallows in face of the forest and in scorn of the outlaws. He little dreamed how swift Robin had been rush to the rescue.

"There is a palmer standing under the walls yonder," said Robin Hood to Little John. "I will send a messenger to him to gain the latest tidings."

A young man was sent to speak with the palmer, and returned with the news that Will Stutely would soon be brought out to be hung on the gallows tree before the wall. Scarce had the young man returned than the gates were thrown open widely and a line of archers and spearmen, bowmen and billmen, came pouring out of the town. Rank after rank they swept forward until the gallows was surrounded by a powerful force of armed men, their spearheads and drawn swords glittering in the rays of the newly risen sun.

Almost last of all came Will Stutely, his arms bound and a white cap on his head. This cap the hangman would pull over the prisoner's eyes before the rope was put round his neck. Around Will marched a band of the sheriff's stoutest fellows, and the sheriff himself rode beside the group which guarded the outlaw.

Will looked up at the gallows and gave a grimace of disgust, then spoke up gallantly to the sheriff:

"Now, seeing that I must die, grant me, I pray you one boon. No man of our noble band hath yet been hanged. Therefore, give me a sword and let me be unbound that I may fight with thy men until I am killed."

But the sheriff would not hear of granting Will Stutely so brave a death.

"No, indeed," replied the sheriff gruffly. "Thou shalt die on the gallows, and thy master, too, if ever it lie in my power!"

Will Stutely laughed the sheriff to scorn on hearing this craven reply, but the sheriff cared nothing for that and only wished to see the outlaw hanging by the neck.

Now near the gallows there was a little thicket of hazels, and just as the rope was about to be placed round Will Stutely's neck, a tall man sprang from this thicket and burst through the guards with the utmost coolness.

"What, Will!" he said, "and are you going to take leave of the world without bidding good-bye to all your friends? Nay, that is unkind of you."

Will looked up with a gasp of delight. He could not fail to know that voice and to recognize the huge form. It was Little John who stood before him.

In the surprise and confusion following the moment in which the giant burst through the ring of guards, Little John was quick to act. He cut Will's bonds and snatched a sword from the hands of one of the sheriff's men and gave it to his friend. "Now, Will guard thy head!" he cried, and the two outlaws stood back to back and defied the whole throng to seize them.

All this had passed so quickly that the sheriff sat on his horse gaping in silent wonder and scarce able to find his voice. Then voice and rage burst from him together.

"'Tis he! 'Tis he!" yelled the sheriff. "Yonder great rogue is the fellow who hath cozened the king and me. 'Tis the false messenger. Seize him on your lives! But, nay. Slay him! Slay him! That is the surer way."

It was all very well for the sheriff to call upon the guard to slay Little John, but to do it was another matter. For the giant stood there, his buckler on one arm, his huge, gleaming sword waving above his head, his ruddy face lit with joy of battle, ready to crush to earth any who should dare to venture within reach of that mighty broadsword.

Then arose a still wilder shout of surprise and a louder cry of dread, for a long, clear bugle note rang out, and a band of archers sprang from cover of the forest and rushed upon the force which the sheriff had gathered.

"Robin Hood's men! Robin Hood's men!" shouted the foresters. "Bows and bills, comrades! Bows and bills! Have at them! Have at them!"

"A Hood! A Hood to the rescue!" roared the outlaws and charged home with Robin at their head.

The onset of the outlaws was so fierce and unexpected that the sheriff and his men were borne back into the very gates of the town. This advantage lay to the credit of the brave and wily Little John. He made his venture alone into the midst of the enemy in order to draw their attention and give his comrades a chance of taking them unawares, and he had succeeded nobly. In the uproar of the combat he cut his way easily through the ranks of the enemy and rejoined his friends, with Will Stutely at his side.

Robin Hood had his eyes everywhere at once. No sooner did he see that the prisoner and Little John were safe than he sounded the order for retreat to the forest. He had gained his end, and there was no further need for bloodshed. Besides, the sheriff's men were beginning to rally and recover from the surprise, and they formed a powerful and well-armed force, outnumbering the outlaws by at least three to one. So Robin, like a prudent leader, thought it wise to draw back in time.

The outlaws obeyed at once, and began to retreat, shooting steadily as they went, and holding back their foes with shower after shower of keen shafts. But there were brave fellows, too, among the sheriff's force, and these burst after the outlaws in hot pursuit. On the edge of the forest a sad mischance befell, for down went Little John on his face with an arrow through his knee.

"Master!" cried Little John. "I can neither fight nor fly. Take, I pray thee, thy good broadsword and smite off my head that I may not fall alive into the hands of the sheriff, who will triumph over me."

"By the rood, Little John, but I will not!" cried Robin Hood. "I would not lose thee for all the gold in Merry England," and he turned to hold back the foremost of his pursuers while Little John was carried off. This was done by Much, who swung the huge fellow on his shoulders and bore him away, heavy as he was, with ease.

So the running fight and retreat went on, ever growing worse for the outlaws, for seven men were wounded sorely, and not one was left to the tender mercies of the sheriff. Many fell on the other side, but these did not hinder the pursuit, which pressed hotter and hotter on the forest outlaws. Robin Hood was a host in himself that day. Every time his bow twanged, one of the sheriff's men reeled to earth, and so far was the range of his whistling shafts that he held them at bay long after they would have closed on poorer bowmen. Nobly did his men second him. Will Scarlet, Stutely, Hal, and Hobb, and the rest fought beside him, and the "iron sleet" of their keen shafts held back the fierce pursuers, while others toiled ahead with the load of wounded men.

And so the tide of retreat and battle surged along a forest road and into a wide clearing, where a fair castle raised its gray walls above a deep moat.

At sight of the combat the warder blew his torn and aroused the inmates of the castle. Among the first to reach the walls was the knight who was the lord of the castle. He cast a single glance at the retreating men, then rushed to the drawbridge, crossed in, and hurried towards them.

"In, in!" he shouted. "Carry your wounded in, and retire thither every man. My house is thine."

It was Sir Richard of the Lea, not forgetful of benefits received, and never was invitation more welcome. In trooped the outlaws to the shelter of the strong stone walls, and the sheriff and his men dashed up to hear the portcullis clang down, and the drawbridge go creaking up, and to find themselves on the wrong side of the deep, dark moat.

The proud and disappointed sheriff cried out, "Thou traitor knight, thou'rt succoring the enemy of the king! Thou'rt breaking the law!"

Then Sir Richard looked over the wall and replied, "Sir, I will avow the deed that I have done, even to the loss of my lands. Go now to the king, and learn what is his will in this matter. Till then Robin Hood and his men are safe with me."

So the sheriff went to London and told the tale to the king.

"By my faith as crowned king and belted knight," said Richard Plantagent, "but these fellows hold together truly and stanchly. The more I hear of them, the greater grows my wish to see them. Go back, sheriff, and stir no more in this matter at present. I myself will come to Nottingham shortly and look into these things myself."

Now the sheriff had been hoping to get orders from the king to raise the whole country on Sir Richard's castle, and so he was greatly disappointed. Still, there was nothing for him to do but go home in dudgeon and wait for the king, while Sir Richard feasted Robin and his men to the full, and his lady nursed Little John and the wounded men back to health and strength.

King Richard Comes to Sherwood ⌒

AFTER a time King Richard came down to Nottingham in hopes of meeting with Robin Hood. He marched into the forest attended by a strong body of knights and expected to encounter the outlaws very shortly. But he marched hither and thither and found the forest empty and silent as far as all human life was concerned. He saw the deer bounding over the greensward, the great oaks waving their boughs in the wind, but never a glimpse had he of the stout fellows in Lincoln Green.

Day after day passed, and Richard traversed the glade and woodland all in vain; he seemed no nearer to coming to speech with Robin Hood than he had been when seated in his palace in London.

"By my halidom," said Richard, "but this is passing strange. I was told that these fellows so haunted the forest roads that a beggar could not pass unnoticed, and yet I see naught of them.

259

The reason was simple: it was Robin's own doing that Richard saw nothing of the outlaws. Robin loved his king, and was not willing that a hand should be raised against Richard and his followers, so he gave strict orders that his men should keep out of the way.

He was faithfully obeyed. Time and again the outlaws lay hidden in brake and shaw* as the glittering train swept by, and smiled to see the king and his lords pass within easy bowshot, but never an arrow was placed on string and never a sign was given of their presence.

One day Richard was lamenting that Robin Hood seemed to have vanished from the face of the earth when an old forester who stood by his knee smiled and said, "Nay, my Liege Lord, he is in the forest as surely as I stand here, and ye may easily see him."

"How?" demanded the king.

"Why, my Lord, you go in armor and with a train of soldiery: think ye that the outlaws will set green jacket against coat of mail? I trow not; but should ye go in guise of a fat abbot, whose mails would yield rich plunder on rifling, I warrant me that Robin would appear fast enough."

King Richard saw the force of these words and nodded gaily. The adventure was just to his liking, and the very next day he slipped secretly from Nottingham, in abbot's dress, with half-a-dozen followers, dressed as monks, and a couple of led horses, heavily laden with stores and baggage.

Sure enough he had not gone three miles into the forest

---

*Copse.

before he was called upon to stand. At a bend of the way, a man, handsomely dressed in Lincoln green, bow in hand and quiver full of shafts, stepped from a thicket and laid his hand on the abbot's bridle.

His sunburned face and bright eyes were full of amusement as he said, in courteous tones, "Sir Abbot, by your leave, you must bide awhile with me and my men." He waved his bow, and at once a score of hardy, active fellows burst from the bushes and surrounded the party. At their head was a huge yeoman, grinning at sight of this rich haul, and on him Richard's eyes were at once fixed. It was easy to know Little John again.

Then Richard looked at the first man and knew that Robin Hood stood before him at last.

"And who are ye who bar my way?" asked the king quietly in his deep, rich voice.

Robin Hood started slightly at hearing those commanding tones and looked keenly at the stranger. But the great hat and hood which Richard wore quite concealed his features. Then Robin replied:

"We be yeoman of this forest. We dwell 'neath the greenwood tree and we live on our king's deer, for we have no other means. But ye have churches, rents, and gold; give us of your plenty, for Saint Charity's sake."

"In truth, good yeoman," said Richard, "I have brought to the greenwood no more than forty pounds. For I have lain at Nottingham with the King's Court and spent much on feasting these great lordlings who follow the king."

"Art thou a true follower of the king?" asked Robin.

"That am I," replied Richard. "I love him with all my heart.

"Then for that speech thou savest half thy money, Sir Abbot," said Robin. "Give me twenty pounds for my men, and keep the other twenty for thine own needs."

"Gramercy," said Richard, "but thou art a very gentle yeoman. And thou must know that my errand into this forest is to search for thee and bid thee come to Nottingham to meet the king; he is full of longing to see thee, and he sends thee a safe conduct, and here is his seal to assure thee."

Richard now drew the royal seal from beneath his cloak and showed it. Robin bent his knee in respect before it, and every yeoman pulled off his hood.

"Why," said Richard in surprise, "I was told, yeoman, that thou wert a disloyal fellow who set the king's law at naught and did all kinds of evil."

"Nay, Sir Abbot," replied Robin. "I hate unjust sheriffs and greedy monks, but I love no man in all the world so well as I do my gallant king, and if thou art his messenger and bear his seal I make thee welcome to the greenwood, and today thou shalt dine with me for the love of our king under my trysting tree."

So Robin led the abbot's horse until they came to the camp pitched under a mighty oak which was the trysting place of Robin and his men. Here Robin sounded his horn, and his men ran to the spot, company by company, bright, brisk, alert fellows, well dressed and well armed, and every man bent his knee in courtesy to his leader.

"By my faith," thought Richard, "these fellows are more at his bidding than my men be at mine."

Swiftly a fine feast was made ready, and the disguised

abbot and his men were set down to it. Richard was hungry, and he ate and drank and enjoyed the noble fare of the greenwood to the full.

When the dinner was over Robin Hood said to his guest, "Now ye shall see what life we lead in the forest that ye may report our doing to my lord the king." So the yeomen fell to their sports, wrestling, playing with the quarterstaff, and, above all, archery, the dearest sport of all.

At the foot of the glade they set up a long, slender wand, and Robin bade his men split it with their arrows. Another mark was a rose garland, through which the arrows had to be shot without touching leaf or flower.

"By my faith!" cried Richard; "but those marks are set full fifty paces too far away, good yeoman."

"Nay," smiled Robin. "Of what use to practice at an easy mark? And, i' faith, should any man miss, he must take a stout buffet on the ear in penalty."

"But does not such an exchange of buffets breed ill-will among them?" asked Richard.

"Content you, Sir Abbot, but that is foreseen and guarded against. Every man receives his buffet at the hand of our Father Confessor, Friar Tuck, and the punishment received from the Church must ever be taken in meek obedience. Stand forth, Friar Tuck, for shooting is about to begin."

Friar Tuck came up from the spot where he had just been polishing off a huge venison pasty and murmured a greeting in very bad Latin to the captive abbot, who replied with the utmost correctness.

"And dost thou smite them in earnest, brother?" demanded Richard.

"Ay, verily I do," replied Tuck, his small, bright, black eyes rolling mischievously above the forest of black beard which almost swallowed his face, "for if our men shoot carelessly we are like to be undone: so that the bad shot must be paid for by a good blow."

The shooting now began, and Richard marveled at the wonderful skill shown by yeoman after yeoman. The wand was split or the arrow threaded the garland with astonishing precision. But at last Much was so unlucky as to miss the wand. He was at once forced to stand up before the powerful friar, who sent him rolling with one swing of a brawny arm. Then Little John, to the wonder of all, failed at the garland, and even the giant was now felled by the arm of Friar Tuck.

The yeomen roared with laughter to see the huge lieutenant measure his length on the greensward, and then a still louder shout arose, for Robin Hood himself now missed the garland and must pay the penalty of failure.

"If I must be chastised by the Church," laughed Robin, "let me make my choice. Sir Abbot, serve me out my blow."

"Nay, master," protested Friar Tuck, "that is to slip aside. What can yonder fat, lazy abbot do? His blow were no more than a tap with a bulrush."

"Say not so, friar!" cried Richard. "Thou art not today the only man in a churchman's gown who hath a little pith in his arm."

"A fig for the pith in thy arm," said Tuck scornfully. "I

would take a cuff from thee and scarce know what had tickled my ear."

"And wouldst thou so!" cried the supposed abbot, leaping from his seat. "Then here is a fair offer, friar. I will abide thy blow if thou wilt abide mine."

"And I to have first blow?" cried the stout friar eagerly.

"Yes," said the other.

"Agreed, agreed!" roared Tuck joyously. "By the mass, if I do not save my own head, then e'en let it sing."

Thus promising that the abbot would be struck helplessly down, Friar Tuck rolled up the sleeve of his gown and showed a brawny arm, on which the muscles worked in knots and ridges as he closed and unclosed his huge fist. The yeomen formed an eager ring, and the abbot stepped quietly into it and stood erect to receive the friar's blow.

"By our Lady," murmured Robin to himself, "but yonder abbot is a goodly figure."

Head and shoulders above the burly figure of the friar rose the stately form of the Lion Heart, and when Friar Tuck loosed at him a terrific blow which would have hurled a heavy man flying, naught was disturbed save the abbot's great hat, which flew twenty yards away.

The yeomen raised a great shout of applause in honor of the first man who had ever held his own against Tuck's mighty fist, and then the abbot said quietly, "My turn now, brother," and Tuck, without a word, stood manfully forth to take the return cuff.

But what a shout was raised when the abbot, folding up his sleeve, bared a muscular arm, and dealt Friar Tuck such a blow that the burly priest went head over heels as if a thunderbolt had smitten him. Every man who had felt the weight of the friar's fist shouted with glee at thus seeing him paid back in his own coin, but Robin Hood did not laugh.

"An evil choice I have made," he thought. "This stranger is a more terrible boxer than our own Tuck." But he stood forth to take his cuff, and received so hearty a one that Robin measured his full length on the greensward and the abbot's hood flew back as he struck.

"In truth, Sir Abbot, thou art a stalwart fellow," said Robin, getting up and rubbing his head ruefully. "There is more pith in thy arm than ever I dreamed a churchman had."

He looked up into the abbot's face and wondered if this man could be a churchman, for never had Robin seen an abbot with such a bold, handsome face, with such bright, sparkling, honest blue eyes, with such a merry smile, so merry and gay, that Robin could not help smiling in sympathy. But Robin's wonder was turned to astonishment when he saw Little John fling himself on his knees before the abbot, and call out, "Pardon, Sire, pardon!"

"Pardon for what, Little John?" cried Robin. "Thou hast had thy cuff. There is no need to fear that this abbot of the mighty arm will deal thee a second blow."

But again Little John cried, "Pardon, Sire, pardon!" and at the next moment the wonder of the onlookers grew. For their good friend Sir Richard of the Lea now rode down to the glade to pin them, and no sooner did he see the abbot than he hasted to leap down from his horse and fall on his knees beside Little John.

*No sooner did he see the abbot than he hasted
to leap down from his horse and fall on his
knees beside Little John*

"Is there any service a loyal knight may render to his king?" said Sir Richard. "If there be, I am Your Majesty's command."

"The king!" cried Robin in wonder.

"The king!" echoed the yeomen, and everyone bent the knee before that stately figure in abbot's weeds.

"Mercy, Sire," cried Robin Hood to the king. "Mercy for my men and me, I crave, under our trysting tree."

"Mercy you shall have," said Richard smiling; "for surely such a brave band of yeomen were better employed in my service than exiled in the forest here. What say you, Robin Hood? Will you be my man, and serve me henceforth?"

"I will, My Lord!" cried Robin Hood. "I am your man from this day and forever!" and his men echoed the words, and, with a loud shout, gave their fealty to Richard of the Lion Heart.

"Hast thou any green cloth to spare, Robin?" asked the king, "for, by my faith, I would rather wear a forest jerkin than these dark weeds," and he threw his abbot's cloak aside.

"Plenty, My Liege Lord," replied Robin Hood, and hastened to dress the king and his followers in Lincoln green such as the outlaws wore.

In this guise they returned to Nottingham, the king and Robin Hood and the whole band of outlaws. But when the people of Nottingham saw this great band of men in green drawing near to the town they were greatly frightened.

"The king is slain," they said, "and here come the outlaws to seize the town and kill us all." So at first they fled in dismay.

But soon the truth was discovered, and then all crowded to see the king enter the town in triumph among the forest outlaws—outlaws no longer, but free men who could smile in the face of the sheriff. And, I promise you, the sheriff looked on very sourly at sight of this friendship of King Richard for Robin Hood.

That night there was a merry banquet in Nottingham town, for the king now feasted the outlaws as they had feasted him, and there was the best of good cheer, and Alan-a-Dale sang his gayest songs and struck the sweetest strains on his harp, so that Richard was full of delight and swore that for good fellowship and mirth and music his new followers surpassed all.

Before Richard went back to London there was a gay wedding in St. Mary's Church, and Maid Marian became the bride of Robin Hood. The king graced the wedding with his presence, and raised Robin to the rank of a noble, with the title of Earl of Huntingdon.

And so Robin Hood entered the service of the Lion Heart, and left the greenwood glades of Sherwood, as he thought, forever.

Robin Hood Shoots ❧
His Last Arrow

For some time Robin Hood was very happy in the service of the king. Then Richard left England again, and Robin found life at court very dull. More than that, he was not on friendly terms with Prince John, that false, cruel, cowardly man who later became King John, the most worthless king that England has ever known.

Now Prince John was always plotting to seize the throne, and he sent messengers to sound Robin Hood to find out if Robin and his bold archers would be willing to support Prince John against his brother Richard. But Robin was full of rage at the thought of such base treachery and sent back a reply which caused Prince John to hate him bitterly.

One lovely morning in May, Robin was walking through the streets of London and thinking how beautiful his beloved forest of Sherwood would look on such a day as this and how wearisome it was here, cooped up inside the walls of London town. He walked on to Finsbury Fields, and there stood to watch the young men shooting at the butts. The twange of the bows, the whistle of the arrows, sweetest music in his ears, fired his blood, and he resolved to go once more to Sherwood and hunt in its glades. So he and Maid Marian, with Little John and Will Scaret, slipped secretly from London and set out for the forest. They had to leave the city quietly or Prince John would have prevented them from going, and now that his brother was abroad, John held great power in the land.

Oh, how delightful it was to regain the old haunts, where the great harts and the dun deer ran through the woodland glade, and the sun seemed to shine twice as brightly as amid the dirty city streets!

Forth they went to hunt, and Robin, with a single shaft, slew a mighty hart and felt himself once more a woodman gay and free. And so they spent some happy days, when one morning a man came running frantically through the trees to the camp under the trysting oak, and they saw it was Much, their old and trusty comrade.

"Save you, master, and beware!" cried Much to Robin, "for King Richard is dead in France, and King John is now the ruler of the land."

"Ah!" said Robin. "And is he King John at last? This tidings bodes no good to me."

"You speak truth, master," said Much, "for one of his first commands has been that you are to be seized and cast into hold. And of this I have hastened to tell you."

"A thousand thanks, my faithful Much!" cried Robin.

"Then once more am I outlaw in the greenwood. Welcome to our merry old life! 'Tis a thousand times happier and more joyous than to live in the gayest palace a town can afford. Hail to the forest glade! Hail, Sherwood!"

And Little John and Scarlet echoed their master's cry and waved their bows for joy to think that the old days had come back again, for both were weary of guard room and city street.

So Robin Hood became an outlaw once more in the depths of Sherwood Forest, and swiftly his men slipped back to rejoin him until all the old faces were seen in the ring about the evening fire, as Alan-a-Dale thrummed to them on the harp and sang the sweet songs of the North Countree.

But a time of fierce storm and stress followed, for King John was a far more terrible enemy than the Sheriff of Nottingham had ever been. He sent force after force of trained soldiery to beat the forest recesses and drive the outlaws out. Many a wild skirmish was fought out among the great oaks: sometimes the outlaws won, sometimes they lost and were compelled to flee before the king's men, but conquered they never were. Year after year passed, and still they lay in hiding among the thickets, and not one failed in faith and devotion to the dauntless Robin Hood, their trusted leader. Then King John died, and all England was full of joy to think that the hated tyrant had gone, yet was none so joyous as the hunted outlaws, who had lost their worst and bitterest enemy and could now have a little peace.

So time passed on until, as the old ballad says, "Robin

dwelled in greenwood twenty years and two," and in this time Robin saw many changes. He lost his beloved partner, Maid Marian, and many an old comrade had been laid to rest beneath the mighty oaks, but still Little John, his faithful lieutenant, was at his side, and master and man hunted the dun deer over hill and dale.

Then came a time when Robin Hood felt that his strength was failing. His great yew bow became too stiff for him to bend, the whistling shaft did not travel to the old range, and he felt listless and ill at ease.

In this state of mind and body he remembered that he had a cousin, the Prioress of Kirkley, who was deeply skilled in the medicine of the time. So he said to Little John that he would go the nunnery over which his cousin ruled and ask her to bleed him, for in those days people believed that many diseases could be cured by letting blood.

He set out at once for fair Kirkley, but on the way he was taken ill, and he was very weak when he arrived at the door. His cousin welcomed him with open arms and offered food and drink, but Robin replied that he would neither eat or drink until he had been bled.

So the prioress led Robin to a small room high up in the house, and there she opened the veins of his arm with a lancet, and the blood ran freely. Now Robin thought he was in the hands of a friend, but in truth he was in the grip of a treacherous enemy. The prioress was a close friend of some of Robin's bitterest foes and had promised them to do him an ill turn if ever she had the power. Her chance had now come, and the wicked woman made the most of it. She bled her helpless guest until he lay weak and fainting. At length Robin revived a little and tried to leave the room to which the prioress had conducted him. But he found the door was locked, and no one answered his outcries and knocking. And now he began to suspect the truth: that he had been shut up there to bleed to death.

He dragged himself to the window and flung open the casement, but he was so weak that he could not leap down. Still, there was one thing at hand, the thing that had so often brought strong hands and stout hearts to his rescue when sore bestead—his bugle horn. He knew that Little John was awaiting him in the forest near at hand, and he raised the horn and blew it thrice, but ah! such short, feeble blasts, the faintest echo of the full, rousing notes with which he had so often caused the woodland to ring. But his faithful follower was on the alert and caught the faint sounds.

Sitting under the tree Little John barely heard the horn. "I fear my beloved master is near death," he said, "he blows so weak a blast."

So up he sprang and ran to Kirkley Hall as fast as he could put his feet to the gound. He came to the great door and knocked loudly. No one answered, no one came even to look out at the lattice beside the door to parley with him. Again he knocked until the place rang again with his heavy blows. No answer. Then the giant felt sure that there was foul play somewhere, and he glanced about for means of entry.

He looked at the windows, but they were very small

and iron-barred. Then his eye fell on a great log of oak, a piece of timber which two ordinary men could scarce lift. The giant sprang at it, caught it up, and smote the door a thundering crash of a blow which burst all locks and bars as if they had been straws and sticks, and beat the door from its hinges. As the door clattered on the pavement of the hall, Little John leapt in and rushing about shouting, "Master! Master! Where are you?"

He listened, but the silence was perfect; the nunnery seemed as quiet as a house of the dead. He called again, and now a faint voice answered him from above. He rushed upstairs, and again heard the call, and ran to the door of the room whence it came. The door was locked, but Little John burst it open with his knee and sprang in.

"What is this, master?" he cried. "Treachery, I fear me. Thou art bleeding to death!"

"Ay, Little John," said the dying man slowly. "My time has come."

Little John fell upon his knee beside his beloved leader. "Then one last boon, I crave of thee, dear master!" he said sternly.

"What boon is it thou dost beg of me, Little John?" asked Robin Hood.

"It is that I may burn Kirkley Hall and its nunnery and consume this nest of traitors with fire."

"Nay," quoth Robin Hood, "I cannot grant that boon, for never have I injured a woman or a man in woman's company. Give me my bow and I will shoot a broad arrow. Where that arrow falls I would have my grave dug."

Little John raised his master and bore him to the open

window. Long and fondly the dying man looked on the
woodlands he had loved so well, and then, with a last
effort, he collected all his remaining strength and placed
an arrow on the string, drew the feather home, and loosed
it. He smiled as the bow twanged full and deep, and his
ear caught the sound which had been the sweetest music
in the world to him.

"Lay me where the arrow drops," he murmured. "Bid
my true hearts dig me a deep grave, and lay a green sod
under my head, and my good bow at my side." Little
John nodded, for he could not speak, and with his eyes
fixed on the greenwood, Robin Hood died in the arms of
his faithful follower.

So died Robin Hood. But his fame did not die with
him. Age after age and generation after generation his
memory lingered among the common people, who loved
to recall his famous exploits and the doings of his great
followers. Kings and nobles were forgotten or their deeds
recorded only in musty books which none but scholars
read. But minstrels and rhymers made ballad after ballad
of the doings of Robin Hood, and these ballads lived on
the lips and in the hearts of the people. They were sung
or recited on holidays and at merrymakings, and no
rhymes were so popular as those which told of this true
English hero—a protector of the poor, a foe to the tyrant,
brave, gentle, and chivalrous, a man after the English peasant's own heart.

Tradition says that he was buried at the spot where his
last arrow stood in the turf. A stone was set up at his
head, and on it was graven the inscription:—

He smiled as the bow twanged full and deep

"Here, underneath this little stone,
Lies Robert, Earl of Huntingdon;
Never archer as he so good,
And people called him Robin Hood.
Such outlaws as he and his men,
Will England never see again."

After Robin's death his company was broken up and no
record is kept of the end of any among them save Little
John.   And the grave of that famous outlaw is a disputed
spot.   England, Scotland, and Ireland contend for the
honor of his death and burial.   In each country a site is
pointed out as that of Little John's grave.   Some authorities give the pride of place to the village of Hathersedge, in
Derbyshire, where there is a long and wide grave, which,
when once opened, was found to contain some bones of
uncommon size.   It is marked by a great stone at the head
and foot, and tradition declares that, should any one be so
daring as to move the bones, he would become a most
unlucky man until they were restored, when his troubles
would cease.   And so, peace to the ashes of those famous
yeomen and mighty outlaws, Robin Hood and Little John!